LOVE TAKES WING

JANETTE OKE

BETHANY HOUSE PUBLISHERS
MINNEAPOLIS, MINNESOTA 55438
A Division of Bethany Fellowship, Inc.

Cover illustration by Dan Thornberg,
Bethany House Publishers staff artist.

Published by Bethany House Publishers
A Division of Bethany Fellowship, Inc.
6820 Auto Club Road, Minneapolis, Minnesota 55438

Printed in the United States of America

Library of Congress Cataloging-in-Publication Data

Oke, Janette, 1935–
   Love takes wing.

   (Love comes softly series ; bk. 7)
   I. Title. II. Series: Oke, Janette, 1935–
Love comes softly series ; bk. 7.
PR9199.3.038L56   1988   813'.54   88–19276
ISBN 1-55661-035-1   CIP

To Aunt Laurine—
with love and thanks
for who you are
and what you mean to me.
God bless!

JANETTE OKE
PRAIRIE LOVE STORIES

SEASONS OF THE HEART Series
Once Upon a Summer
The Winds of Autumn
Winter Is Not Forever

LOVE COMES SOFTLY Series
Love Comes Softly
Love's Enduring Promise
Love's Long Journey
Love's Abiding Joy
Love's Unending Legacy
Love's Unfolding Dream
Love Takes Wing

CANADIAN WEST Series
When Calls the Heart
When Comes the Spring
When Breaks the Dawn
When Hope Springs New

JANETTE OKE was born in Champion, Alberta, during the depression years, to a Canadian prairie farmer and his wife. She is a graduate of Mountain View Bible College in Didsbury, Alberta, where she met her husband, Edward. They were married in May of 1957, and went on to pastor churches in Indiana as well as Calgary and Edmonton, Canada.

Janette's husband is president of Mountain View Bible College, Didsbury, Alberta. The Okes have three sons and one daughter and are enjoying the addition to the family of grandchildren.

Edward and Janette have both been active in their local church, serving in various capacities as Sunday-school teachers and board members.

Table of Contents

Characters in the LOVE COMES SOFTLY Series

Clark and Marty Davis—partners in a marriage in which each had lost a previous spouse.

Nandry and Clae—foster daughters raised by Clark and Marty. Nandry married Josh Coffins and they had Tina, Andrew, Mary and Jane. Clae married Joe Berwick. Their children were Esther Sue, Joey and Paul.

Missie—Clark's daughter from his first marriage, married Willie LaHaye and moved west to ranch. Their children—Nathan, Josiah, Melissa (who came east to live with Clark and Marty while she finished high school, then went on to train as a schoolteacher) and Julia.

Clare—Marty's son born after her first husband's death, married Kate. They lived in the same farmyard as Clark and Marty. Their children—Amy Jo, Dan, David and Dack.

Arnie—Clark and Marty's first child. He married Anne and had three sons—Silas, John and Abe.

Daughter Ellie—married Lane Howard and moved west to join Missie and Willie. Their children were Brenda, William and Willis.

Son Luke—trained to be a doctor and returned to the small town to practice medicine. He married Abbie. Their children were Thomas and Aaron—and, now, new baby daughter Ruth.

Jackson Brown—the schoolfriend who greatly impressed Melissa, Amy Jo and Belinda when he first arrived at the country school. Melissa was the one who really carried a torch for him, though Jackson preferred Belinda.

Chapter 1

The End of a Long Day

Belinda pushed wisps of gold-brown hair back from her flushed face and took a deep breath. It was "one of those days"— again! The whole week seemed to have been filled with emergencies. One right after the other.

Why are people so careless? Belinda asked herself a mite crossly.

She tossed her soiled white apron aside and began to clean up the blood-stained operating table.

The last case of the day was a boy who had caught his hand in a piece of farm machinery. Luke had worked hard and long to try to save all his fingers, but neither he nor Belinda were too hopeful about the outcome. She felt tired, overworked and anxious about young Jamie's fingers.

I should be getting used to such things by now, she admonished herself. After all, hadn't she been assisting Luke in surgery for over a year? But she hadn't gotten used to the suffering she felt when she looked at the pain in another's eyes—especially when it was in the eyes of a child.

She sighed again deeply and breathed another prayer for Jamie.

"I'll do that," said a voice from behind her.

She hadn't even heard Luke enter the room. She turned to protest that cleaning up was part of her job, but he continued.

13

"I know you're in a hurry. It's only an hour until the train will be in."

Belinda's thoughts focused on the event that had been filling her with excitement this whole week. She had been counting the days—the hours. How could it have slipped her mind? It must have been the injured boy. He had taken her complete attention while they worked to save his hand. But now with Luke's reminder, Belinda's excitement flooded her mind again. *Melissa is coming home!* She now was finished with her teacher's training in the East and would be spending a few weeks at the farm before continuing on to her home in the West.

Belinda glanced down at her soiled dress. She hated to leave Luke with the cleaning, but she did need a bath to freshen up, and she just had to do something with her wayward hair. Missing out on welcoming Melissa on the afternoon train was unthinkable. It had been a long time—a long, *long* time since she had seen her.

She gave Luke a warm, appreciative smile and turned reluctantly from the untidy surgery.

"Sorry," she apologized, but he assured her, "No reason for you to be sorry. It isn't your carelessness that has been filling our office with accident cases."

Belinda reached up and pulled the pins from her hair and let it tumble down about her shoulders. She eased her slender fingers through the curls and shook them gently to shake out the tangles.

"Have ya ever seen a week like this one?" she asked her brother soberly.

"It's been a bad one, all right," Luke admitted. Then he went on with deep thoughtfulness: "I sure hope it's about to come to an end."

Belinda agreed.

"Now you'd best hurry," urged Luke. "You don't want to be late for that train."

Belinda scurried from the room. She did want to be there when the train pulled in to the local station. Her whole family would be waiting for Melissa. Would she have changed much? Would the two of them still be able to share secrets and understand—sometimes even without words—how the other was feeling? Was Melissa still pining over Jackson Brown or had she found another young man? What was teacher's training like? Did she like the city? Belinda had so many questions.

Yes, they had written frequently, but it just wasn't the same. There were some things that were not easy to say in letters. Belinda did hope that there wouldn't be any awkwardness between them. She was filled with anticipation and yet felt some apprehension.

She set the portable tub on the mat in her small upstairs room at Luke and Abbie's house and carried pails of warm water to fill it. As she settled into it, her thoughts went back to the first time the family had gathered to wait for the arrival of Melissa. That time she had been coming from her home in the West. None of them had known what to expect as they waited for the stage to arrive. Belinda could still remember the butterflies and the questions. What would she be like? Would they like each other? Would they be able to get along? Maybe it would be like having a sister her own age.

And so it had turned out—Melissa had been like a sister even though she was in fact a niece. Belinda had grown to love her dearly and had missed her greatly when she went away to Normal School. And now the days had slowly ticked by and Melissa was coming home again—this time by train.

The Davis family had never gathered to meet the train before. This was a new and welcome luxury to the people of their small town. They were getting used to hearing the whistle and the clickity-clack of the metal wheels on the iron tracks, but Belinda still had not quite gotten over the thrill of having their very own train. Often she dreamed of boarding the passenger car and being taken to some far-away place that she had only seen in picture books. But so far it only remained a dream for Belinda.

She did not allow herself the pleasure of a long soak in the tub. There just was not time. The train, though sometimes late, was far more dependable in its travel than the stagecoach had been, and Belinda knew that if she did not hurry she would miss the excitement of Melissa's arrival.

She rushed around as she dressed and hurriedly pinned up her hair. With each glance toward the dresser clock, her heart beat faster. She was going to be late in spite of her scurrying about. She still had the tub to empty and—

She called an answer to a gentle knock, and Abbie opened the door only wide enough to poke her head in the room.

"My, don't you look nice," she smiled, then quickly added, "Luke said to tell you to leave the tub. We'll take care of it when we get back."

Belinda glanced sideways at the tub. She did hate to leave things undone, but Luke was right—there just wasn't time before going to the station. She sighed resignedly and nodded to Abbie.

"Everyone ready?" she asked, and Abbie indicated that they were as she pulled on a glove.

Belinda grabbed her own gloves and a small handbag. She took one last look in the mirror to be sure that her hat was on straight, smoothed the hipline of her skirt and hurried downstairs after Abbie.

Thomas and Aaron had already left the house and were waiting at the end of the walk. Aaron, the younger of the two, was giving Thomas a ride on the front gate even though both boys had been told not to swing on it. As soon as their mother appeared, Thomas dropped quickly to the walk and turned his attention to the ants that were scurrying back and forth across the boards, as though he had been studying them the whole time.

Abbie was not fooled. "Thomas," she said sternly, "what have we told you about swinging on the gate?"

Thomas just lowered his head and did not answer.

"There's a nice swing in the backyard," Abbie continued. "I've told you before that the gate will sag if you swing on it."

Still Thomas did not respond. Abbie hurried down the walk and when she reached the small boy, she laid a hand on his shoulder.

"No dessert for dinner," she said quietly but firmly, and Belinda saw the small boy's eyes quickly lift to his mother's face. Thomas loved desserts.

"Now, let's hurry along," Abbie prompted both boys, dismissing the matter of the gate. "We don't want to make Aunt Belinda late for the train."

"But Papa—" began Aaron.

"Papa says for us to go ahead. He'll join us at the station."

Belinda felt another pang—she should have been cleaning up the surgery room instead of leaving it for Luke. Abbie must have sensed her hesitation, for she quickly added, "Papa says that it's more important for Aunt Belinda to be there on time. She has missed Melissa more than any of us."

So saying, Abbie herded her charges toward the train station at a brisk pace; Belinda didn't protest further and fell into step.

Clark and Marty, already waiting on the wooden platform near the tracks, had come into town from the farm. Beside them stood Amy Jo, her brownish-red hair swept rather carelessly into a loose knot on the top of her head. Her green velvet hat looked none too secure to Belinda's eyes, but Amy Jo wore her apparel in the same lighthearted fashion that she did everything else. She smiled and waved exuberantly at Belinda in greeting.

"Isn't this jest too exciting?" she enthused. "Imagine traveling by train—all by yerself. Wouldn't you jest—jest *die*?"

Belinda doubted that she would die—but there was something inside that did yearn to have such an experience. She greeted Amy Jo and then turned to her mother and father.

"I was afraid ya'd been held up," said Marty, "an' I knew how special this is fer ya."

"We *were* held up," responded Belinda. "In fact, I should be back scrubbing the surgery—but Luke let me go."

"Isn't he gonna make it?" This time Marty's question was directed to Abbie.

"He hopes to," Abbie answered, "but he did need to do the surgery first. He never knows when he might need it again, and one can't stop and do the cleaning up then."

Marty nodded in understanding and Clark asked, "Would it help iffen I were to—?"

He didn't have a chance to finish his question. Abbie knew

what he was about to ask and answered quickly, "No. No, he wouldn't want that. No use you missing the train too."

"I *should* have stayed—" began Belinda, but Abbie reached out to give her shoulders a quick squeeze. "He wouldn't have let you and you know it," she said firmly, closing the matter.

Amy Jo moved over and crowded in against Belinda. "Isn't this—isn't it jest—jest—?"

For a moment Belinda's mind flew back many years, and she could imagine Amy Jo finishing her sentence with "vibrant," a word Amy Jo had chosen to describe almost everything during her early teen years. But this time Amy Jo picked another word, one she had recently discovered. In Belinda's view it too was a little overdone.

"—Jest wondrous!" she finished excitedly.

Belinda smiled. Amy Jo had not changed. She still gushed and glowed over most of life. Things would never be dull as long as Amy Jo was around. Belinda reached out to clasp Amy Jo's long slender fingers and gave them an affectionate squeeze. Amy Jo pressed closer, her excitement spilling over and making them both almost tremble.

"What do ya think she's like?" she prodded.

Belinda looked a bit blank. Amy Jo knew Melissa as well as she did.

"She'll have changed, ya know," Amy Jo bubbled. "Be more grown up, more sophisticated. More—more—worldly."

Marty turned to the two girls, a slight frown on her face. She did not care for the word *worldly* in regard to her dear Melissa, and Amy Jo sensed it immediately.

"I—I mean—more—more knowledgeable of the world. More—more—" She faltered to a stop, grasping Belinda's hand until her fingers hurt.

A distant train whistle drew all eyes to the track. Somewhere out there, around the curve hidden from view by poplar trees, the train was making its way, far too slowly, toward their town, their station, the platform where they all stood. And sitting sedately and educated all alone on one of the upholstered seats was their Melissa. A stir of excitement ran through the little cluster on the wooden planks of the platform.

"It's comin'!" shrieked Aaron, and Thomas answered with a long hooted whistle of his own.

Just as the train rounded the bend, Belinda noticed Luke take his place beside Abbie. She sighed with relief that he would not miss out on the excitement, and then forgot everything and everyone except for Melissa.

Would she have changed? How much? Belinda fervently hoped that her niece hadn't become too sophisticated—too worldly-wise.

And then the huge engine was rattling along beside the platform, and smoke and soot were wafting out over the afternoon air, making people step back sharply and cast anxious glances at their Sunday-best clothing.

The metal wheels squeaked and squealed as the train ground to a halt, and the loud hiss of steam spilled out into the quietness of the springtime air. The train gave one last shudder and settled into quietness.

A conductor soon appeared, methodically setting into place a wooden step and opening doors. There was movement at the windows as passengers started to shift about inside, putting on coats, gathering belongings and preparing to exit. Others stayed seated. This was not their destination, so they had no reason to stir. They looked with little, if any, interest at the crowd on the little platform and the wine-red station behind them. There was nothing much noteworthy in this small town, much like most every other stop on the tedious western journey.

Belinda saw one elderly lady glance carelessly out the window and then raise a gloved hand to her mouth to cover a yawn. Belinda found herself looking quickly around her. Were they all really that boring? Was the little town truly that unexciting? Perhaps so. Belinda had never known anything else with which to compare her surroundings. Briefly she visualized herself stepping up onto the iron steps and entering the passenger car, bags in hand, traveling to wherever the train might take her.

The thought was fleeting, for, coming toward them, arms filled with small packages, was a more mature and even prettier Melissa.

At her glad little cry, the group surged toward her. Belinda too moved forward, then realized that Amy Jo still held tightly to her hand.

Melissa passed from one to another, tears unashamedly sliding down her cheeks as she greeted each family member with hugs and kisses.

"Oh, Belinda!" she exclaimed when it was Belinda's turn. "Look at you! You're so—so grown-up. And so pretty! Oh, I just—" But Melissa didn't finish her statement. Instead, she threw her arms about Belinda, and the two girls held each other tightly.

When the whole group had expressed their welcome, the family cluster moved from the platform with Melissa's luggage to the wagon, all talking at once.

Belinda thought back again to the first time Melissa had been met by the family. In so many ways this was the same. And yet so very, very different. There was no reserve here now—not from anyone. Amy Jo, who had felt left out of the conversation the first time, made sure she was not left out now.

Questions and answers filled the air until it was difficult to sort out who was answering what. Even the two young boys fired rapid questions at their older cousin, most of them in regard to the train. How fast did it go? had she seen the coal being shoveled into the engine? had the train—? Melissa laughed and hugged them both with a promise to tell them all about the train trip.

"Are ya all ready to come home?" Clark was asking Belinda.

"My things are all packed and waiting. We jest need to stop off at Luke's and pick 'em up," Belinda answered, savoring the pleasure of a whole week off to enjoy Melissa's company.

"Ya sure you won't need me?" Belinda asked Luke one more time as he tucked her things in beside Melissa's luggage when the wagon stopped at the house.

" 'Course I'll need you," Luke responded, but at the flicker of concern in her eyes, he was quick to add, "But for a few days I'll manage—somehow. And if I really get into difficulty, I'll send for you."

"Promise?" asked Belinda.

"Promise," Luke assured her.

Belinda turned to give each of the boys a quick hug and climbed up into the wagon beside Melissa and Amy Jo.

The trip to the farm was filled with more chatter—and this time it wasn't just Melissa who talked nonstop. Belinda soon began to feel that the conversation was almost as exhausting as the surgery. She hoped she soon would have Melissa to herself for a more quiet talk. Belinda was sure that she wouldn't really know if Melissa had changed until then, when the deeper thoughts and feelings of the two girls could be expressed.

Until that time, Belinda knew she must be patient. The rest of the family wanted to have time with Melissa, too. She belonged to all of them. When they got to the farm, there would be a family dinner to welcome back Missie's little girl. After dinner there would be a large stack of dirty dishes to be dealt with. There would be no time for a girlish chat on this night.

Belinda allowed a small sigh to escape her. It was hardly audible with the grinding of the wagon wheels and the chattering of Melissa and Amy Jo, but it brought Marty's head around as she studied the face of her youngest.

She didn't ask the question, but Belinda could sense it. She smiled at her mother to reassure her.

"I'm a bit tired," she admitted. "It's been a very long day. Started even before sun-up with the Norrises rushing their baby in with croup."

Marty nodded in understanding. Clark overheard and turned his head.

"A week's rest will do ya good," he said, then turned back to guide the team. "You've been workin' awful hard. Yer lookin' a mite pale," he threw over his shoulder.

"I'm fine—really," insisted Belinda and suddenly felt uncomfortable as the chattering stopped and all eyes rested on her.

"One good night's sleep and I'll be right as rain," she insisted, hoping that folks would forget her and get on with the catching-up again.

Chapter 2

Girl Talk

When the last family wagon had left the yard and the last dish had been returned to the cupboard, Belinda was far too weary to suggest a chat with Melissa. She looked weary too, in spite of the fact that she still was chattering away about her year out east and her excitement with being back.

Amy Jo reluctantly wrapped her light shawl about her shoulders and headed for the log house across the farmyard, promising that she would be back again first thing in the morning.

Belinda tried to stifle a yawn, but it was getting hard for her to keep her eyes open.

"Ya be needin' yer bed," Clark commented and Belinda could only nod in agreement.

"You must be weary, too, dear," Marty said to Melissa, giving her granddaughter an affectionate pat.

Melissa smiled. "I am," she admitted. "Terribly! But I'm still not sure I'll be able to sleep. It's just so good to be back with you all."

Marty smiled. It was good to hear that sentiment from Melissa. Marty had been afraid she would be so taken with town life that she would almost forget her country relatives.

"Ya best git on up to bed—both of ya," Marty went on, looking from one girl to the other. "Plenty of time to catch up on all the news."

They climbed the steps slowly together and did not even pause to visit at the doors to their rooms, but with a promise of a "good talk" on the morrow they hugged their good nights and went to bed.

Belinda was so weary she could hardly lift her warm flannel gown over her head. Kneeling to say her evening prayers, her brain refused to function and they were shorter than normal. With a slight apology to her God, she slipped between the soft sheets and was soon sound asleep.

Belinda slept much later than usual the next morning. She was oblivious to the sounds of the stirring household, unaware that Amy Jo had already made her appearance to a "sh-h-h" from her grandmother and that the sun was climbing higher and higher into the late spring sky.

Melissa, too, had slept late, though she did awaken before Belinda. After eating one of Marty's hearty breakfasts, she left with Amy Jo to go look at some of her recent sketches and drawings.

It was almost ten o'clock before Belinda stirred. As she looked at her little clock on her dresser, she could scarcely believe her eyes—she couldn't remember ever sleeping so late. A bit embarrassed, she hurriedly dressed, made her bed and tidied her room. She couldn't resist a peek through Melissa's open door and could see for herself that Melissa had already left a neat room and gone out to enjoy the new day.

As Belinda descended the stairs, her face flushed slightly as she heard Marty stirring busily in the kitchen. What would they all think of her?

Marty's head turned from her churning when she heard Belinda, concern in her eyes.

"My churnin' didn't waken ya, did it?" she asked.

"Oh, my no," responded Belinda. "Fact is, I guess nothin' wakened me. I jest slept on and on."

"Ya had a lot of catchin' up to do," insisted Marty. "Ya likely shoulda' slept longer."

"Mama," said Belinda in unbelief. "Look at the time. It's 'most ten. I'll be willin' to bet ya never slept this late in yer whole life."

"Nor do I have my sleep interrupted night after night either," Marty said in Belinda's defense. She began to scurry about her kitchen to get Belinda's breakfast.

"It *has* been bad recently," Belinda admitted, "but it's not always like this."

"Well, ya need a few nights of good sleepin'," Marty went on. "I'm glad thet ya got ya one to start out with."

Belinda smiled. It was nice to have her mother fussing over her again.

"Not much breakfast," Belinda quickly said as she realized what Marty was doing. "Let me jest get myself somethin'. Ya sit down and finish yer churnin'."

"Ya need to eat," Marty insisted. "Yer gittin' thin."

Belinda looked down at her slim body. Perhaps she had lost a few pounds—but nothing much.

"It's 'most dinner time. If I eat a big breakfast now, I won't want any dinner."

Marty's eyes rested on the clock. She finally nodded in agreement.

"Fix what ya like then," she said, sitting back down at her butter churn and starting the handle humming.

"Where's Melissa?" asked Belinda as she sliced some homemade bread for toast.

"Oh, my! I promised the girls thet I'd let 'em know the minute ya stirred!" Marty jumped up from her chair to head for the door.

"Let them be," Belinda stopped her. She laughed softly. "As late as I've slept, a few more minutes won't hurt anything. Amy Jo was most anxious to get a chance to talk to Melissa anyway. We'll jest give them a few more minutes while I have my breakfast, and then I'll go on over."

Marty settled down again for a few quiet moments alone with Belinda.

"Ya do look a mite better this mornin'," she observed as Belinda brought her slice of toast and glass of milk to the table.

"I feel better, too," admitted Belinda.

"Ya looked terrible tired last night. Thet nursin' be too hard on ya, I'm a thinkin'."

"Oh, no," Belinda was quick to defend her work. "Usually we get lots of sleep. Well—anyway, enough sleep. But recently we've had so many emergencies—accidents and illnesses. It's been a bad time for Luke, too. He really is far too busy. This town could use another doctor."

"I never thought on thet," remarked Marty, surprised at Belinda's comment.

"Luke says it himself," went on Belinda. "And Abbie—well, she says it often."

"Well, maybe Jackson will come back here to practice," commented Marty. "His mama would sure like thet."

It wasn't the first time Belinda had thought about that possibility. Jackson had changed his mind about banking and had now completed two years of his training toward becoming a doctor. Luke had mentioned Jackson's name several times when he talked about the town needing another man. Belinda hardly knew her own mind on the issue. She did hope fervently that Jackson had not decided on a career in medicine simply because of her own interest in nursing. But she couldn't help but wonder.

When Jackson first left their area, he had written Belinda often. Belinda enjoyed the newsy letters telling of his new experiences, the long recitals of what he was learning in his classes and from the library textbooks. But soon the letters started to become more personal than Belinda was comfortable with. She thought that Jackson was taking too much for granted. As difficult as it had been for her, she wrote Jackson, telling him that she felt they were unwise to keep up the distant relationship. Jackson had written back a very kind and understanding letter. Still, Belinda had some misgivings. Jackson's words had implied a good measure of "for now."

"How much longer does Jackson have?" Marty was asking.

Belinda's attention jerked back to her mother.

"Ah—ah," she stammered and then got her thoughts back in order. "Luke says he will be ready in two years, I think," she responded.

"Can Luke wait thet long?"

"He might have no choice. It's hard to find doctors willin' to work in small towns."

"Has he talked to Jackson?"

Belinda thought about that one. She wasn't sure, though one night she had heard Abbie urging Luke to get in touch with the young man before someone else spoke to him.

"I don't know," she said, "but I think he may have."

"I hope so. Fer Luke's sake. An' fer the sake of Abbie and the boys. Luke doesn't see nearly enough of 'em."

"Thet's what worries Luke," Belinda said thoughtfully. "He doesn't seem to tire like I do, but he does hate to be so busy. He enjoys the boys so much and says they are growing up far too fast. He'd like more time to do father-son things. Take them fishin' and play ball and such."

Belinda rose slowly from the table, reluctant to break off the visit with her mother but anxious to see Melissa—and Amy Jo too. Though not far from each other, they seemed to have few chances to really talk anymore.

"I'd better go," she told her mother. "The girls will think I've gone and died in my bed."

Marty smiled.

"I'll be back to help ya with dinner."

"No need," said Marty. "I've got it all ready to jest put on the stove. You go ahead and enjoy a visit. The days will go fast enough."

Belinda knew that was true enough. She stacked her dishes on a corner of the cupboard and left the house.

The morning sunshine felt warm and welcome on her hair. She turned her face to it and breathed in deeply of the spring-smelling air. Above her, birds twittered and frolicked, thankful to be alive. It was nest-building time.

Belinda found Melissa and Amy Jo on the lawn swing sipping lemonade and chatting excitedly. Both girls called to her and motioned her over to join them.

"Yer lookin' better," said the frank Amy Jo. "Ya looked awful last night."

Belinda smiled.

"Not awful," corrected the more tactful Melissa, "but awfully tired."

"Thet's what I said," hastened Amy Jo. "Awful!"

The three laughed.

"So are ya caught up on all the news?" Belinda asked Melissa.

"Oh, my, no," Melissa countered. "That will take much longer than we've had. I doubt we'll get it all said in the next two weeks."

At the mention of "two weeks," Amy Jo's face fell and she hastened to cut in. "Don't talk about it. I don't want to even think about Melissa leaving again."

"I do," said Melissa almost defiantly. "I haven't seen Mother or Papa for almost three years."

Amy Jo immediately became sympathetic. "Have ya missed them terribly?"

"I've missed them. Sometimes a lot. Other times not so much. But I've missed them. And Nathan and Joe and Julia." Melissa's face became very thoughtful as her mind went back to her home and those she loved. "I've even missed the ranch hands and my horses," she admitted.

"If I left home, I don't think I could stand it," said Amy Jo, shaking her head. "I'd miss everyone so much."

Melissa nodded. "I'm glad I came," she informed the two girls. "Really glad I came. But I will be glad to get home again, too."

"I'm glad ya came, too," said Belinda softly. "It would have been a shame not to get to know ya."

"It would have been jest awful," wailed Amy Jo. "Jest awful!"

"Even more awful than I looked last night?" teased Belinda, and they all laughed again.

"I think it's good to see more of the world than your own little nook," Melissa said. "I love the West, but I'm glad I dared to leave home for a time and get to know a bit more about our country. One can get so—so—ingrown."

Ingrown, thought Belinda. *Guess that's what's happening to me. I know nothing about the world except these few miles around where I was born and live. Nothing!*

"An' ya never would have met *Jackson!*" squealed Amy Jo and the girls laughed merrily.

"Jackson," Melissa chuckled. "You know, there was a time when I thought that life just wouldn't be worth living without Jackson."

"Is it?" wailed Amy Jo in mock surprise.

Melissa laughed again. "Well," she said evenly, her large brown eyes rolling heavenward, "if I learned nothing else at Normal School, I did learn this. There are lots of young men out there. And some of them—a few of them are even as exciting as Jackson."

"No-o-o!" groaned Amy Jo.

"On my honor," said Melissa in mock seriousness, raising her right hand.

From there the talk went on to Melissa's year at the school and the school parties and church functions that she attended and the escorts that she had had for such occasions.

Amy Jo clasped her hands together and groaned openly at the very thought of being a popular young lady in such a circumstance. Belinda listened quietly, though she did have a few questions of her own that she wished to ask Melissa. She wasn't sure if she would enjoy so many beaus or not, but it was interesting to think about it. One thing for sure was that she was no longer concerned about Melissa being heartbroken if Jackson should choose someone else.

Chapter 3

A Neighborhood Party

A party in Melissa's honor was planned. It was really Amy Jo's idea, but Marty saw it as an opportunity for the youth of the community to get together for a fun and fellowship time and heartily endorsed it. Belinda, who usually wasn't too keen on parties, found herself looking forward to the Saturday evening event.

The guest list included past school friends and young people of the local church. The invitations went out with some concern as to how many would be able to come on such short notice.

But on the evening of the party, the teams and saddle horses began to arrive shortly after seven, and the farmyard soon was filled with tethered animals and various kinds of horse-drawn vehicles. It had been some time since so many of the girls' schoolmates had been together, and there were lots of excited greetings and laughter as the group gathered in the large Davis backyard.

The festivities began in the nearby pasture with a game of softball, the fellows playing and the girls wildly cheering them on. Then a few girls joined the game, Amy Jo one of them. She was used to playing most of the games that her younger brothers played and saw no reason to be left out. She coaxed Melissa and Belinda to play but Belinda declined. She had never cared much for sports of any kind and did not want to embarrass herself by showing her lack of ability.

Melissa hesitantly joined the game. Her sports skills were no greater than Belinda's, but she had the sense to make the most of her lack of expertise. Joe Parker coached her running. Tom Rankin helped her to cover third base, though his spot was really short stop, and Sly Foster showed her how to hold and swing the bat. Melissa was actually enjoying the game of softball.

The game continued until almost sundown. When it became too dark to see the ball, the group switched to other running games. Belinda excused herself, saying that she would prepare the fire for the corn roast to follow.

She was laying the kindling wood in the open brick pit Clark had built in the backyard for just such occasions when a voice spoke to her from the soft twilight. "May I help?"

It was Rand O'Connel, a young man Belinda hadn't seen since school days. Belinda flushed slightly and moved aside so that Rand could take over the task.

"Hear you've been nursin'," he commented as he carefully placed the wood.

Belinda nodded her head and then decided that in the near-darkness a question should be answered aloud. "Yes," she said. "Helpin' my brother Luke."

"Do ya like it?" he questioned further.

"Oh, yes. Least most of the time. Sometimes it can get a bit hectic."

"Pa says yer good at it," went on Rand, and Belinda puzzled for a moment and then remembered that Mr. O'Connel had been in to have stitches because of an axe-cut on his foot.

"How is yer pa's foot doin'?" she asked.

"Fine now. Doesn't even limp."

"That's due to Luke—not me," said Belinda.

"Pa knows thet. But he also said thet ya took his mind off the pain, knew what to do until Luke got there, and how to help Luke when he did the sewin' up."

Belinda flushed at the praise and dropped her eyes.

"Do ya farm with yer pa?" she asked to cover her embarrassment. "I haven't seen ya around since—since grade school."

"Jest got back. Been helpin' my uncle down state."

"Oh."

"He has him a dairy farm and needed a hired hand."

"Are ya goin' back?" asked Belinda to keep the conversation from dying.

"Nope. Not to milkin'," he said simply.

"So, what do ya plan to do now?" asked Belinda.

Rand lit a match to the kindling and watched as the small flame began to lick at the fine wood splinters. Around them the darkness was closing in. The shrieks and calls of the players filled the air all about them, making the evening feel friendly and warm.

"Fer now, I plan to jest look around here fer a job," responded Rand, his eyes still on the growing fire.

"What kind of job?" Belinda asked.

"Can't be choosey," he acknowledged. "Take whatever I can git. Heard of anything?"

"No-o. Not that I remember. But it shouldn't be hard to find something. Yer big—an' strong. Should be lots of work—" And then Belinda realized what she had just said about him and stopped in embarrassment. Rand said nothing. She wondered if he had even heard her foolishness. Much to her relief, he seemed totally taken with tending the fire.

The firelight was casting dancing shadows over his features. She had forgotten what he looked like. She had even forgotten Rand O'Connel. Not that she had ever really noticed him much in the past. He had been just a boy—a fellow student at their small school, neither stupid nor brainy, loud nor shy. He had just been there. By the light of the fire, she took a good look at him now.

His dark hair fell boyishly over his forehead, and he brushed it back impatiently with a work-toughened hand. The hair at the nape of his neck curled over his shirt collar, and Belinda realized that if the rest of it hadn't been cut short, it would probably curl over his whole head. His eyes were deep-set and fringed with dark curling lashes. His nose had the slightest hump, suggesting that it might have been injured at some time. There was a small indentation in his cheek that looked almost like a dimple—though, looking at the young man, Belinda dared to think he'd not take kindly to anyone calling it such.

He must have felt her eyes upon him, for he turned to look at her. Belinda shifted her gaze quickly away and pretended to be busy brushing the wood chips from her long skirt.

"I hear Melissa's been away at school an' is a full-fledged teacher now," he said after a brief silence that hung awkwardly between them.

Belinda, glad for something to break the spell, answered in a rush, "Yes, that's right. She loved Normal School—but she's glad to be home, too."

"Is she stayin'? Here, I mean? I thought her home—"

"Oh, it is. I mean, she's jest here for a brief spell. Two weeks in fact—and part of thet's already gone. Then she's going home. To her real home. I have jest gotten used to thinkin' of this as her home. I mean—this seems like home for her—to me. She was with us for more'n two years and then back for visits an'—I really will miss her," she finally finished lamely.

Rand just nodded his head. He seemed to have been able to follow her rambling.

"She excited about teachin'?" he asked.

"Oh, yes. She's always wanted to be a teacher. And they need lots of teachers in the West, too."

"I'm glad she likes it."

He seemed so sincere, so genuinely pleased for Melissa that Belinda looked at him intently, wondering. *Is this another of Melissa's secret admirers? Is he wishing her well even though his real desire is for her to stay in the area?* Belinda concluded that he well could be. She felt a strange sympathy for Rand. He seemed like such a nice young man. Belinda was sorry he might suffer over Melissa's coming departure.

But Rand went on in a matter-of-fact voice. "Glad she's found what she wants to do. Must be nice to decide an' then jest go on out an' do it." He laid a bigger stick of wood on the fire.

Now Belinda was puzzled. Perhaps he *was* smitten by Melissa—but he also sounded almost wistful about her goal of teaching. Was there something Rand wished to do—to become—that seemed beyond him? Belinda hardly knew what to say next. This turn in the conversation was a surprise, a puzzle to her.

Before she could think of what response to make, Rand looked at her and smiled. In the firelight she saw his eyes lighten, his cheek crease into a deep dimple.

Now that is definitely a dimple, she caught herself thinking and shifted her weight from one foot to the other in an effort to hide her embarrassment over the unbidden thought.

"Have me the feelin' thet nursin' or teachin' jest isn't in the same class as milkin' cows," he laughed good-naturedly.

Belinda smiled back and took a minute to answer. "Maybe it is," she said slowly. "If one enjoys milkin' cows."

He sobered. Then nodded his head. "Might be at thet," he agreed, "if one enjoyed milking cows."

The fire crackled and the calls and laughter reached out to them from the nearby game. But a silence fell between them as each studied closely the orange-red fingers of the flickering flames.

Belinda gathered from his statement that he had never been fond of farming. She also sensed that there was something else that he felt he would enjoy. Whatever it was, he seemed to consider it unobtainable. Was it? Or was that just Rand's assessment of the situation? Belinda knew that it really was no business of hers—and yet she was interested and concerned for him. She really did care. Would he feel she was interfering if she pressed further? She finally decided to risk asking, hoping that Rand would not see it as prying into his personal life.

"What *might* ya like to do?" she asked softly.

Rand laughed quietly as though his dream were too far-fetched to even mention. Then he turned and studied Belinda carefully to see if she really was interested in hearing. From the look on her face, he could tell that she was.

When he answered, he spoke softly as though his words were for her alone.

"Had me this crazy dream, ever since I was a kid, of makin' things—buildin' with my hands," he said, stretching out his hands before him.

Belinda's gaze fell on the out-stretched hands and she saw

there strength and creativity in the long fingers and broad palms.

"Thet's not one bit crazy," she responded before she could check herself. "No reason in the world why ya can't do thet."

Rand swung to face her. "I ain't got no money to train," he said rather stiffly, "an' I wouldn't know where to go to git trainin' even iffen I did have the money."

"Then learn by doin'," Belinda put in quickly. "Try! Be willin' to try! You might fail—but you'd learn from yer mistakes. Next time you'd know how to go about it better. Watch others and learn from them. There's lots of ways to learn if you really want to. I couldn't go off to school either, so I'm learnin' from Luke. Maybe a builder would let you work with him—" Belinda might have gone on and on had not Rand stopped her.

"I never thought on thet," he said, shaking his head in wonderment. "Never once thought on it. Do ya really think someone might—?"

" 'Course! Why not?"

The voices of the others were drawing closer. Belinda could hear the chatter of Amy Jo and the ladylike laugh of Melissa as they all came to take part in the roasting. But before they reached the yard and the crackling fire, Rand reached out and gave Belinda's hand a quick squeeze.

"Thanks." He spoke simply, and Belinda gave him a brief smile.

She was surprised at the amount of empathy she felt for him. It must be tough to be a young man with dreams and little hope of seeing them realized. If he did become a builder, then there was Melissa who would be hundreds of miles away—

Before Belinda could stop herself she said, "And I'm—I'm sorry," her voice almost a whisper, "thet Melissa is goin' back west. She is very sweet—an' terribly pretty, an' I know—"

Rand looked puzzled. "Melissa? Why? I think thet she should go where she feels home is—where she is needed."

"But—" began Belinda.

Rand seemed to catch on then. "Ya thought I—I liked *Melissa*?"

Belinda just nodded.

"Why?" he asked simply.

"Ya asked about her—talked about her. I—I thought—"

He shook his head. "She seems nice—sure—an' pretty, too, I guess, though I really hadn't noticed." For a moment he hesitated. The group was entering the yard. Taking a deep breath, he hurried on. "Guess I've only been seein' one girl tonight. For a long time, in fact." And Rand gave Belinda such a meaningful look that she flushed with embarrassment. Mumbling something about seeing to the lunch, she fled to the security of the farm kitchen.

Chapter 4

Such a Short Time

As the girls put the clean dishes back in the cupboard, they discussed the party.

"We should do it oftener!" exclaimed Amy Jo. "I haven't had so much fun for jest—years."

Melissa looked dreamy. "Me, too," she admitted. "It was even more fun than the parties in town."

"Really?" demanded Amy Jo. "Ya really had more fun?"

Melissa nodded. "Part of it was having you and Belinda with me," she admitted. "You make everything more fun."

Amy Jo sighed.

"Did I say something wrong?" asked Melissa quickly.

"No—it's jest—well—it's never as much fun when yer not here. Belinda works an' I—I jest help Ma and hang around—an'—"

Melissa stopped to put her arms around Amy Jo's neck, and Belinda felt an odd stab of guilt. *Life must be hard for fun-loving Amy Jo.* She loved people and parties and all of the merriment that went with them. Belinda didn't really miss the fun and excitement of parties. Oh, she liked people, too. But she was usually too tired to even think of social events and companionship, with her nursing taking so much of her time and energy. Maybe—maybe if Jackson did come back to help in the medical practice, some of that would change. Maybe there would be time for other things.

Tears had formed in Amy Jo's eyes. "I—I jest wish ya didn't have to go."

Melissa's eyes filled also. She shook her head slowly. "Oh, I'm so mixed up," she said frankly. "So mixed up. I want to go and I want to stay. I—I just wish there weren't so many miles between here and home. If only we could visit more—could stop in for a week here or there whenever we took the notion. I miss the folks—but I know that I'll miss you just as much."

Belinda too had joined in the tears. All three girls stood wiping eyes and noses. The joy of a few moments before had simply melted away with the sorrow at the thought of soon parting.

"I shouldn't *ever* have come here," sniffed Melissa. "I didn't miss you all one bit before I got to know you."

Amy Jo began to giggle. At first Belinda could see nothing funny and then the thought of how the three of them must look, all huddled together wiping tears and moaning over the fact that they had gotten to know and love one another, struck her as funny also. She joined the laughter and Melissa, thinking of her absurd words, laughed harder than anyone.

"We're silly, aren't we?" ventured Amy Jo. "We all know thet we wouldn't have missed these years fer the world—an' yet— it's so hard to think thet they're over."

Belinda poured out three glasses of milk and nodded toward the table. She helped herself to a slice of Johnny cake and moved to a chair.

"I don't know about you," she said, "but I was so busy servin' that I scarcely ate a thing. I'm hungry."

The other girls followed suit. Melissa chose two gingersnaps and Amy Jo helped herself to sugar cookies.

"But it was a good party," insisted Amy Jo, intent upon getting them back in a festive mood.

"I had quite forgotten there are so many charmers around here!" exclaimed Melissa.

"Charmers!" wailed Amy Jo. "Don't ya mean farmers?"

Melissa doubled over in laughter. Even Belinda smiled.

"Get serious, Amy Jo," giggled Melissa. "Some of these fellows are so-o good looking. And strong. And they are so—so anxious to help a person."

"Help *you*, ya mean," insisted Amy Jo, even though she had had her share of "help" in the games as well.

Melissa giggled again, then sobered.

"I'm sure there won't be nearly as many young men back home," she said quietly.

"See! Thet's another reason ya should stay here," insisted Amy Jo.

Melissa seemed not to hear. "In fact," she went on slowly, "I can't really remember much about the boys at all. They all seemed like such kids."

"They *were* kids when you left," Belinda reminded her. "Don't forget that they have been growin' up too while you've been gone."

Melissa nodded. "Still—I can't really think of a single one that I would be interested in."

"Stay here!" Amy Jo put in. "There's no future in being an ole-maid-schoolteacher."

Melissa made a face and dunked a cookie daintily in her milk. She took a bite and rolled her brown eyes heavenward. "There *are* a number to choose from here, I will admit!" she exclaimed around the mouthful.

"So stay!" said Amy Jo.

"Amy Jo," scolded Melissa good-naturedly. "I didn't come to find a beau. I came to get my teacher's degree."

"So-o," said Amy Jo, "who's to complain iffen ya get lucky?"

Belinda smiled and Melissa laughed heartily. Amy Jo did have a tendency to speak her mind, but she was a lot of fun.

"Talking about young men," said Melissa, finishing her cookie and turning her eyes toward Belinda, "What about that 'wondrous' young fellow"—she flicked a playful glance at Amy Jo—"giving you all the unneeded help with the fire?"

Melissa rolled her eyes again and Belinda felt her face coloring and quickly got up to pour herself another glass of milk. Amy Jo waved a hand carelessly in dismissal.

"Thet was just Rand," she stated.

"Just Rand? What do you mean '*just* Rand'? Where did you find him anyway?"

"He's a neighbor. At least was." Amy Jo stopped answering the questions meant for Belinda and turned to ask one of her own.

"I haven't seen him around fer ages. Where's he been?"

"He was workin' for an uncle—someplace," Belinda said as evenly as her voice would allow.

"Is he back to stay now?"

"Didn't say. He's lookin' for work wherever he can find it."

"Don't tell me you're going to let him get away?" asked Melissa with a teasing smile. "Where'd you meet him anyway?"

"He went to our school."

"I don't remember him. And I'm sure I wouldn't have forgotten—" began Melissa but Belinda interrupted.

"I had forgotten thet ya didn't know him. Guess he was through by the time you came. He was a couple of grades ahead of me."

"Oh! What a shame!" said Melissa, her brown eyes exaggerating her disappointment.

"Ya wouldn't have noticed him anyway; ya were too busy moonin' over Jackson," Amy Jo reminded her, and Belinda was thankful that the conversation went another direction.

"Dear old Jackson," said Melissa. "Wonder what he's going to do with himself after he's done his training?"

Amy Jo was quick to answer. "Might even come back here iffen Uncle Luke can talk him into it. I heard Uncle and Pa talkin'. We really need another doctor here, they said."

Melissa turned her eyes back to Belinda, unasked questions in them. Belinda pretended not to notice.

"Here?" Melissa mused thoughtfully. Then she turned to smile at Belinda. "So-o, you might win after all."

"Don't be silly," began Belinda. "I never wanted Jackson."

"That was the strange thing about it," Melissa said slowly. "I did. At one time, I did. But I couldn't even get him to *look* at me."

Belinda felt the color rising in her cheeks.

"Belinda never wants anybody," put in Amy Jo, "but none

of 'em seem smart enough to notice thet. They all chase her anyway."

"Don't be silly," Belinda said again.

"It's true," insisted Amy Jo. "Jest look at Jackson—an' Walt Lewis at church, an' Tyler Moore, an' this here Rand. I bet ya we'll see him hangin' around in the future an'—"

Belinda couldn't think of anything else but, "Don't be silly," and went to rinse the milk from her glass.

" 'Me thinks thou doth protest too much,' " spoke Melissa, slipping an arm around Belinda's waist, and Amy Jo laughed at Belinda's discomfort.

Then Amy Jo's eyes went to the wall clock and she jumped up from the table. "Wow!" she said. "Look at the time. I've got to git home before Pa comes lookin' fer me. I'll never be able to git up fer church in the mornin'."

Belinda grinned. "I'll just bet ya you will," she countered. "If yer pa has to carry ya."

"Yer right," admitted Amy Jo. "He'll see thet I'm there all right."

She hurried out the door, and Melissa and Belinda put out the light and climbed the stairs by the light of the moon through the window.

Belinda tried to hang on to each precious day, but each one just flew by. Melissa swung between excitement and melancholy, but Amy Jo seemed to have just one mood. She was down—really down. She just *knew* that she would lose all interest in her world when Melissa stepped onto that westbound train.

Belinda was working in the kitchen when Kate came to share afternoon tea with Marty.

"I'm worried 'bout Amy Jo," she admitted. "She jest dotes on Melissa, an' I'm afraid what it will do to her when Melissa goes off home."

Marty had also sensed the loss Amy Jo was facing.

"Clare an' me have talked an' talked about it. It would be so much better fer Amy Jo iffen she had some kind of work, like Belinda, but she ain't at all interested in nursin'. I've talked to her about tryin' to git a job in town, in the store or some such. She has no interest. She's never wanted to teach. Jest likes to draw an' paint—an' I don't see much future in thet fer a girl way out here."

Marty nodded solemnly.

"We've been thinkin' thet she needs to git away from home fer a bit. She's always known jest us—jest life here on the farm. She needs to—what do they say?—'expand her horizons,' get acquainted with somethin' more." Kate twisted her empty cup in nervous hands.

"I came to talk to ya about it. Clare an' me jest don't know whether it be wise or not, an' we'd like yer honest opinion. Clare is talkin' it over with Pa." Kate stopped to take a deep breath. "Ya know thet Amy Jo has always teased 'bout goin' off to Art School, an' me an' Clare jest have never felt right 'bout it. Well, we still don't. But maybe—jest maybe a girl has to try her own wings a bit."

Marty was about to shake her head. She knew little about the big cities that offered art classes, but she wasn't sure that a strong-willed, impulsive girl like Amy Jo should be away on her own.

"Well, we still don't think thet Art School be the place fer her," went on Kate, much to Marty's relief, "but we been wonderin' if maybe a trip west would be good fer her."

"West?" asked Marty, surprise showing in her voice and face. Belinda jerked around from the cupboard, wondering if she had heard Kate correctly.

"Well, she's got lots of kin there an' Melissa has already done a fair bit of travelin' on her own and could look out fer her, an' she could jest spend some time drawin' an' paintin' new things, an'—"

"Ya mean, let 'er go on out with Melissa?"

Kate nodded, her face still full of questions.

Marty thought for a few minutes and then her eyes began to shine. "I think thet's a good idea," she said, and a small smile began to play around the corners of her mouth. "Never did care fer the idea of Melissa travelin' thet far all alone."

Kate let out her breath. "Ya don't think thet me an' Clare are bein' foolish?"

"No."

"Spoilin' her jest because she's our only girl?"

"Oh, no. Like ya say, it should be good fer her to see another part of the world. She needn't stay long." Marty thought for a minute, then went on. "We'll all miss her. She has her own way of makin' things seem more fun."

"I know," sighed Kate. "I can hardly bear me the thought of givin' her up—even fer a short time."

Belinda moved forward. The two ladies at the table seemed to have forgotten all about her. Kate looked up, her eyes misted with tears. "We haven't said anything to Amy Jo yet," she hastened to tell Belinda.

"Of course," Belinda assured her. "I won't mention it."

"Thanks," Kate murmured and rose from the table. "I'd best git back. I left Amy Jo doin' one last sketch of Melissa." She stood for a moment deep in thought. "Iffen Pa thinks thet it's not foolish—then I guess we'll let her go," she stated. Belinda wondered if Kate was secretly praying that Clark would veto the idea.

But Clark did not. He heartily approved of Amy Jo being given the chance to see the West.

"I jest wish thet ya was free so thet ya could go on out with 'em," he told Belinda.

"Oh, I couldn't—not now," Belinda was quick to inform him. "Luke is just so busy. He needs me so much. It will be different if another doctor comes."

And then for the first time Belinda let herself think about how much she would like to be going with the other two girls. It would be so much fun to travel together—to see another part of the world. It would be awfully lonely with both of them gone. Belinda was glad she would have plenty of work to fill her days. She didn't know how she would ever bear Melissa and Amy Jo both leaving her behind if she wasn't so busy.

When Amy Jo was told the good news, she went wild with excitement, just as Belinda had known she would. Melissa was glad for a traveling companion and immediately began to share with Amy Jo all the things they would see and do together. Both girls begged Belinda to try to get some free weeks so she might join them, but Belinda answered firmly that until another doctor arrived, she was needed here.

A wire was sent off to Missie and a reply came back directly, saying that they would be thrilled to have the company of Amy Jo for as many months as her parents would be willing to let her stay.

Bags, trunks and boxes were packed in a flurry of excitement. Belinda missed out on some of the commotion. She had to go back to Luke's to take up her responsibilities in the practice. But she had the afternoon off to see the girls board the train. Never had she seen anyone so enthusiastic as Amy Jo.

"Oh, I wish thet ya were comin' too," she bubbled. "Then it would be jest—jest *wondrous!*"

Belinda nodded. "I wish I were too," she admitted.

"I'm going to miss you so-o much," sniffed Melissa. "You've been just—just like a sister. I wish that we weren't so many miles apart."

There were tearful goodbyes all around. Even Clark wiped a trickle of tears off his cheeks. The girls had many messages to convey to the loved ones out West and were told over and over how to behave themselves among strangers. At last, all too soon for those who stood on the wooden platform once more, the westbound train was chugging off, its whistle sounding shrilly on the afternoon air. Belinda waved her handkerchief with tears running down her cheeks as two excited passengers leaned from the window to wave back.

As the train rounded the distant bend, Belinda turned from her family and the dusty platform, glad that Luke needed her.

Chapter 5

Back to Work

After her two nieces departed, as before, Belinda's days—
and often nights—were filled with assisting Luke. But the
weekends at the farm no longer seemed as inviting and pleas-
urable. Being home with Clark and Marty was a nice break
from the medical practice. But it certainly was not the same
without Amy Jo breezing cheerily in and out of the farmhouse,
and no longer could Belinda tell herself that "soon Melissa will
be back" to share the big house.

The boys in the nearby log house missed their big sister,
too, though Dan and David were reluctant to admit it. Dack
had no inhibitions about it and expressed his feelings openly,
often lamenting the fact that his folks had allowed Amy Jo to
leave.

"She will be home again in a few months and you will appreciate her even more," his mother assured him more than
once.

Kate now visited Marty far more frequently. Often she
brought handwork with her. She could hardly bear the "empty
nest," and left it with the least excuse. Some days she even
went to the fields with Clare, driving the team while he pitched
hay or loaded rock.

Marty, too, missed the energetic Amy Jo. The days slipped
by with no Amy Jo bouncing in and out asking favors, eating
cookies, running errands or bringing bits of news. Marty won-

dered if she should take to the fields herself, but as it was, she had all she could do to keep up with her housework and garden.

When summer had passed into fall, the family began to count the days until Amy Jo would be back home. Then one of her fat, newsy letters had an unexpected request. "Please, please," she begged, "could I just stay for a few more months? I just love it out here. The people are so friendly and there is so much to draw and paint. I've learned so much more about color. You wouldn't believe the colors out here. They are *wondrous*! So different than around home."

Much to Dack's disappointment, Clare and Kate reluctantly agreed that she might have a bit more time and come home for Christmas.

Belinda was disappointed as well. She had been looking forward to getting her cousin back and hearing all about Amy Jo's adventures.

Belinda took a few days off to help Marty with the fall preserving. Marty, thankful to have her at home even for a short time, chatted with her youngest as they worked, catching up on their talks since Belinda had been busy with her nursing duties.

The snow came early, and Marty was doubly glad that she'd had Belinda's help to get in the garden. The menfolk had not been so fortunate with the crops. One field was still unharvested and probably would remain so until spring, with the look of the late fall storms. Clark and Clare discussed the situation and decided to turn the cattle into the field. The herd could forage for what was there; then at least the whole planting would not be lost.

Minor farm accidents and a nasty flu had kept the surgery full. Now measles had visited the neighborhood, and many children and a few adults were down with the disease. So Belinda had little time to really mope about. Still, she looked forward to Amy Jo's letters and read and reread every incident until she had them almost memorized.

Christmas was approaching and Belinda began to count the days again. Amy Jo's return would not be long now. Belinda expected news of her arrival date with each new letter that came, but each time she quickly scanned the pages, the homecoming news was missing. Belinda was sure Clare and Kate would never agree to Amy Jo missing Christmas.

When another bulky letter arrived, Belinda tore open the envelope, quickly looking for a date, but again it was not given.

She was very surprised to read: "Remember when Melissa said there weren't many fellows to choose from out here? Well, she was wrong. One of them is calling on her. She might have forgotten about the young men out here, but believe me, they didn't forget about her! And it didn't seem to take her long to remember Walden when he asked if he could call. Walden came to see her almost as soon as she got home. I guess he was just waiting for her to get back."

So Melissa had a beau! Belinda was not surprised. "Bet Missie was glad ya waited 'til ya got home," Belinda muttered to her faraway niece, then continued on with Amy Jo's letter.

"And just listen to this!" Amy Jo went on. "Walden has a younger brother named Ryan. He is just *wondrous*! I could write pages and pages about him. They are the sons of a neighborhood rancher. Their pa helped Grandpa build the little church. And Ryan is calling on me. Isn't that just wondrous! They usually call on us together. Walden and Ryan both plan on ranching with their pa. Melissa says that the ranch is plenty big enough to support three families. They have a sister, too, but she is crippled. Was thrown from a horse when she was a child and has never had proper use of her legs since. It is really sad, but she is a nice person and doesn't let it get her down. She loves art too and I have spent some time helping her to learn to sketch. She really isn't awfully good at it yet, but she does her best."

Belinda smiled. Amy Jo was as candid as ever. Belinda couldn't help but wonder about the crippled girl. Would she have been able to overcome the fall if she'd had proper medical attention?

"Well, I've got to go," Amy Jo's letter finished up. "Wally and Ryan will be here soon and I must get ready. I will tell you more about him next letter. I would love for you to meet him, but until you do I'll describe him the best I can in a sketch.

"Oh, yes. Please, *please* don't say anything to the folks yet! I don't want them getting all upset about this. I'm not sure yet how Ryan really feels about me, and until he makes his intentions known, there is no use causing any fuss. You understand!

"I guess I should say that I wish you were here. I do miss you—terribly—but I'm afraid I don't wish you were here. If you were, then Ryan likely would have picked you, and I just would have died if that had happened.

"I love you. Amy Jo."

Belinda stood with the letter drooping in her hands. *Amy Jo has a beau—little Amy Jo—and she doesn't want the fact known!* Belinda's thoughts whirled. *Is it dishonest for me to keep it from Clare and Kate?* she wondered. But if she were to tell, what could she say? "Amy Jo likes a young man but she isn't sure yet if he likes her?" That would accomplish very little. No, she'd keep quiet, at least until more facts were known. No good would come of her telling now.

She turned her eyes back to the letter and then remembered the last page—Amy Jo's sketch of her "wondrous" Ryan.

Belinda's eyes looked at an ordinary yet pleasant face. Amy Jo's drawing had even seemed to capture a joyful twinkle in his eyes, and his mouth parted slightly with a hint of a smile. He was boyish-looking, but Belinda reminded herself that Amy Jo was not much more than a girl. But youthful or not, they suited each other somehow, this young man and Amy Jo. Belinda could see why they might take to each other.

Carefully she folded the paper and tucked it and the letter into her top dresser drawer. Deep inside she felt a stirring of loneliness like she had never felt before.

The news did not need to be kept secret for long. Amy Jo's next letter to her folks told them all about Ryan Taylor. She begged and pleaded for them to please, please, give her one more extension of her visit. She wanted to spend Christmas with Ryan and his family. She would be home early in the new year—at least by Easter, she promised—and she sent her love to each one of them, thanking them for their patience and understanding.

Clare and Kate were dumbfounded. They had not realized that their little girl was so grown-up that she might fall in love on her trip out West. Belinda was quite sure they would have kept her closer to home if they had even considered such a possibility. Now the harm was done. Amy Jo was miles away and felt herself deeply in love with a young man that her parents had never seen.

A long letter from Missie, which soon followed, helped the situation a bit. She wrote to Clare and Kate, giving them a detailed account of Ryan and his family. He certainly seemed to be an upright and worthy young man, but that fact did not move him one mile closer to the Davis farmstead. Still, it did manage to reassure Clare and Kate to some degree. It did nothing for Dack. He fretted and cried and declared that Christmas just wouldn't be Christmas without his big sister.

Belinda felt the same way, but she didn't add to the gloom of the family by stating so.

Three days before Christmas, Luke's Abbie had a baby girl. The precious little bundle added new meaning to the season for all of them. She had arrived two weeks early, but though she was tiny, she was wiry and healthy. Belinda felt that she had never seen anyone so small and so sweet.

So they missed Luke's family at the Christmas dinner table too, but the rest of the family gathered as usual. Belinda did not linger for long. If Luke should be called out on an emergency, someone would need to be with Abbie and the children. She ate as hurriedly as she dared, shared in the opening of the gifts and then saddled Copper and headed for town. Marty hated to see her go but knew that Belinda's responsibilities made it necessary.

"Yer first Christmas," Belinda crooned to the tiny Ruth Ann as she held her that evening. "What did ya think about it? Oh, it was a little different this year. No big dinner for ya with all of the cousins and aunts and uncles. Not much fuss and bother in presents because we didn't know ya were coming quite so soon. But the real Christmas—that was the same. This is Jesus' birthday, Ruth Ann. Ya *almost* shared His day. I wonder if He was ever as tiny as ya are." Belinda's finger stroked the soft cheek. "His mama didn't have much of a Christmas either, thet first year. No presents—until later when the Wise Men came—no warm room or fancy dinner. But she did have some guests. Strangers—not family. Shepherds. Not too polished, I would think.

"But I'm sure she was happy. Because she had her little Son. She knew He was special—but she didn't know then jest *how* special. And she didn't know all about the heartache she would suffer because of what people would do to her Son. She just loved and enjoyed Him that first Christmas.

"We don't know what lies ahead for you either, but we know God loves ya—and we all love ya, and I hope and pray that everything waiting for ya in life will be jest good things."

And so saying, Belinda kissed the soft little head and tucked the baby in her crib until her next feeding. Christmas really had been rather special after all.

Chapter 6

Rand

Belinda was getting Ruthie ready for bed when she heard a rap at the door and Luke answer it.

"What now?" moaned Belinda. She had been looking forward to a free evening. But instead of another emergency call for the doctor, Belinda heard a male voice say, "Good evening. Is Miss Davis in?"

Luke replied that Belinda was.

"I'm Rand O'Connel," was the reply. "May I speak to her, please?"

"Come in," invited Luke, and Belinda found her heart skipping and her mind in a flurry.

My, I must look me a sight, she admonished herself and couldn't resist a quick peek in the mirror. She heard Luke seat the guest in the parlor, and then he came through to the kitchen to inform Belinda that she had a caller. "I'll finish with Ruthie. You go ahead," he told her.

"I'm 'most done," replied Belinda, her head still whirling. "I was jest ready to take her on in to her mama."

Luke gently eased the baby from Belinda's arms and walked toward the bedroom, whispering sweet-talk to her. Belinda stood in the middle of the kitchen floor watching him go and wondering what on earth she should do next.

Awareness that someone sat in the parlor waiting for her to make an appearance finally spurred her into action, and she rushed upstairs to her own bedroom, stripping away her soiled apron as she went.

There wasn't time for a thorough cleanup. She pulled off her wrinkled dress and slipped into a fresh one, then attacked her hair with a brush. Its unruly curls gave her some trouble, but Belinda managed to get most of it tucked into the pins. Taking one final look at herself in the dresser mirror, she drew a deep breath and went down to meet her caller.

Rand was seated where Luke had left him on the parlor sofa, twisting his hat nervously back and forth in his hands. At the sight of Belinda he quickly rose to his feet and managed a smile that showed his dimple. Belinda smiled in return, though her nervousness refused to leave her.

"Good evening," she greeted him in proper fashion.

Rand nodded his head slightly and responded in kind.

Belinda didn't know what to say next. Scrambling through her whirling thoughts, she eventually stammered out, "Please—please be seated." She held her hand toward the sofa and then moved to a parlor chair to seat herself.

"I was wondering iffen we might walk instead," Rand answered. "It's a lovely evenin'—an'—I thought thet ya might like some fresh air."

"Thet—thet would be nice," Belinda said in relief. It would be so much easier to walk and chat than to sit and chat. "I'll just grab a shawl."

On her way she informed Luke and Abbie of her plans.

"I—won't be long," she promised.

She was turning to go when Abbie stopped her. "Belinda— feel free to help yourself from the kitchen to serve your young man refreshments."

It was meant sincerely and Belinda appreciated it, but the phrase "your young man" brought the color to her cheeks. Rand was not "her" young man. She scarcely knew him. They had been children in the same country school—nothing more.

She murmured a thanks to Abbie, determined to straighten out the misunderstanding on the morrow, and went to join Rand.

He was still standing, waiting for her. As soon as she appeared, he moved forward to help her with her shawl, then opened the door to allow her to pass out into the twilight.

Rand was right. It was a perfectly beautiful evening. The warmth of the day lingered just enough to keep it from being chilly. The promise of another spring was in the air, and off in the distance Belinda heard a bird singing.

Rand fell into step beside her and they walked a few paces in silence. Breathing in the evening air, Belinda looked skyward where the stars were just beginning to make an appearance, and sighed.

"Long day?" asked Rand solicitously.

Belinda shook her head and laughed slightly. "Not particularly. Just routine things. But the evening always affects me this way. I guess it's my favorite time of day—but I haven't been seeing much of it recently. Baby Ruthie always needs her bath then and the boys need to be tucked in."

"I thought you were a nurse," spoke Rand good-naturedly, "not a nursemaid."

"Oh, I am," Belinda quickly explained. "It's just thet Abbie hasn't really gotten her strength back since Ruthie arrived. Luke still sends her to her bed early—and I love to help with the little ones. Ruthie is such a dear and the boys are no problem at bedtime—much." She finished her speech with another little laugh. "Sometimes they test me," she admitted.

Rand was watching her as she spoke. He nodded his head and gave her a smile.

"I—I haven't seen you around," Belinda said to change the direction of the conversation away from herself, and then bit her tongue. He would think she had been watching for him, expecting him to call. *What a foolish thing to say!* She berated herself silently.

But Rand answered matter-of-factly, "I've been away." He added softly, "I took yer advice."

"My advice?"

"After givin' it some thought, I remembered a man down near my uncle who was a builder. I decided to go see him. He put me right to work—jest like ya said. I learned a lot over the past months."

By the time Rand had finished, Belinda was beaming with pleasure.

"Really? I'm so glad!" she exclaimed and it was clear to Rand that she was.

He smiled warmly, but from the look on his face, Belinda sensed that he really would have rather tossed his hat in the air and whooped, as though he couldn't believe he was actually going to have his dream come true.

"I'm so glad," she repeated.

"I owe it all to you, ya know."

"Nonsense!" said Belinda. "Yer the one who had to take the risk and—and do all the work. And yer the one who had the ability in the first place. I really had nothin' to do with it."

"Not true," insisted Rand. "I would never have tried iffen it hadn't been for you. When we talked thet night, suddenly you made me realize thet it all depended on what I was willin' to do 'bout it. Dreams are fine—iffen they don't jest stay dreams. But they git ya nowhere iffen ya don't put some effort 'long with 'em."

They walked on in silence, each deep in thought. Belinda was truly pleased that Rand had found the courage to take the first step toward becoming a builder. He did seem like a nice young man.

"So now what?" she asked softly, hoping that he wouldn't misunderstand the question and give her interest greater importance than she intended. "What will you and the man down south be building next?"

"I won't be buildin' down there anymore. He kindly taught me all he could—then gave me his blessin' an' sent me on my way to build on my own."

"Here?" asked Belinda in surprise.

"Here," he laughed. "And thet's why I came to see ya first. I wanted to properly thank ya."

Belinda flushed slightly. "But there's no—"

He held up his hand to stop her. "I know what went on in my head," he laughed, "an' I had already given up the dream until ya urged me to try and suggested a way to start. So I know thet I owe ya a heap of thanks."

Belinda smiled and nodded her head teasingly. "Fine," she said. "I accept yer thanks. I'm mighty glad to have had a part in yer decision. I think thet you made the right one."

Rand chuckled along with her.

"Now, fer a proper-like thanks, I'd like to take ya out to supper," he continued.

"To supper?"

"Over to the hotel dinin' room."

"There be no need fer thet," Belinda hurriedly replied, unconsciously dropping to the speech of her parents.

Rand stopped walking and placed a restraining hand on Belinda's arm. He looked down at her, his eyes studying her face in the soft dusk. "I'd like to," he said intensely. "Please?"

Belinda was flustered. Yet what harm could it do to go to supper with a young man in the local dining room? Especially if he felt honor-bound to express his thanks. She swallowed and nodded her head in agreement.

"Fine," she managed. "Fine. If ya like. It would be very nice to go to supper."

Rand released her arm. "Thank ya," he said fervently. "Tomorra?"

Belinda nodded again, trying hard to think ahead to what day "tomorra" was and what commitments she might have. She could not think of any, but she hoped she wasn't making an arrangement she would need to break. "Tomorra," she agreed.

She could scarcely see Rand's face now in the gathering darkness, but she did see him smile.

"I'd—I'd best be gettin' on back," Belinda said, and they began to retrace their steps.

It was a quieter walk back through the darkness. Rand reached out a hand to her elbow on occasion to steady Belinda as they walked over the uneven planks of the boardwalk. She knew the familiar walk like her own bedroom, but she didn't pull away from the offered assistance. Rand was a mannerly young man and would offer the same kindness to any lady he accompanied, she reasoned.

"What will ya build first?" she asked in the darkness.

"I start on a house tomorra. The fella who has the hardware

don't wanna live above it anymore. His wife wants her own house—an' own yard. So he's havin' me build it for 'em."

"That's wonderful! What is the house like?"

Rand chuckled softly. "I wish I knew. That's the only—the only 'fly-in-the-ointment,' so to speak. His wife still hasn't made up her mind, so the next few days are gonna be spent tryin' to get 'er settled on what she wants."

"I wish ya well," laughed Belinda.

They reached the doctor's house and Rand opened the door for Belinda. She suddenly remembered Abbie's proposal.

"Would ya care for some coffee—or—or lemonade? Abbie said we could use the kitchen."

"Not tonight, thank ya. I still have lots of work to do on buildin' plans iffen I'm gonna be ready to show Mrs. Kirby some ideas tomorra."

Belinda's eyes fell to the parlor clock. "Oh, my!" she exclaimed. "It's already late. I'm sorry we took so long."

"Nonsense," cut in Rand. "I won't sleep tonight anyway," and he chuckled.

"I s'ppose, yer pretty excited," agreed Belinda. "Guess I would be, too, if I was about to build my first house."

"The house has little to do with it," Rand informed her, leaving Belinda to puzzle over his statement.

"See ya tomorra night," Rand went on. "What time?"

"I—I guess we should make it—say six-thirty. If thet's okay with you."

"Six-thirty," agreed Rand. "I'll be here."

Just before he closed the door, he turned back to Belinda. "Thank ya," he said sincerely, "for agreein' to walk on such short notice. It was bold of me to jest drop over—but I didn't know how else to see ya."

"It was nice to see you," Belinda heard herself saying and wondered at her frankness. Then with a smile and a tip of his hat, Rand closed the door and was gone.

Chapter 7

Supper

Belinda rushed through the surgery cleanup the next day so she might have plenty of time to make herself presentable. She had never been out to supper with a young man before and her stomach was so knotted up just thinking about it that she wondered if she even would be able to eat.

Over and over she reminded herself that this was simply an opportunity for Rand to say "thank you" for what he considered to be her part in nudging him toward his dream. Belinda quite successfully talked herself into its "common courtesy" aspect rather than seeing it as a social occasion, even though she still felt she deserved no such thanks.

Luke and Abbie didn't look quite as convinced when Belinda explained to them the reason for her not sharing in their usual evening meal. They said nothing but Belinda noticed the sparkle in Abbie's eyes as she nodded a bit knowingly toward her husband.

Aaron and Thomas, along with their older cousin John who was there for a visit, didn't seem to catch the lack of special significance in the event either.

"Why are ya goin' ta eat with a man?" asked Thomas.

"Because—because he has asked me," responded Belinda. "He wants to say 'thank you' by taking me to supper."

"Can't he talk?" inquired Aaron.

"Of course," Belinda answered, her cheeks flushing.

"Then why don't he jest say it?" demanded Aaron.

"Well, he has said it."

"Then why do ya hafta eat over there? Why don't ya eat here with us?"

"Well, he—he—wants to say it again—in another way." Belinda felt flustered. How could one explain such a thing to children?

"I think it's dumb," put in Thomas.

"I think it's dumb," echoed Aaron.

"It's not dumb. It's—it's a—a social nicety," argued Belinda. "A—a kindness. Mr. O'Connel is bein' a gentleman."

The boys thought about that for a moment. Belinda was hoping she had finally succeeded in making them understand and was about to shoo them from her room so that she could finish pinning up her hair in peace.

"Can I come, too?" asked Aaron.

Belinda stopped her pinning and spun to look at the young boy. His earnest eyes looked intently into her face.

"Not—not this time," she answered, trying not to sound unkind.

"Why not?" he insisted.

"Because—because—ya haven't been asked," Belinda said evenly.

Thomas reached out a hand to draw his younger brother back. "He don't got nothin' to thank *you* for, Aaron," Thomas reminded him.

Aaron reached a hand into a trouser pocket and pulled out a fistful of childish treasures. "I'll give him my blue marble," he offered.

"Don't ya understand nothin'?" put in the older, wiser John who had been quietly listening to the whole exchange. "Aunt Belinda is goin' to eat with him 'cause she wants to. It's called courtin'. Pa told me. O'Connel says 'thanks' an' takes her to supper, then she says 'thanks fer the supper' by invitin' him to tea, then he says 'thanks fer tea' by takin' her on a buggy ride. It's called courtin'.'" John finished his factual recital while Belinda stood with her mouth open. She wanted to protest, but

John already was gathering his two younger cousins and herding them toward the door.

"I still wanna go," insisted Aaron.

"People what's courtin' don't take nobody with 'em," explained John patiently.

"Why?" demanded Aaron.

"I dunno. They jest don't. They always jest—"

The voices faded down the staircase and Belinda could hear no more. She turned back to her mirror not knowing whether to laugh or cry. Her brush was still in her hand, and with trembling fingers she finished her hair. She noticed that her cheeks were flushed and prayed that she would regain her composure before Rand arrived.

Rand was there promptly at six-thirty. Belinda heard Thomas answer the door and hurried from her bedroom before the young boys might have a chance to question him or make any inappropriate comments.

Only a few minutes' walk brought them to the town hotel, and as Rand had already spoken to the dining room host, they were quickly seated. Belinda then had the difficult task of deciding what she would like for supper. Her head was not working well. Over and over the words of her nephews chased around her brain.

"Might I suggest the fresh lake trout?" Rand asked and Belinda quickly nodded. Fish would be a nice change and it would also save her the task of deciding.

After their order was given, they had too much time to just sit and feel uncomfortable, to Belinda's way of thinking. Rand seemed perfectly at ease and Belinda couldn't help but wonder where he had found his confidence.

She could think of absolutely nothing to say and felt very foolish just sitting there studying the hands that fluttered nervously in her lap.

"Did ya have a busy day?" Rand questioned and Belinda drew a deep breath, thankful for something to talk about.

She explained briefly some of the events of her day and then asked him about his activities. Rand smiled as he described how he and Mrs. Kirby had gone over and over the houseplans.

"Things are far from settled," he informed her. "She still isn't sure jest what she wants."

"Best not to rush her then, I guess," spoke up Belinda. "Buildin' a new house takes a great deal of thinkin'-on fer a woman. She'll want to be sure it has all the things she's been dreamin' of. If they are left out, she will keep thinkin' of them after she's all moved in, and wishin' that they'd been added. Ya wouldn't want yer first customer to be eternally dissatisfied."

"Where'd ya git so smart?" Rand teased with a chuckle. Then he went on, "I've been thinkin' the same thing. In fact, I talked to Mr. Kirby. Said thet it might be wise to give his wife more plannin' time. Wilson wants a storage shed built and they need a new barn at the livery. Maybe I'd best start there before I take up on thet house."

"What did Mr. Kirby say?" asked Belinda.

"He agreed—rather reluctantly. I think he's jest anxious to git this buildin' over. I'm sure thet he's heard nothin' but 'new house' fer the last several months."

From then on conversation was much easier. In fact, Rand was interesting to talk to and soon had Belinda completely at ease. They talked about the small town, the new developments, the hope for the future, the need for another doctor, and laughed over some of the memories of their shared school days in the little country school.

In no time, it seemed to Belinda, their plates of food arrived; as they enjoyed the tasty meal, the conversation continued. All too soon supper was over and there was really no reason to linger.

"Thank ya," Belinda said sincerely as Rand led her from the dining room. "That was very nice. And now yer 'thank you' is more than paid in full."

Belinda's thoughts went back to John's comment. Her simple "thank you" did seem inadequate. She felt she owed Rand more than that. But even as the invitation to tea lingered on her lips, she refused to utter it. This was not a courtship. This was one friend expressing gratitude to another. She would not consider it to be any more than that.

They walked home slowly, enjoying their chat and the warmness of the evening.

"Where are yer two nieces?" Rand asked. "Wasn't one going back West?"

"Yes. Melissa. But it turned out that Amy Jo went too. She was to be gone only a few months but it has extended on and on. She still isn't home."

"You must miss 'em."

"Oh, I do."

"Will Amy Jo be back soon?"

"I hope so. It seems such a long time—but I fear—I fear that she might not come back at all."

"She likes the West?"

"More than the West. She's found a young man out there," Belinda said simply.

"Is she thinkin' of marryin'?" Rand asked in surprise.

"She hasn't said—but I'm thinkin' she is."

"Isn't she younger than you?"

"A little."

"Do her folks think she's ready to be married?"

Belinda laughed softly, a complete change from her former mood. "Do one's folks ever think a girl ready to be married?" she quizzed teasingly.

Rand smiled, then surprised her by asking, "Do you—*you* think she's ready?"

"I don't know," responded Belinda slowly. "She was always kind of flighty—carefree—but she sounds more serious now. Maybe she is."

They walked in silence for a few more moments.

"Are you?" asked Rand quietly.

"Me? What?" pondered Belinda. She had entirely lost the thread of the conversation.

"Ready fer marriage?" he said simply.

"Oh my, no!" exclaimed Belinda, her cheeks flushing and her composure fleeing. "I—I haven't even thought on such a thing. I'm nowhere near ready. I—I—"

Rand did not press her but, seeing her embarrassment, quickly changed the conversation.

"Luke has him a nice house. It has lots of special features. Thet's the kind of houses I want to build—'stead of just straight

box-type. Wonder iffen he'd be so kind as to let me peek in his
attic someday to study the rafter structure."

Belinda was surprised at the sharp turn in subjects but
mumbled that she was sure Luke wouldn't object. His house
had been purchased, along with the practice, from the late Dr.
Watkin.

With the talk back on safer ground, Belinda regained her
composure and enjoyed the rest of the walk home.

She thanked Rand for the meal and the lovely evening, but
she did not extend an invitation to tea.

"May I see ya on the weekend?" Rand asked and Belinda
was quick to turn him down.

"I go to the farm for the weekends," she said. "It's the only
time thet I get to see the folks."

"I understand," he said kindly. "Then perhaps I will see ya
in church on Sunday."

Belinda nodded.

After he had left, Belinda chided herself for not being more
hospitable. He was a fine young man and she could do with
friendship. *But why, why,* she asked herself as she pressed cool
hands to warm cheeks, *why do I get the feeling that he is thinking differently about it than me?* Was there more to his simple
question concerning her preparedness for marriage than he had
expressed? Surely it was all in her head. She determined to put
it from her thinking completely.

Rand took his place in church on Sunday with a row of
neighborhood young men and did not greet Belinda more than
by doffing his hat and wishing her a pleasant good morning.

She saw him chatting with Clark for some length after service, though, and was careful to keep herself busy with some
of her friends.

On the way home Clark chose to share the earlier conversation with Marty, and Belinda could not help but overhear.

"Thet young O'Connel fella is back. He's been learnin' the
buildin' trade an' wants to do his buildin' here-about now."

"Thet's nice," said Marty agreeably. "Does he think there'll
be enough work?"

"He's already lined him up several jobs. Seems ambitious enough."

"Thet's nice," said Marty again.

"He was wonderin' iffen some of our young fellas might be interested in workin' fer 'im," went on Clark.

"Some of ourn?" asked Marty, taking a new interest in the conversation.

"Yeah. Clare's or Arnie's. Promised I'd ask."

"They're jest boys," offered Marty.

"Old enough to work. I was doin' a man's job by the time I was their age."

Marty nodded. That was likely true. It was easy for her to forget how quickly time marched forward and how quickly her grandsons were growing up.

"Do ya think any of 'em might be interested?" she asked.

"Don't know," responded Clark. "But I'll mention it like I promised. Clare's Dan might be. Don't think he has him much interest in farmin'."

It was true. They had all sensed it.

"What do ya think Clare will say about it all?" asked Marty next.

"S'ppose he'll want Dan to be a-doin' what brings 'im pleasure," Clark responded, and clucked to the team to hurry them up.

Belinda thought that the conversation was over. But Clark continued, "Good to see thet young fella back agin. Seems like a fine young man. I'd be right glad to see Dan workin' with the likes of 'im." And then as an afterthought, "Now why ya s'ppose Amy Jo couldn't have stayed on here an' taken up with 'im 'stead of goin' off west an' meetin' someone we don't even know?"

"Who knows the ways of the heart?" asked Marty, and the conversation was finally dropped, much to Belinda's relief.

Chapter 8

Amy Jo

A wire from Amy Jo simply stated that she would be home for Easter as promised. They should meet the afternoon train on Good Friday. She did not mention her young man, and the family wondered if the little romance had ended. Secretly, Kate prayed that it might be so, though she did hope her impetuous daughter had not been hurt by the whole experience.

The wire arrived only two days before the noted Friday, and the whole family was in commotion preparing for Amy Jo's return.

Belinda was glad that she was busy with patients and chafed impatiently when things slowed down for the day. To get herself through the long evening waiting for the morrow, she busied herself in Abbie's kitchen doing some special baking. Thomas and Aaron pulled up chairs and leaned on the counter, watching the dough taking shape in the blue mixing bowl.

"Whatcha makin'?" Aaron began.

"Cookies. Can't ya tell," observed Thomas. "See, she's got sugar an' eggs an' butter all stirred together."

"It might be cake," defended Aaron. "Mama puts all them things in cake."

"This time it is cookies," put in Belinda.

"What kind?" asked Aaron.

"Apple-sauce cookies," answered Belinda.

"Ummm," said Aaron. "My favorite."

"You say thet 'bout any kind," rebuked Thomas.

"That's 'cause I like 'em," said Aaron with a stubborn set to his chin.

"They're not yer favorite, then, iffen ya like 'em all," argued Thomas.

Belinda was in no mood for childish spats. "They are Amy Jo's favorite. Her *real* favorite," she hastened to inform the children.

"Are ya bakin' 'em jest fer her?" asked Aaron dolefully.

"Yes—but no. Not all fer her. We'll give her some—but you can have some, too."

Aaron seemed satisfied.

"When's she comin'?"

Belinda lifted her eyes to the clock. "In about—about forty-two hours," she responded.

"Forty-two? Thet's a long, long time!"

"Does two days sound better?" asked Belinda.

"Two is better'n forty—forty-what?"

"Forty-two."

"Yeah, forty-two. Two's better'n that."

"Ya silly," cut in Thomas. "She comes when she comes. Don't make no difference what ya call it." Then he thought of his statement for a moment and directed a question to Belinda. "Is forty-two and two days the same long?"

Belinda smiled. "Two whole days are forty-eight hours, but it's not quite two whole days now. Instead of forty-eight, it's about forty-two," she explained to the boy.

"It still seems a long time," insisted Aaron.

"We only got the message this mornin'," Belinda reminded them.

"Forty-two is still a long time," Thomas agreed with his brother.

"Bet the cookies'll all be gone by then," Aaron said, eyeing the dough as it was placed on the cookie pans.

"We'll hide some," suggested Belinda.

Aaron grinned. He loved secrets. Then he sobered. "But only a few many," he cautioned.

When the first cookies were taken from the oven, Belinda

poured two glasses of milk and sat the boys at the table with three cookies apiece. They chattered contentedly as they ate, and Belinda found their company a help in filling the long evening hours.

"Ya gonna hide some fer 'Connel?" Aaron surprised Belinda by asking.

"Fer what?" she asked.

"Not 'what,' " corrected Thomas. "People aren't 'whats.' Papa says."

He stopped to dip a corner of his cookie into his milk and then sucked the moisture out.

" 'Connel," repeated Aaron.

"Oh, you mean Mr. O'Connel."

"S'what I said," remarked Aaron, then followed his brother's lead in dunking a cookie. Not quite as adept at dunking, a soggy piece of his cookie fell into the glass and he ran to the cupboard for a spoon.

"Are ya?" he asked as he returned to the table.

"No-o-o. He lives at Mrs. Lacey's boardinghouse. She cooks for him."

"Bet he doesn't git cookies like this."

"Aaron," spoke Thomas impatiently. "Jesus didn't say we gotta share with ever'body."

"That's not what I meant," hastened Belinda. "God wants us to share with others. It's jest that sometimes—" Now she was talking herself into a corner. She would never know how to explain to the two boys. She quickly changed her tack.

"How would ya like to take a couple cookies to yer papa? He is busy in his office, but I think he would like some cookies and milk."

The boys loved the idea, and Aaron was given a small plate with the cookies and Thomas a glass of milk and they hurried off to take the offering to Luke.

By the time Belinda finished her baking, "hid" a few cookies to present to Amy Jo, and cleaned up the kitchen, it was late and she was ready for bed. She mentally scratched this first long day of waiting from her calendar and hoped the next day would be filled with jobs that needed to be done. *I'm awful glad,* she told herself as she climbed into bed, *that Amy Jo didn't send that wire any sooner!*

The next day was quiet in the office, so Belinda asked Abbie if there were any errands she could run. Abbie did need a few things from the store, so Belinda donned a light shawl, her spring hat, and set off with a basket over her arm.

The purchases did not take long, and she whiled away a few more minutes looking in shop windows. The afternoon still stretched on before her and she did not look forward to trying to find something to fill it.

She strolled home, studying neighborhood gardens and the spring flowers beginning to make their appearance. She was so preoccupied that she went right on by Luke's house without even realizing it.

"Out for an afternoon stroll?" The nearness of the voice startled her and she jumped. "I'm sorry. I didn't mean to catch ya off guard," the voice apologized. "You were jest so deep in thought."

Belinda looked up to see Rand smiling down on her. "I—I guess I was," she admitted, looking about her to get her bearings. "I—I was off doin' some errands fer Abbie and coming home I was—was admirin' the spring flowers an' I 'most forgot what I was about, I guess." She laughed at herself and turned to head back in the right direction.

"May I walk along with ya?" he asked. "I'm headin' fer the hardware store."

"Certainly," answered Belinda and shifted her basket only to have it gently taken from her hands.

"I heard around town that ya have some good news."

"Oh, yes! I can hardly stand the wait. I guess thet was why my thoughts were so far off a moment ago."

He nodded and fell into step beside her.

"What happened to the young man?" he asked after they had walked a short distance together.

Belinda lifted her eyes to look at him. "We don't know," she said honestly. "Amy Jo said nothin' about him in the wire. Perhaps—perhaps it wasn't so serious after all."

"That's unfortunate," said Rand. "I hate to hear of love affairs gone sour."

Belinda wasn't sure if the comment was teasing or serious. She could think of no response, so she held her silence.

"What's Melissa doin' these days? Teachin'?"

"Yes," Belinda answered, wondering again if Rand might be interested in Melissa. "She got a school the very first term after she got back home. It's close enough that she can stay at home and ride horseback to classes each day."

"That's nice," responded Rand. And then he added as an afterthought, "I don't suppose she'll do thet fer too many years."

Belinda looked at him questioningly.

"Must be lots of ranchers out there who can see how pretty she is," he explained. "One of 'em is bound to catch her eye one of these days."

"She—she already has a beau," Belinda offered, carefully watching Rand's face.

He brightened. "Has she now?" he said. "Thet's nice." Then he quickly added, "Is Melissa older or younger than you?"

"Older," said Belinda. "A bit."

They had reached Luke's gate and this time Belinda had no intention of missing it again. She reached for her basket and said that she must be getting in to see if she could be of any help to Abbie.

Rand reluctantly gave up the basket and tipped his hat, saying he hoped to see her again soon. Then he was gone, and Belinda went around to the back door and into the kitchen.

I never even thought to ask him how his building is goin', she chided herself. *He'll think me most uncarin'.*

The next morning Belinda and Luke were so busy that she began to fear they would still be in the office sewing up cuts and administering medication when Amy Jo's train whistled its way into town. Why couldn't some of the cases have been spread out over the past two days?

Luke must have read her agitation.

"Don't worry," he soothed, "when it's time for that train,

you'll be on the station platform. Anything that's going on here I can handle alone."

Belinda still fretted. She had already missed the morning Good Friday service in the little church. *If only patients could be regulated,* her thoughts whirled around unreasonably, *instead of coming by bunches at the wrong times!*

But she said nothing out loud. She turned her attention back to the task at hand and hoped that by the time the train was due, the office would have cleared out.

At last the final patient was on the way out the door, and Belinda took a deep breath and looked around her. There was cleaning up to be done, but the clock on the wall said there were still forty-five minutes until train time. If she hurried she would make it just fine.

"I would like to say I'll do the cleaning," said Luke, "but I promised the Willises that I'd drop by. Mrs. Willis hasn't been able to shake that nasty cough she developed when she was carryin' her last child."

"It's fine," responded Belinda. "I have plenty of time."

"Do you mind giving Abbie a bit of help with the youngsters?" asked Luke. "I know she wants to meet the train, but it's kind of hard for her to carry the baby and watch two rambunctious boys."

Belinda smiled. "I'll be glad to help," she assured him. "Those boys and I have a few cookies to deliver."

Belinda hurried to clean the room and sterilize the instruments. Amy Jo would soon be back home where she belonged. Belinda hoped that her niece would never be tempted to leave home again. It was far too lonely without her.

Belinda finished her duties and rushed up to her room to get ready. She took the remaining apple-sauce cookies from their hiding place and carefully placed them in a small decorated tin. *Aaron will want to carry them,* she noted to herself. Leaving them on the kitchen table, she went to see what assistance she could give Abbie.

Abbie was just putting the blanket around the baby. The two boys were already on the front step. Belinda gave the cookie tin into Aaron's care and offered to carry the baby. It was only a brief walk to the station, but by the time they arrived Belinda's arms were tired. She couldn't believe how much little Ruthie had grown in such a short time. She wished they had one of those baby prams she had seen pictured in a Sears Roebuck catalog.

When they joined their excited family on the platform, Clark took Ruthie and Belinda was glad to give her arms a rest. Cousins shouted at one another and raced about. Scoldings followed and then threats and finally the younger members were firmly seated on the bench beside the station and told to remain there until the train arrived, much to their chagrin.

Finally the far-off whistle was heard and then the distant thunder of the metal wheels told them that the train would soon be there.

Kate stood with white face and hands clasped tightly together. "Oh, I can hardly wait to see her," she said to the little cluster of family. "I never dreamed when we let her go thet she'd be gone so long. When she kept stayin' an' stayin', I felt so frightened—so frightened thet she wouldn't be comin' back. I'm so glad—so glad thet she is. I jest hope thet she isn't hurt over thet there boy. But there are lots of fine young men around here fer her. She's still so young—so young."

Belinda had never heard Kate go on so. She accounted it to nerves.

"I jest hope thet she won't miss the West too much. Maybe she'll have it all outta her system by now. Same with thet young man. My, I hope thet she doesn't moon over losin' him. I scarce could bear a mopin' girl." Kate turned to Belinda, her thoughts tumbling over one another in her excitement. "You'll have to watch out fer her. You always was good at talkin' her outta her dark moods. You could introduce her to some of the young people in town here—like thet O'Connel boy. Pa says he's real fine. Dan's gonna go work fer 'im as soon as school classes are out."

That was news to Belinda, though she wasn't surprised. She was surprised, however, at her feeling of reluctance to be a matchmaker between Amy Jo and Rand. She felt hesitant. Were they right for each other?

Then the train was pulling up beside them, and they all

moved back a step so Kate might be the first one to greet her girl.

Will she have changed? wondered Belinda. Might she have had her heart broken by the young Ryan? Belinda hoped not. Amy Jo had seemed so taken by him. Yet Amy Jo was impetuous. Perhaps she had now forgotten all about him.

And then Amy Jo was stepping down from the passenger car. Radiant, her brownish-red hair was swept atop her head becomingly and her light-green traveling dress fit her to perfection. Her complexion was flawless with no longer a trace of the hated freckles. She walked with poise and decorum. Amy Jo had left a girl and had come back to them a young woman. Belinda held her breath.

Kate swept Amy Jo into her arms and held her closely, weeping with joy. It seemed a long time until Belinda had her turn.

"You look wonderful," she said with a slight laugh. "Jest— jest so—so—vibrant!"

Amy Jo laughed merrily.

"That's what love does for one," she whispered in Belinda's ear.

Belinda pulled back to look into the violet eyes.

"Ya mean ya still—? But yer home now—many miles from—"

But Amy Jo silenced her with a little shake of her head. She turned glowing eyes to the family group.

"Everyone!" she called excitedly. "Everyone! I want ya to meet Ryan. We've come home to be married."

Belinda hardly heard the gasps around her she was so busy trying to get her own startled thoughts under control. She raised her eyes toward the bubbling Amy Jo and for the first time noticed a young man who stood behind her. At Amy Jo's words he took a step forward and reached out a possessive hand to take Amy Jo's arm. He smiled and tipped his hat to Kate, then to Marty, and Belinda saw Kate's face turn white.

"Oh, my!" Belinda said under her breath. "Oh, my!" Then she looked again into the deep-blue eyes and tanned face of the young rancher. Amy Jo had sketched a good likeness. Belinda felt that she would have known the young man anywhere. This was indeed Amy Jo's Ryan.

After the initial shock, the family was quickly captivated by Amy Jo's young man. Even Kate, who hated the thought of losing her Amy Jo to the West, had to admit that Ryan would make a wonderful son-in-law.

"Iffen she had jest given us a bit of warnin'," Marty kept saying, shaking her head, "we wouldn'ta all stood there with our mouths a'hangin' open."

But warning was not Amy Jo's way. That would have spoiled her "surprise." The young man Ryan did apologize several times to Clare and Kate. "I wanted to ask for her hand properlike," he informed them, "but Amy Jo wanted to make the announcement herself."

It seemed that he was willing to let Amy Jo have her own way in all matters concerning their wedding.

"I want to be married on June first," Amy Jo insisted. "Thet is the day Melissa and Wally have chosen, and Ryan and I decided thet as we couldn't have a double wedding, the family being scattered so, thet we'd do the next best thing and be married on the same day, here."

Kate was sure she would never be ready for a wedding by the first of June, but Marty and Anne and even Nandry all pitched in, and things for Amy Jo's trousseau began to take shape.

"Why don't we git Mrs. Simpson to sew the gown?" asked Marty. "She does a wonderful job and she is so quick with her stitchin'."

Mrs. Simpson was still very much in demand as a seamstress and had even purchased her own machine, so Marty saw very little of her. But arrangements were made and Amy Jo's cream-colored wedding gown began to take shape under the skilled hands.

At first it didn't seem real to Belinda. But as item after item—two new everyday dresses, a travel outfit, snowy white underthings as well as two quilts, dish towels and other household linens—was spread out on the bed in the spare bedroom at the farm, she had to admit that it was indeed true. *Our Amy Jo is getting married!* Amy Jo, their little girl. Amy Jo, their bit of sunshine. And many miles away, somewhere out West, Melissa too was excitedly preparing for her big day. Belinda felt as if she was being left behind.

The frantic preparations kept Belinda more than occupied until June the first arrived. The day was beautiful, and she slipped the cool mint-green dress over her head as she got ready to join her lovely niece at the front of the church where she would solemnly declare her love and commitment to Ryan.

"Oh, my!" Belinda couldn't help but exclaim when she caught her first glimpse of the bride standing in the middle of her family's living room. Kate was fluttering around her, making sure the dress was hanging properly on the slim figure.

"That soft, creamy material an' the lace trim are jest *perfect* with your hair," Belinda commented, giving Amy Jo a careful hug. "It's truly *wondrous!*" And they laughed together.

Later, Belinda could not keep the tears from forming in her eyes as she listened to the two young people make their promises. Amy Jo was no longer theirs. She belonged to Ryan now, perhaps at the same moment Melissa too was repeating her marriage vows.

It was a lonely and rather subdued Belinda who went up to bed that night after the festivities of the day were all over and the wedded couple had left for their honeymoon trip, home to their West.

Belinda wondered who would shed the most tears that night, she or Kate? She knew they all would miss Amy Jo, their "vibrant" one, something awful.

Chapter 9

An Accident

Belinda sure had missed Amy Jo while she was out West, but it was always with the hope that she soon would be coming home. Now Amy Jo was making a home of her own many miles away from Belinda.

Melissa too! she mourned. *And all at the same time!*

"I know ya miss the girls," Marty said to Belinda. "Maybe Luke could get along without ya for a few weeks an' ya could go on out ta see 'em."

"Mama," Belinda reminded her, "a few months ago I woulda jumped at the chance. I was so lonely for them both, and I'da given anything to be able to see them. But not now. Now they're both new brides. They wouldn't want me hangin' around. Besides, I would feel out of place. It's not the same as it used to be. We wouldn't have the same—the same closeness as before."

Marty nodded in agreement. Belinda was right. It wasn't the same anymore.

Belinda looked about at her world. Why did things have to keep changing? Spring, without slowing down even for a minute, turned to summer and summer to fall. Why, one hardly had time to turn around and things were all new and different again. In the fall little Thomas would be off to school. The next thing they knew it would be Aaron's turn—and then wee Ruthie's. Already she was sitting up alone, reaching for things and pulling herself up in her crib. She had scarcely even been a baby at all.

Things had seemed so simple, so secure when Belinda had been a child going to school and sharing girlish games with Amy Jo, her constant companion. But life went on and no amount of "digging in one's heels" seemed to slow it down.

Belinda had never been so lonely in her life. She would have had a most difficult time of it had she not been so busy. Luke was right—they certainly needed another doctor in the town.

The thought of another doctor immediately turned Belinda's attention to Jackson. What was Jackson like now? He had been a nice young fellow when they had been schoolmates. Was it possible that after all this time she might be drawn to him? Belinda allowed herself a few minutes of imagining and then sharply rebuked herself; by now Jackson likely had another girl. *Perhaps he's even married,* she told herself.

But Belinda didn't really think that Jackson had married. She saw his mama every Sunday at church, and Mrs. Brown spoke often of her son and his medical career—she had never mentioned anything about his marrying or even having a young lady, to Belinda's knowledge. Belinda pushed the thoughts of Jackson aside and thought instead about Rand.

Rand dropped by occasionally and in Belinda's loneliness she welcomed his company. The little town seemed so confining and the farm home that she had loved so very lonely. Rand was awfully busy, working from sunup to sunset every day of the week except Sunday, and there was very little time for him to make calls. He had been to the Davises for Sunday dinner on a few occasions, but Belinda hesitated to offer an invitation very often lest he get the wrong idea.

When summer had turned to fall, Rand stopped by one evening and suggested a walk. Belinda was only too glad for the diversion. He apologized for his busyness and asked Belinda how her days had been filled.

" 'Ills an' spills'," Belinda responded. "That's what Luke calls it. Sickness and accidents. That's about all I see or do."

Rand looked thoughtful. "Is nursin' losin' some of its charm?" he inquired.

Belinda flushed. "No. No, not really. Fact is, I don't know how I'd ever bear livin' without it. I'm jest—jest restless I guess."

"Still missin' Amy Jo?"

Belinda nodded. She didn't trust her voice.

"Maybe you've outgrown nursin'," said Rand. "Maybe it's time fer ya to take on a new challenge."

"Like what?" asked Belinda innocently.

"I can think of one," admitted Rand. When Belinda did not question him, he went on slowly, "But I promised myself thet I wouldn't speak of it yet. Not 'til I have this Kirby house finished and the cash in the bank."

Rand's statement puzzled Belinda, but her thoughts dashed ahead to the Kirby house. "Mrs. Kirby finally got worked out jest what she wants?"

"I've been buildin' on it fer the past two weeks."

Belinda's eyes began to shine and she imagined the excitement of watching something take shape under one's hands.

"Oh, I'd love to see it sometime. Could I?"

Rand laughed at her enthusiasm. "I'd love to show ya," he promised, "but not yet. There's not much to see now. But jest as soon as I have somethin' to show I'll give ya the grand tour— how's thet?"

Belinda smiled her thanks in anticipation. *Just think of havin' your own house,* her thoughts raced. *Melissa and Amy Jo both have their own . . .*

"Dan likes working with ya," she said, to slow down her imaginings.

"He's good," said Rand. "Fer a fella so young, he catches on real fast. An' he isn't afraid of work either."

They had reached Luke's front gate. Belinda stood silently gazing at the night sky. She was about to say that she should go in, but she lingered, enjoying the lovely evening and the company.

Rand surprised her by reaching for her hand. "I'm sorry I've been so busy," he said softly. "Once I git a house or two built an' git some cash on hand, I can slow down some."

"I understand," said Belinda, touched that he would care

about her loneliness. He was really very kind.

"Could we go for a drive on Sunday?" asked Rand, and Belinda assured him that she would enjoy that.

"See ya then," Rand whispered, lifting her fingers to his lips before releasing her hand. Then he was gone, his long strides taking him quickly toward the boardinghouse.

Belinda stood watching him go, her heart fluttering and bewilderment on her face. She looked down at her slender fingers as though expecting his kiss to show there, and her breath caught in a little gasp. What might that Sunday drive hold for her, she wondered. She opened the gate quietly, and thoughtfully made her way up the walk.

But the Sunday drive was not to be. After the morning service the family had gathered at Clark and Marty's for dinner. Nandry's Mary and Jane had both married and now had homes of their own, and on this Sunday Mary was with her Jim's family and Jane was down with a bad cold. So Belinda was the only girl there. The boys played their games in the yard as usual and the men talked on the back veranda until the call for dinner.

Belinda was about to give the signal when there was a commotion in the yard. Someone was running and there were frantic calls and yells of "Come quick! Come quick!"

"What is it?" Belinda heard Clark call, and young John screamed back in fright, "The bull's got Abe. Quick! He'll kill 'im. Quick!"

Clare was on his feet in a flash. The bull was a new one to the farm and no one knew his temperament. All the youngsters had been warned to stay away from his pen until he was declared safe. Now Clare was running toward the barnyard with Arnie and Luke right behind him.

It was then that Belinda heard the farm dogs barking and the cattle bawling. The whole place seemed to be in an uproar.

"Grab a pitchfork!" Clare shouted over his shoulder, and Luke veered toward the barn to comply.

Clare flung himself over the bullpen fence. Belinda could see nothing more after he entered the corral, but she could hear shouts and dogs barking and angry bellows from the bull.

"Oh, dear God, no," Belinda heard someone say beside her and realized that her mother had joined her on the veranda, her eyes fixed on the fence beyond.

"Mama, go back in," warned Belinda.

But Marty held her ground and soon Kate and Anne had joined her. "What is it?" Kate choked out.

Belinda could not answer. Her eyes on the bullpen, she prayed that Clare would be there in time. Arnie, too, had climbed the fence to face the enraged bull, and Luke was running toward them, pitchfork in hand.

It was Arnie who came back over the wooden fence, the limp form of his young son in his arms, while Clare and the dogs distracted the bull. Only when Luke challenged the bull with the pitchfork did he break away from Clare and run bellowing toward the far end of the pasture.

Dinner was forgotten as Abe was placed on the living room sofa and a white-faced doctor-uncle bent over him, checking his vital signs and feeling for broken bones.

Belinda could see that Clare, too, needed a doctor, but he waved her aside and lifted the rifle from the back porch.

"I won't have a critter on the place that endangers children," he mumbled through still lips, and a few moments later they heard the crack of the gun.

Arnie sat silent, head in his hands and his shoulders shaking. He could not bear even to look at Abe.

"He's dead," he kept muttering. "I know he's dead."

There was too much happening for Belinda to sort it all out. Youngsters were wailing, women were crying, grown men were trembling with the tragedy.

Then Belinda's training and experience as a nurse suddenly took over. Luke needed her. This was an emergency. She was supposed to know how to act in an emergency.

True, it had never been a loved one before. That made it so different. She remembered many years before when she had heard Luke say that it was always so much harder when it was a child, and that he hoped and prayed he would never need to tend one of his own family.

And now Abe lay deathly white and blood-spattered, and

Luke would need to fight with all that he knew to try to save him. Belinda braced her shoulders, wiped away her tears and steeled herself to join him.

Luke's hand was still on the boy's pulse. Belinda could not voice the question she knew she should ask, but Luke sensed her presence and without looking up spoke to her. "We need to get him to town. He needs attention immediately. I have nothing here. He shouldn't be moved, but we have no choice. He's in bad shape, Belinda."

"Have ya—have ya—found where he's hurt?"

"He has some broken ribs. I hope his lungs are okay, but I'm worried. His left arm is badly broken. His neck and back seem all right, thank God."

Belinda looked down at the ashen face of her nephew. It all seemed so unreal—like a nightmare.

"Clare needs some tendin', too," she said, "but he wouldn't stop fer me to check him. I don't know where he's hurt, but I saw blood, and his shirt is all torn and dirty and—" Suddenly the tears were streaming again, and Belinda wanted to throw herself onto her bed and let the sobs shake her body. She fought hard to control herself and finally managed to stifle the flow.

"I'll tell Pa we need the team," she said to Luke and turned back to the family members who crowded in about them, hankies to faces and tears flowing.

"We need to get him to town," Belinda said as calmly as she could. "Luke has nothin' here."

"Then he's—he's still—" sobbed Anne, unable to finish her question, and Belinda reached out a hand to ease her into a chair.

"He's hurt—bad," Belinda said honestly, "but we'll do all we can."

It was a long trip into town. Anne was so distraught that Arnie had left her in Marty's care. Belinda prayed silently all the way as she sat beside the boy on the floor of the wagon. She knew Luke was praying too and that those at the farm would be doing the same. Abe roused on the way and cried out because of the intense pain, then slipped into unconsciousness again.

At last Clare pulled the team up before the doctor's residence, and Luke and Arnie gently carried the youngster in to the surgery table. While family members waited outside, Luke carefully went over the young boy once more. Though the ribs were broken, Luke thanked God that there was very little blood showing on the young boy's lips. Perhaps the internal injuries were not too great. A careful check of his pulse and breathing told Luke that he had not gone into shock.

Luke administered drugs and, with Belinda assisting him, set the mangled arm the best he could. He let Arnie and Clare in to see the boy before sending them back to the farm with the latest news of his condition. Then began the long vigil.

Abe was in and out of consciousness. When he awoke he murmured pleas for his mother, and Anne was soon there to whisper soothing words through trembling lips. Luke did not want Abe stirring because of the broken ribs and so kept the boy sedated much of the time. Family members came and went quietly, suffering with Abe as their hearts ached for his parents. But eventually the boy began to improve, and by the time a week had passed, Luke was gently propping him up with pillows to discourage pneumonia. By the end of two weeks the family was confident that Abe would get better. He still had a long way to go, but daily they prayed their thanks to God that his life was spared.

Clare had a multitude of bumps and bruises, but miraculously no broken bones. He said the farm dogs took the brunt of the bull's charges, finally distracting the animal from him.

When Abe was well enough to be moved on home, Luke and Belinda were able to again get a full night's sleep. But it wasn't over yet. Luke's doctor-eyes told him that. He would need to have a chat with Arnie—and how he dreaded it.

Chapter 10

Concern

Luke watched young Abe closely, making regular house calls to Arnie's. He said he was pleased with the boy's general progress. Still, Belinda had a strange feeling that Luke was looking for something and was not completely satisfied with how things were going. She didn't quite dare ask him about it, afraid of what he would say.

Arnie hardly let Abe out of his sight. He was constantly reminding the lad to be careful, to watch his step, to slow down when running. Belinda wondered if Arnie's worrying would turn his son into a sissy.

"What was Abe doin' in thet bullpen anyway?" she asked Dack one weekend when she was home. "Didn't he hear Clare say that everyone was to stay away from thet bull?"

"Our ball went in there, an' Abe thought thet he could jest climb in and out real quick an' no one would ever know," Dack explained.

Belinda shook her head. "When adults make rules, they have reasons," she continued. "Abe is sufferin' because of his disobedience—and the rest of the family has suffered, too, because of him. Besides thet, yer pa lost an expensive bull."

"I know," said Dack, his head lowered. Then his eyes came up. "But it wasn't my fault, Aunt Belinda. Honest."

Belinda reached out to ruffle the mop of red hair. "I'm not blamin' you, Dack," she said. "And I shouldn't scold ya. I jest

80

don't want ya to forget the lesson."

Rand came one Sunday to take Belinda for the promised drive. She bundled up warmly against the brisk fall wind and settled herself on the high buggy seat beside him.

"Where would ya like to go?" he asked her.

"I can't think of anyplace in particular," Belinda responded with a shrug. There was really nothing that scenic to see. Belinda had seen the neighborhood farms dozens of times. She was not aware of anything new to see in the whole area unless some farmer had put up a new hog barn or machine shed. True, the fall leaves could be beautiful, but most of the color of the fall already lay strewn over the pastures and fields.

"We could drive into town and see the Kirby house," he suggested.

"Is it ready?" she asked in excitement.

"No, not finished yet. But at least there is enough of it fer ya to get some idea of what it will be."

"Oh, let's!" cried Belinda. "Unless it's too far to go."

"Yer sure ya'll be warm enough?" he wondered.

She assured him that she would and the team was turned onto the road to town.

"How's Abe?" asked Rand, and Belinda answered that he seemed to be recovering nicely. The talk was of little bits of news from town and community. Belinda noticed again that Rand was an easy person to talk to.

When they reached the building site, Rand tied the horses securely and gave Belinda a helping hand down over the buggy wheel.

"It's a bit awkward to get into the house yet," he admitted. "I was goin' to wait until the steps were in place before bringin' ya on over."

Belinda laughed. "I'll manage fine," she said, eyeing the makeshift stepping blocks.

The house was bigger than Belinda had imagined. She wandered through the main-floor rooms, trying to picture in her mind's eye what they would look like when they were completed and furnished, with a family living in them. *It must be fun to have a house,* she mused. For a moment she almost envied Mrs. Kirby.

"This must be the parlor," she commented as she walked. "And the dinin' room and kitchen through there, with a pantry over there. But what's this?"

"Mrs. Kirby wants a mornin' room," answered Rand.

"A mornin' room? I've never heard of such."

"All the finer homes used to have them—accordin' to Mrs. Kirby. The ladies of the house sat in them and did needle work while the maids cleaned the rest of the house."

Belinda looked at Rand in surprise. "Is Mrs. Kirby going to have herself maids?"

Rand laughed. "Not thet I know of—but she will have her mornin' room."

Belinda smiled. "Maybe it'll give her a sense of well-being," she offered, feeling that she should defend Mrs. Kirby for her little quirk.

"Maybe so," responded Rand.

"And what's this?" asked Belinda, indicating another room off the main entry.

"Well," smiled Rand, "tit for tat. Iffen Mrs. Kirby was to git her mornin' room, then Mr. Kirby insisted on a library."

"My," said Belinda. "It will be a grand house, won't it?"

Belinda's eyes traveled upward. There was no stairway to lead to the second floor, only a ladder leaning against the opening. Belinda did not wish to attempt it in her Sunday skirts.

"How many bedrooms?" she asked.

"Four—and a nursery."

"I didn't know the Kirbys had any family thet young," Belinda noted.

"They haven't. Their youngest is eight or nine. But I guess it didn't sound right to Mrs. Kirby to have a fine house without a proper nursery. Maybe she'll use it for a sewin' room or somethin'."

"My! It must be nice to have ya so many rooms thet ya can

have one jest fer sewin' in," reasoned Belinda.

She continued her wanderings from room to room, running her hand over the smoothness of polished wood or studying the delicate colors of stained-glass inserts over the windows.

"It's goin' to be one grand house," she said with awe in her voice. "Mrs. Kirby is a lucky woman."

She hadn't realized the high praise she was giving to the builder, but Rand took her words to heart and smiled softly to himself. It was all he could do to hold his tongue—but he had promised himself that he would not rush ahead. He was not as yet in any position to declare his true feelings to Belinda.

"I'd like to see it again—when ya get nearer to bein' finished," said Belinda. "Do ya think the Kirbys would mind?"

Rand smiled. He couldn't have been more pleased with Belinda's enthusiasm for the house. "Guess it's mine fer the time bein'," he said. "I'll be glad to show it to ya as many times as ya wanna see it," and so saying he took Belinda's hand to help her down the improvised steps.

Belinda was in the office when Arnie brought Abe in for another checkup. His Uncle Luke looked him over thoroughly and declared the ribs as good as new. He then sent Abe in to have cookies and milk with Thomas and Aaron. There was nothing unusual about that, so Belinda was unprepared when Luke pulled a chair up beside Arnie and haltingly began, "Arnie—there's something we need to talk about."

Arnie's eyes swung to Luke's face, and Belinda could read fearful questions there.

"He's not healin'?" Arnie asked quickly. "But you said—"

"He's healing. He's doing fine," Luke interrupted.

"Then what's the problem?" Arnie demanded.

"The ribs are great, the lungs just fine. All the bumps and bruises are completely healed—but I'm worried about the arm."

"Hasn't it healed?"

"It's healed—sure. But it was a bad break—and I didn't have the equipment to set it properly. It needed care that I couldn't give and—"

"What are ya tryin' to say?" Arnie cut in. "Yer talkin' riddles. Ya set it, didn't ya?"

"I set it—like I told you. I did the best I could under the circumstances, but—"

"What circumstances?"

"That arm needed the care that only a large hospital could give to make—"

"Then why didn't ya say thet before?" Arnie interrupted, his voice harsh with emotion. "Why'd ya let us think thet everything was goin' to be jest fine?"

"Arnie," said Luke as patiently as he knew how, "Abe was badly hurt. I was concerned about saving his *life*! I knew at the time that the arm needed special care—better care than I could give it in my simple office, but I did the best I could here because Abe was not fit to be moved to a hospital at the time. The trip might have killed him. Can you understand that?"

Arnie nodded slowly.

"Well, it's done now," he said, working hard on swallowing. "Guess we made out okay. Abe is alive an' seems fine an' iffen the arm has healed all right—"

"But it hasn't," replied Luke carefully. "That's what I'm trying to tell you. Abe still needs special care for that arm."

"But ya said it's healed."

"It is," Luke answered slowly, "as far as the break itself—"

"Then what needs doin'?"

"It's healing crooked, Arnie. Crooked."

Arnie just sat staring into space, trying to understand the words.

"What's thet mean?" he asked finally.

"It means if it doesn't get treated properly, the arm will get worse. Abe won't have full use of it. In time it might not function well at all."

Belinda looked first at Arnie and then at Luke. So that was what had been bothering her doctor brother.

"What—what can be done?" asked Arnie, his voice tight. "It's already set."

"That's not a big problem. They re-break it. The only thing

is, the sooner it is done, the more successful it—"

But Arnie swung about to face Luke, his eyes black with anger. "Are ya suggestin' thet I take my son to some city hospital and put 'im through his pain all over again—on *purpose*?"

For a moment Luke was shocked to silence.

"Well, forget it," rasped out Arnie. "The boy has suffered quite enough. Iffen you'd a'set it properlike in the first place—" But Arnie stopped short. He wasn't being fair and he knew it. Luke had done his best. He had saved the life of his son. Arnie wished he could take back his words but it was too late.

"Arnie," said Luke gently, "I don't blame you for feeling that way. Honest, I don't. And I wouldn't even suggest such a thing if there was any other way. But I've been watching that arm. It's getting worse. It needs to be fixed and the sooner the better. I know a good doctor. He does amazing things in corrective bone surgery. He would take Abe's case, I'm sure he would, and there's a good chance—a *good* chance that the arm would heal properly—be almost as good as new. This doctor—"

"I said no." Arnie's voice was low but the tone unmistakable. "I won't put him through all thet."

Luke took a deep breath. "If you don't," he said firmly, "you'll have a crippled boy."

The tears spilled down Arnie's cheeks. He brushed them roughly aside. "He's been through enough pain already," he insisted. "What kind of pa would I be to put him through more?"

"A loving pa," Luke said, laying a hand on Arnie's arm, his voice little more than a whisper.

Arnie spun around to face him. "You doctors!" he cried, choking on his words, "all ya wanna do is play God. Ya don't think anythin' 'bout the pain ya cause. Ya jest gotta fix, fix, fix. Well, I won't have them experimentin' on my son jest to git glory in the doin', ya hear? The matter is closed. I never wanna hear of it agin. An' one more thing, I don't want ya sayin' a word of this to Anne. She's suffered enough havin' to watch her boy fight to live. It would jest make things worse.

Ya hear?" And Arnie slammed out the door, calling for Abe as he went.

Belinda took a deep breath and looked over at Luke. He stood leaning against the wall with his head down, his face in his hands, and he was weeping.

Chapter 11

Bitterness

Belinda could sense the heaviness in Luke as he went about his daily medical rounds. She longed to share his burden in some way. She knew Luke had done his best, but she also knew he felt that he had failed a child—and a family member at that.

One wintry day when the foul weather seemed to be keeping away all but the emergency cases, Belinda decided to broach the subject of young Abe. She knew there was no way for her to ease the pain that Luke was feeling, but reasoned that even talking about it might help some.

"Have ya talked to Pa and Ma about Abe?" she asked softly.

Luke's head raised from the column of figures he was adding. He shook his head, his face thoughtful.

"Do ya think ya should?"

"I don't know," Luke hesitated. "Some days I think that I've just got to talk to them and on other days—I don't know. It might just make things worse."

"Worse how?"

"Arnie already avoids me."

Belinda nodded in agreement. She had noticed it too the last time the family had gathered for Sunday dinner. Quiet and morose, Arnie hadn't entered in with the usual mantalk and good-natured banter. In fact, Arnie seemed to have retreated from the warmth of the entire family. Marty had noticed it also and worried that he might be coming down with something and should be taking a tonic.

"Abe seemed chipper enough," Belinda went on.

Luke was still deep in thought. He turned his eyes back to Belinda as she spoke.

"He's chipper," he responded, "but he's not using that arm well. If you watch him, he handles almost everything with his other hand."

Belinda hadn't noticed, but then she hadn't been as attentive as Luke. Thinking back she realized now that Luke was right.

"What happened, Luke?" she asked softly.

"One of the bones that was broken was in the elbow and it was pushed out of proper position. I figure that the bull must have caught the arm between his head and the hard-packed earth and twisted as he ground it. You've seen certain critters do that. They aren't content to just butt things. They grind at them with those rock-hard heads of theirs."

Yes, Belinda had seen them do that.

"Well, this bone was dislocated, so to speak, as well as broken, and I couldn't get it to line up properly. I hoped—and prayed—that it might adjust itself as it healed, but deep inside I knew it would really take a miracle for the bone to align on its own." Luke sighed deeply, his eyes troubled. "Well, this time we didn't get our miracle," he stated simply.

"And ya think they can do thet in the city—set it right?"

"I'm sure they could. They have a team of doctors and all the latest equipment. I'm sure they could do a good job for the boy. I got to watch a doctor do a procedure very similar when I was in training. I couldn't believe what he accomplished."

"Is it—is it terribly painful?" went on Belinda.

"There's pain—of course. After all, it is a break. And also surgery. But they have good sedatives. Good medication for pain. And the main thing is that the patient is whole again. It's worth the additional suffering if Abe gets his arm back."

Belinda understood Luke's reasoning. If it were his son, he would do all he could to give him a whole and usable body. But this wasn't Luke's son, but Arnie's. And Arnie had never been able to stand to see suffering of any kind. He shrank back from it, hating it for its very sake. Arnie would find it hard to make a decision that would cause suffering to anyone, especially his child, even if the purpose was to bring healing.

"What happens if nothin' is done?" Belinda continued.

Luke shook his head. "It'll get worse and worse. He may lose use of the arm entirely as time goes on. It might not grow with the rest of the body. Might even begin to shrivel some. At best, the elbow will be stiff and unbending. To say it simply—the boy will have a crippled arm."

Belinda cringed. She remembered, years ago, seeing such a boy. She had gone to another town with her ma and pa, and they were riding down the street in an open carriage when they were halted in the street for some reason. Belinda had looked about her as the horses had fidgeted and impatiently tossed their heads.

At first she had enjoyed looking in the windows of the nearby shops and watching the people in their colorful garments as they hurried back and forth on the sidewalk. And then her eyes had fallen on a young boy on the street corner selling papers. In his one hand he held high the latest edition as he called to the passers-by the headline and urged them to buy their copy. But it was the other hand that drew Belinda's attention. The whole arm was twisted off to the side in a strange way, the hand small and the fingers bent.

She had been shocked at the sight and unable to understand why the boy's arm looked like that. Even at her young age her heart was tender with sympathy. She had tugged on her pa's coatsleeve and pointed a finger at the young boy, asking what was wrong with him.

Concern in his eyes, her pa gently pulled her arm down and turned to look at her intently.

"He's crippled, Belinda," he had said softly. "I don't know how or why, but his arm's been damaged somehow. Like my leg was damaged," and he tapped on his wooden one. Belinda stared up at her pa with wide eyes. She was so accustomed to his handicap that she didn't even notice it.

At just that moment three young boys came around the

corner. Belinda saw them stop before the newspaper boy. *Maybe they're goin' to help him,* she thought. But they didn't help him. They began to dance around, calling out such things as, "Claw hand, claw hand," and "Crooked arm!" Then they had snatched his papers and begun throwing them about on the street. Clark too saw it all and before Belinda could understand what was happening, her pa had jumped from the carriage. Seeing him coming, they turned and ran from the scene.

It had taken Clark many minutes to help the young lad gather his papers back in the stack, and then Belinda had seen him slip the young boy a bill, pick up a paper and join the family, his jaw set and his eyes filled with anger.

By then Belinda was in tears and Clark reached out to draw her close while Marty fished in her handbag for a fresh handkerchief, clucking all the time over the injustice of it all.

"Why—why did they do thet—be so mean?" Belinda had quavered out.

Shaking his head, Clark said, "I don't know, little one. I don't know," he soothed. "Our world is full of unkindness. It wasn't meant to be—but it is. Thet's why it's so important that we, as God's children, never add to the grief of any of His creatures. He put us here to love an' help an' heal, an' we need to be extry careful thet we're a'doin' thet. Not hurtin' or harmin' our fellowmen."

But Belinda still was unable to understand why the boys would taunt and tease the boy, and she could not erase the scene from her young mind. There followed a time when she had bad dreams about it and would waken in the night crying, and Marty would come to her bed and comfort her.

And now—now their own Abe was destined to be crippled. Belinda felt she understood Luke's concern. Surely—surely there was something to be done about it—some way to make Arnie see reason.

"Well, I think we have no choice," she said firmly. "Ma and Pa have to know. They are the only ones who can talk some sense into Arnie."

Belinda placed the sterilized instruments in a sheath of clean gauze and returned them to the cabinet.

"But Arnie would be angry—I know he would," Luke said thoughtfully.

Belinda nodded. "Fer a time. But surely in the end he would see thet we've done the right thing. Surely—surely when young Abe is—is whole again, he will be thankful thet we persisted." Belinda lowered herself to a chair near Luke and allowed herself a few moments of deep thought. "It's a terrible thing to be handicapped if it doesn't really need to be," she finished sadly.

Luke lifted his pencil back to the paper before him. He shook his head and sighed again deeply. "Maybe you're right," he said wearily. "Maybe I shouldn't give up so easily. If only there was some way to do it without hurting Arnie further."

Strange! mused Belinda. *It's Abe's accident, Abe's pain, but it's Arnie who's sufferin' the most.*

"It's too cold for you to be riding horseback," Luke said on Friday afternoon after the last patient had been sent on his way. "I'll get the team and drive you home."

Belinda did not protest. The buggy wasn't a lot warmer, but if she were to take Copper, by the time she reached the farm her feet and hands would be numb and her cheeks tingling. Besides, this would give Luke an opportunity to speak to Clark and Marty, and Belinda was convinced that such a talk was a must.

The two rode most of the way in silence. They were both weary and had already discussed the main things on their minds—and besides, they felt comfortable with silence. Now and then, they would discuss something briefly and then fall silent again.

Marty was at the door to meet them.

"My, my!" she exclaimed. "I was worryin' some 'bout ya comin' on horseback, but Pa said ya'd jest stay on at Luke's fer the weekend." Belinda had often stayed in town for one reason or another.

Marty hurried about the big farm kitchen, putting on the coffeepot and slicing fresh bread for sandwiches.

Clark came in from the barn to join them at the table. He gently massaged his injured leg, hoping to take the sting of the cold from it without attracting too much attention. Luke noticed but made no comment.

Belinda knew without Luke's saying so that he would talk to his ma and pa about Arnie and little Abe. She didn't particularly wish to be involved in the conversation, knowing it would be difficult for all involved. Excusing herself to "change into a housedress," she left the kitchen and climbed the stairs to her room.

She spent some time changing from her office clothing, puttering around tidying her dresser, straightening a few drawers, and at last she went back down to the kitchen. All during this time she had been praying for her family.

Luke and her parents were still seated at the table when Belinda entered the room. The coffee cups were empty and pushed to the side. Belinda read concern and distress in the three faces. Marty's eyes were red from weeping, and she held a damp handkerchief in her hands, abstractedly twisting it back and forth. Clark's hand rested gently on the worn family Bible, and Belinda knew that they had been drawing counsel from its pages.

Belinda poured herself a glass of milk and joined them at the table.

"We've got some money laid aside," Clark was saying softly, "an' we'd be glad ta help. I s'ppose, sech an operation would cost a great deal."

Clark reached out and took Marty's hand, and Belinda saw them exchange silent messages—Clark seeking her agreement and she giving it without hesitation.

"It would cost, to be sure—the trip, the hotel, the surgery. It would cost. But Arnie didn't mention money. That's not what's holding him back. If he was convinced it was the right thing to do, he wouldn't stop to consider the money. He'd take Abe tomorrow. Even if he had to sell his farm to do it," said Luke.

Clark nodded. Arnie would, he knew.

"We jest have to convince 'im thet there's more'n one kind of pain," Marty said thoughtfully. "Abe might suffer far more from a useless arm than from the operation."

Belinda wondered if her mother was remembering the young lad on the street corner.

Luke suddenly looked at the kitchen clock and stood to go. "I've got to get home before it gets dark," he said. "Promised the boys we'd play some Snakes 'n Ladders tonight."

"We'll talk to Arnie," Clark promised. "First chance we git, we'll talk to 'im."

Luke nodded, seeming satisfied with that. Surely Arnie would listen to his parents whom he loved and respected. He shrugged into his heavy coat and hastened out to his team.

Clark and Marty did talk to Arnie. Anne was there as well, and she was shocked to hear about the condition of her son's arm. Arnie had said nothing to her.

But though Clark and Marty urged Arnie to take Luke's advice, Arnie held firmly to his position. His young son, just a child, had suffered enough. His own father should not put him through any more. Besides, who knew for sure if the operation would even be successful? Luke himself had admitted that there wasn't one-hundred-percent certainty. What if Abe went through the pain and ended up with no improvement?

Clark and Marty returned home with heavy hearts.

The next Sunday only Anne and the boys were in church, and she offered no explanation. Afterward she simply said that they would not be joining the rest of the family for Sunday dinner.

The pain in Marty's heart grew worse. Besides the anguish over her grandson's arm, her family was no longer a close-knit, openly loving unit. She wiped tears and tried to swallow the lump in her throat as she dished up the fried chicken. Where would it all end?

Chapter 12

A New Kind of Suffering

The situation did not get better. Arnie was not back in church during the next Sundays. Anne came with the boys a few times, and then she too began to miss more often than she attended.

"Surely they will all be there fer Christmas Sunday," Marty reasoned out loud to Clark, but she was wrong. Again they were missing and word came through Clare's children from school that Arnie's family wouldn't be coming home for Christmas celebrations. They would be sharing Christmas dinner with Anne's folks.

The pastor called on them but was given no real explanation for the change. It seemed that things just kept "croppin' up" on Sundays. Then Arnie resigned from the church board.

Hoping that *something* would help, Clark and Marty called at the farm. They were welcomed openly by the children, civilly by Anne and reluctantly by Arnie. After a short and strained conversation over teacups, they left for home, their hearts even heavier than before. There seemed nothing more to do but wait and pray.

Marty's heart ached as she felt the burden of it. "I never woulda dreamed," she confessed to Belinda, "—I never woulda dreamed thet it could happen to us. Ya hear of sech things in families—rifts thet break a family apart, but I never woulda dreamed it could be *our* family."

"Do—do the rest know?" asked Belinda soberly. "Missie and Ellie and Clae?"

"I finally wrote 'em," Marty confided. "I waited an' waited, hopin' an' prayin' thet things would—would heal. Thet Arnie would change—but I finally decided thet they should know." Marty stopped to blow her nose. "They were the hardest letters I ever had ta write in my entire life," she continued, "even worse'n when I had to write on home 'bout yer pa."

Belinda nodded.

"Clare went to see Arnie too—did ya know?"

Belinda hadn't but she wasn't surprised.

"It was way back 'fore Christmas. He didn't git nowhere either."

Marty stopped to think back over the exchange between the two boys.

"What did Arnie say?" asked Belinda quietly.

"Said lots of things. Mean things. Things thet Arnie—our old Arnie—never woulda said."

Marty brushed at more tears.

"He said it was no one else's business. Said he and Anne loved Abe the way he be—crippled in other's eyes or no. Said Luke had no business bein' a doctor iffen he couldn't even proper-set an arm."

Marty's voice stopped in a sob and the tears ran uncontrolled down her cheeks.

"An' then he said thet the whole thing was really Clare's fault. He never shoulda had him an unsafe bull in the first place."

Belinda blinked back her own tears. It was hard to believe that her own brother—tender, sensitive Arnie—could say such cruel things. He had always been so loving—so caring. *Arnie must be deeply hurt to have changed so much—so completely,* she reasoned inwardly.

"I've never felt me so heavy-hearted in all my life," admitted Marty. "To see those I love so much hurtin' and not speakin' is jest 'most more'n I can bear."

"How's Pa doin'?" asked Belinda.

"Never saw yer pa suffer so. Even his leg didn't lay 'im as

low as this has. His leg was jest—jest flesh an' bone—but this—this is—is flesh an' *blood*," Marty sobbed and Belinda understood.

"How's Abe?" asked Belinda after a pause.

"The boys see 'im at school. Say he's fine. Jest fine—though he don't use thet arm much a'tall. They say it's beginnin' to twist off to the side some. Dack had 'im a fight over it last week. One of the other boys called Abe some name. Dack wouldn't even say what it was—but the teacher sent him home with a note to his pa an' ma, after givin' both fighters the strap."

Marty halted her account long enough to wipe her nose again.

"Clare went on over to the school an' had 'im a long talk with Mrs. Brown. Guess she was real nice 'bout it, but Dack has been warned no more fightin'."

Marty shook her head slowly. "Maybe we be in danger of takin' the family fer granted," she said. "When ya have it all together, lovin' an' supportin' one another, ya don't realize how blessed ya are. Iffen ya got yer family—then ya have most of what ya really need."

Belinda wiped her own eyes and rose from her chair to get a cup from the cupboard. She could hear Clark on the porch and knew that he could use a cup of hot coffee to take away some of the winter chill.

Marty finally decided to take matters into her own hands. On the first day the cold let up some, she asked Clark for the team, bundled herself up warmly and set out for Arnie's. The boys were at school and Anne was alone in the kitchen. She seemed genuinely pleased to see her mother-in-law and expressed sincerely how she had been missing their visits.

"Me too," Marty said openly, "an' thet's exactly why I'm here. It's jest not right fer a disagreement to keep the family apart. The boys need their cousins—an' their aunts and uncles—an' grandma an' grandpa, too. An' we need them—an' you an' Arnie. Ain't right nor natural fer a family to be apart."

Anne nodded, but she made no comment.

"I came to talk to my son," went on Marty. "Is he here?"

"He's at the barn," Anne said softly.

"Did he see me comin'?" asked Marty outright.

"I think maybe—he—he might. Yes, he did." Anne hung her head.

"Then I guess I'll jest have to go out to his barn," said Marty briskly and she moved to put her coat back on.

"No. No, don't do that," Anne quickly responded. "I'll go. I'll go get Arnie—tell 'im you want to see 'im."

"Ya think—?" Marty began and Anne nodded. Surely Arnie would agree to see his own mother.

Arnie did come. His face looked drawn, his eyes cold, but he nodded agreeably while seeming to steel himself against whatever Marty had come to say.

He sat down at the table with her and accepted the cup of tea from Anne. Marty made small talk about the weather, the children and asked a few questions about his stock. Arnie appeared to relax some.

Marty reached out a hand and laid it on Arnie's. She had to be careful, very careful in what she said. She knew Arnie so well.

"Arnie," she said, and in spite of her resolve the tears began to form in her eyes. "Arnie, you have always been the tenderest member of the family—have felt things the deepest—an' said the least. I—I know how the hurtin' of young Abe has brought ya deep pain. We have all suffered—we love the boy—but you have suffered the most."

Marty paused. Arnie's eyes were fastened on his cup, but he had not withdrawn his hand. Marty took courage and went on. "We miss ya, Arnie—you an' the kids—an' Anne. We need ya—as a family we need ya. It's jest not the same when yer not there. The family isn't—isn't whole anymore. We all feel it. It hurts. Real bad. It's not as God intended it to be."

Arnie stirred and Marty was afraid she was pressing too far—too fast. She withdrew her hand and sat silently for a moment. Then she said carefully, "We've pushed ya—an' we're sorry. We haven't been—been thoughtful of yer feelin's like we shoulda been. We know thet ya can't stand to see anyone ya love suffer."

Then Marty changed direction, her voice picking up a new lilt.

"Well, we won't push no more. We'll promise ya thet. Abe is a dear, good boy. We got no shame concernin' 'im jest the way he be. An' maybe thet arm will git better 'stead of worse. God has done such miracles before. But whether He chooses to heal our Abe or not won't make no difference to how we be a'feelin' 'bout 'im. He's ourn—an' we love 'im an' miss 'im.'"

Marty waited for some response on Arnie's part, but he said nothing. Anne was standing by her kitchen cupboard crying softly, silently.

"Would ya come back, Arnie?" Marty pleaded. "Would ya come back to yer family? To yer church? We love ya, Arnie. We need ya. Please. Please come home."

Marty's tears were flowing unashamedly as she made her plea and suddenly Arnie's face convulsed, and he laid his head down on his arms and let the sobs shake his body. Marty leaned over to hold her broken son. She soothed and comforted and stroked his hair much as she had done when he had been a child. Then she kissed his cheek and slipped into her coat. She had done all she could.

Arnie did come back. He came to church the next Sunday, though he sat stiffly in the pew. The children were thrilled to be back, and Marty noticed a more peaceful look in Anne's eyes.

Arnie also joined the family at Clare's house for dinner. Marty had warned all of them that not one word should be said about the young Abe and his need for corrective surgery. Everyone was very cautious about the words they spoke—so much so that the conversation often lagged. At times the tension in the air was so heavy that one felt choked by it.

The family was back together—at least bodily. But it wasn't the same, not the same at all. They all tried so hard—too hard—to try to make things seem as they had always been. The chatter, the teasing, the concerns over one another's affairs—all meant to bring back the feeling of family—all failed miserably in doing so. There was a strain about it all that seemed to draw more attention to the fact that there was friction, not harmony, in the family circle. The unity had been broken. The bond had been weakened. They were not as they had been.

Marty talked to Clark about it on the short walk home. She longed for the old relationship to be restored, but she was at a loss as to how it could be done. She didn't have any answers and there seemed to be so many troubling questions. Marty wept again as she walked.

Belinda, too, suffered under the strain of the family rift. It weighed heavily upon her as she went about her daily nursing duties. There were times when she wished she could get out from under it all, even for a brief season. She often thought of asking for some time off so she might go out West for a visit, but she always dismissed the idea. Luke needed her. It sounded like in just a few months they might get their new doctor, and then she would be free to take some time for herself. She would hang on until then.

Rand still called when he was free. He had taken Belinda to see the Kirby house on a number of occasions. Belinda thought it was beautiful and wondered that Rand could build such a lovely home. Rand smiled at her praise, wishing he now could promise her such a home of her own one day. But he would not presume until there was enough put aside to back up the promise.

Once the Kirbys were established in their new home, there was no longer that small diversion. Rand was busy working on another house for the town grocer but not nearly as grand as the Kirbys'.

Belinda got through the days as best she could, finding pleasure in the company of her young nephews and little Ruthie. *Children,* she often thought, *they seem to somehow put the world to right again. If only we could be more like children.*

Belinda ticked off the long winter days one by one, looking forward to spring. But one morning the unexpected broke into the routine of their days. A message was sent from the local station that someone traveling the train had taken suddenly, seriously ill and the doctor should come at once. Luke left hurriedly, telling Belinda to prepare for the patient in his absence.

Belinda at once set about making up a bed on a cot in the surgery. She had no idea what the problem was or if the patient was male or female, young or old, but she did the best she could to be ready.

An older woman was rushed from the train to the surgery, lying quietly in the back of Tom Hammel's wagon. Belinda had never seen anyone quite like her before. Her clothing was very stylish, though the elaborate hat had been laid aside to accommodate the makeshift pillow. Her face was ashen in spite of powder and rouge. A fur wrap lay loosely about her shoulders. She looked to be tall and thin and very regal looking even in her present state, and Belinda felt herself quiver with excitement in spite of her deep concern for the patient.

Chapter 13

The Patient

For the next several days, Belinda's time was taken up with the careful nursing of the woman. Twice Luke feared they were losing her, but each time she managed to hang on to life. Her condition was diagnosed as a stroke, and Luke was concerned that there would be some lasting paralysis to her left side. Belinda hoped not, and daily as she nursed the sick woman she prayed that she might totally recover.

Three days later a gentleman arrived at their door. Abbie had answered the knock. Luke was out in the country making a housecall and Belinda was sitting with her patient. She could hear the conversation from the next room.

"Good day, madam," the man said properly, and Belinda could visualize him doffing his hat.

Then he continued. "I understand that Mrs. Virginia Stafford-Smyth is being cared for at this address."

"That's—that's right," responded Abbie. "She was brought in to us from the passing train." The name of the woman appeared on her luggage and was one of the few things they had managed to learn about her—that and her Boston address.

"I came to see her," said the man simply.

Abbie hesitated. "She's—she's very ill. My husband—the doctor—has not allowed visitors."

Belinda could not help but smile. No one in the small town even knew the woman, much less was interested in visiting

101

her—however, Abbie was following Luke's usual orders in such circumstances.

The silence that followed alerted Belinda to the fact that Abbie might need some help. She checked her patient and rose from the side of the small cot in the already overcrowded little surgery.

"May I help you, sir?" she asked politely when she reached the door. "I'm Mrs. Stafford-Smyth's nurse."

"Oh, yes," said the tall man, standing erect with his bowler hat firmly in gloved hands. He looked relieved to see someone with a position of authority.

"I'm Winsah. Mrs. Stafford-Smyth's butlah," he explained in precise eastern tones. "We received a telegram that she had been taken ill. I've come to take charge."

A butler! thought Belinda. *Whoever would have thought we'd ever see a real one way out here?* Excitement coursed through her, but she kept her professional demeanor and answered firmly, "Dr. Davis is in charge of Mrs. Stafford-Smyth at the present. I'm afraid you will need his permission to see the patient. She has been very ill."

"Oh, deah!" said the man a bit impatiently. Belinda had never heard an accent like his before.

"I came all this way on that abominable train," he explained. "And now you say I can't see Madam."

"I'm sorry," said Belinda. "I'm sure the doctor will allow you to as soon as he returns, but until then I'll have to ask you to be patient."

"Very well," agreed the man and lifted his bowler hat toward his bald pate. Then he hesitated and lowered it again. "I suppose there is accommodation for one in this town?"

"A hotel," responded Belinda. "Over three blocks and down Mainstreet."

"That little building called the Red Palace or some such thing?"

Belinda allowed the flicker of a smile. "The Rose Palace. Yes, that's the one."

"I noticed it on the way ovah," said the man. "It didn't appear to be much of a spot. Palace indeed!" He clicked his tongue in derision. "I suppose it shall have to do." Then he turned to go, placing his hat on his head as he did so.

Belinda stood looking after him, wondering about it all. After farmers and local townspeople, it seemed so very strange to be nursing a woman who had her own butler. And it seemed even more strange that a butler should be coming to "take charge" of her. Where were her family members? Didn't they have time to look after their own?

But Belinda had little time to ponder it all. She turned back to the bedside of her patient.

"Mrs. Stafford-Smyth," she said softly. "Mrs. Stafford-Smyth, do ya hear me? Windsor was just here to see you. He has come all the way from Boston—yer home."

But as in the past there was no flickering of eyelash or indication that Mrs. Stafford-Smyth had heard.

"Keep talking to her," Luke had said. "Maybe one of these times we will break through." So as Belinda nursed her charge, she talked. But to this point there had been no response whatever.

When Luke arrived home he was told about the strange visitor and, after checking the patient, went to see if he could locate the man. Belinda was sure that he would have no problem spotting him in the small inn.

He didn't and was soon home again, Butler Windsor in step beside him.

Luke brought the man directly in to see the patient, and Belinda stepped aside to allow him access. He bent over her solicitously, and Belinda saw his face drain of color.

"She is in a bad way, isn't she?" he said in a hoarse whisper.

He straightened up, shaking his head. "I had hoped the telegram was exaggerated."

He then looked around the room, his eyes taking in the cabinets for medications and instruments, the spotless table that served as Luke's surgical table, the two high stools, the small desk and one oak chair and the corner basket where waste materials were gathered. He looked back again at the cot with its snowy white sheets and woolen blanket.

"Oh, deah me," he murmured. "Madam shouldn't be in a place like this."

Surprised at his own frankness, he hastened to explain.
"Madam has always been in a hospital—in her own private
room."

"There is no hospital in our little town, I'm afraid," explained Luke. "This is the best we have to offer."

"How beastly inconvenient!" the man exclaimed, and Belinda turned to hide her smile.

"She should nevah have gone on this trip to begin with," he
persisted, "but she would have her own way. Madam can be so
stubborn at times." He shook his head in exasperation as
though he were speaking of a wayward child.

"Well, nothing to be done about it now but to make the best
of it, I warrant."

He turned back to Mrs. Stafford-Smyth, his face showing
his concern. "How long did you say she has been like this?" he
asked.

"She was brought to us on Tuesday," Luke informed the
man. "She had taken ill on the train and they stopped to deliver
her to me."

"And she was like this from the beginning?" he asked further.

Luke nodded his head. "There has been very little change,"
he offered.

"Beastly!" said the man again.

As Belinda slipped from the room, she heard Luke begin to
explain Mrs. Stafford-Smyth's condition to the butler and heard
his tongue-clicking in return. He was a funny fellow, but he
certainly did seem genuinely concerned about the elderly
woman.

Belinda busied herself in the kitchen and soon carried a tray
of tea things to the parlor. Putting them down on the small
table next to the sofa, she returned to the room where the elderly woman lay.

"Excuse me," she said softly, "but I thought ya might like a
cup of tea." She looked knowingly at Luke and nodded her head
slightly toward the door. The man looked as though she had
just offered him a ticket back to civilization.

"Oh, my yes," he agreed. "It is long past propah tea time."

He followed Luke from the room.

Belinda poured two cups of the strong, hot tea. Their guest accepted one appreciatively, breathing deeply of the aroma from the cup. She then passed him a plate of Abbie's gingerbread, and he accepted a slice with a slight nod of his head. Belinda, glad to have been able to help restore some order to his world, excused herself and went back to her nursing duties.

Windsor—Belinda did not know if it was his first name, his last name, or all the name that he had—spent the next several days at the local hotel until he was assured that Mrs. Stafford-Smyth, his "charge," was going to recover. He often came to the little room where her cot had been placed and visited with Belinda while she cared for the elderly lady.

Belinda found him most enjoyable in spite of his stuffiness. To her amazement he even had a sense of humor—of sorts. He turned out to be deeply committed to Mrs. Stafford-Smyth, and Belinda could not help but admire that in him.

Still, Belinda did wonder if his frequent visits had something to do with the fact that she always served him tea. The hotel's, he complained, was only lukewarm and weak as rain water.

Belinda smiled and made sure that the pot was boiling, the teapot heated and the tea given a long time to brew.

Belinda did not discover much about her patient from the tight-lipped butler, who considered it poor breeding indeed to discuss one's employer. However, he did give out bits and pieces of information in their chats together over teacups.

He had worked for Mrs. Stafford-Smyth for forty-two years, beginning in her employ as a young man and serving no other. Mr. Stafford-Smyth had been a busy city lawyer, but a heart attack had taken him to an early grave.

"Has the family always lived in Boston?" Belinda asked.

"Oh, indeed, yes," answered the butler quickly, as though to even consider any other locale would be a travesty to all held sacred.

"Did Mrs. Stafford-Smyth have a family?"

The man sat silent for some time as though weighing

whether the question should be considered too personal to answer, but at length said quite simply, "She had two children. She lost one in infancy and one as an adult. She has two grandsons—but they are 'abroad.' "

Belinda understood from his terse answer that she was to pry no further.

It was on their third day of vigil together that Mrs. Stafford-Smyth roused slightly. At first she seemed totally confused. She pushed at Belinda and looked about her in bewilderment and some fear. Belinda was glad that the butler was there to move to her side. The woman quieted when she saw him and settled back again on her pillow.

"Madam must rest," he said gently but firmly. "You have been very ill," and he took her hand and held it until she relaxed again.

Belinda offered the woman some liquid, and she accepted a few sips willingly. One of Luke's greatest concerns was that they had been able to get her to swallow very little.

She did not stay awake for long, but from then on she roused every few hours, and each time she seemed a bit more alert.

Eventually she was able to make her requests known and after several days was even able to form words, though her speech was labored and slurred.

It was at that point that she was moved to a room at the local hotel, and after conferring with Luke and then with Mrs. Stafford-Smyth at length, Windsor decided that he needed to return to Boston to look after the affairs of her house.

"Don't worry—nurse will care for me," the lady managed to say, and Belinda understood that she was expected to stay in her employ. But even Belinda could not nurse twenty-four hours a day, seven days a week. So Mrs. Mills continued on the night shift and Flora Hadley on the occasional day.

Mrs. Stafford-Smyth improved slowly but steadily with each new spring day. Luke was pleased and thankful that she was getting her speech back so quickly—but then Mrs. Stafford-Smyth was not at all like her silent butler and she practiced continually. She loved to chat and she engaged Belinda in conversation most of her wakeful hours.

"What did he tell you about me?" she asked one day, and Belinda knew that she was speaking of Windsor.

"Very little," Belinda replied as she fluffed a pillow. "He seemed to feel thet butlers should be seen and not heard."

Mrs. Stafford-Smyth began to chuckle. "Exactly!" she said. "Exactly! That describes my Windsah perfectly."

Belinda smiled at the word "my." Just how did Mrs. Stafford-Smyth mean the word? she wondered.

"Well, *I'm* not hesitant to talk," the woman said. "What would you like to know?"

Belinda smiled. "Whatever you would like to tell," she responded.

"I'm a widow," she began.

"Windsor did tell me that," said Belinda.

"What else?"

"Thet yer husband had been a noted lawyer. Thet he died quite young with a heart attack. Thet ya lost both of yer children."

"My," said Mrs. Stafford-Smyth. "How did you evah coax all of that from him?"

"He *was* a mite reluctant," smiled Belinda. "But he did like my tea." They laughed comfortably together.

"Mr. Stafford-Smyth was only thirty-nine when he had his heart attack," the woman went on thoughtfully. "So young and with so much promise." She thought for a few minutes and then hurried on, "We lost our Cynthia when she was only two. It was whooping cough that took her. My husband was still with me then, so I had someone to share my sorrow, but when I lost our son, Martin—I had to bear it all alone."

"I'm—I'm so sorry," said Belinda.

"Martin was only thirty-two when he died. He had been to Europe several times with me. He liked it much bettah than Boston, I'm afraid. Then he fell in love with a French girl and they were married. He brought her home to Boston, but she nevah really did care for it, so they were back and forth—back and forth. Finally they bought a new home in Boston and tried to settle down. They had two sons, but they still both loved to travel, so the boys were raised more by nannies than by their parents. I guess there's no harm in that—if one has good nannies. Just because one is a parent doesn't mean that one knows about children."

Belinda found herself wanting to argue the issue, but she kept silent.

"Anyway," Mrs. Stafford-Smyth went on, "on one of their trips abroad there was an accident. They were both killed. They were buried in France. Of course I went over for the funeral. I was devastated. Martin was all I had left. Except for the boys. I brought them to my house and we raised them—my staff and I—with the help of their nannies, of course. They are both grown men now—and I don't see them much. Right now they are in France visiting their family on their mothah's side. Some days I feah that I have lost them, too."

She paused, and Belinda was afraid she might start to weep, but instead she shifted herself on the pillows and lifted her chin.

"So I travel," she said. "Just as much as I can. 'Gadding,' Windsah calls it, and he doesn't approve of it much. Usually I take my nurse with me, but this trip—well, we already had our plans made, our tickets purchased when she took sick. Gall bladder. She had to have surgery. Well, one can hardly travel after surgery, can one? Windsah and I had quite a fuss ovah it. He said I should cancel my plans and stay at home. I said I was old enough to care for myself." She smiled. "So I went."

There was a pause. "Evah been to San Francisco?"

Belinda shook her head.

"Well, I have. All the way from Boston to San Francisco. Just to see what it was like." She smiled again, then sobered. "My, what a long, long dusty trip. And the trains! Some of them are so dirty and appalling and nevah on time." She shook her head again at the thought of it. "But don't evah tell Windsah I said so," she hastened to add. "He already thinks he's been proven right."

Belinda smiled. She did enjoy getting to know Mrs. Stafford-Smyth, but didn't like the thought of this fascinating lady leaving them when she was recovered and would be able to travel home. However, she was a long ways from total recovery yet.

"I think ya should rest a bit now," Belinda cautioned, and without fuss the woman allowed herself to be tucked in and the drapes pulled to shut the sunlight from the room.

Chapter 14

A Busy Summer

"You've been so busy I've scarcely seen ya," Rand lamented, and Belinda had to admit he was right.

"You've been pretty busy yerself," she reminded him.

"I'm hopin' things will slow down some fer me now," he said gently. "Now thet I have the house fer the grocer done, seems I should catch my breath and look to other things as well as buildin'."

Belinda wasn't sure what "other things" Rand was referring to. Perhaps he meant that he didn't want to build every waking minute, she reasoned.

"How's yer special patient?" he asked her.

"Oh, she's doing much better. Luke feels thet she should get completely well. Well, almost completely—she may always have a bit of trouble with her left side. But it's jest a matter of time now."

"Time?" said Rand with just a trace of agitation. Then he softened and added slowly. "Seems to me such a long time already."

"I suppose it seems thet way to Mrs. Stafford-Smyth, too," Belinda responded.

"Yeah," agreed Rand with a sigh. "I reckon it does."

They walked in silence. Belinda was enjoying the warm summer evening. She didn't get out nearly as often as she'd like, and Marty had commented on her paleness the last time she went out to the farm.

"So ya think ya'll be needed fer some time?" Rand was asking.

"Oh, she's not nearly well enough to travel yet. Especially alone."

"Couldn't thet there butler fella come an' get her?" Rand suggested.

"Thet would be awkward. She still needs help with dressing and all."

"What about her old nurse. The one ya said had her gall bladder out?"

"We haven't heard from her for some time," explained Belinda, since one of her tasks was to assist Mrs. Stafford-Smyth with her mail.

Belinda wondered why Rand had so many questions about her patient, but before she could inquire, he had switched the topic entirely.

"Hear there's a church picnic on Saturday. Sure would like to take ya iffen yer free to go."

Belinda thought for only a moment. "I'd love to go!" she responded enthusiastically. "It's a long time since I've done anything like thet. I'll see if I can work out the schedule with Flo."

For the first time, Rand gave her a full smile. She noticed again his deep dimple. She had been missing Rand's company, she realized, surprised at the discovery.

"You've already finished yer second house?" Belinda commented to keep the conversation going.

"Jest this week," said Rand.

"I didn't even get to see it," Belinda bemoaned.

"Ya haven't been seeing much of its builder lately either," teased Rand. "I was about to hit my thumb with my hammer or fall off a ladder or some such thing jest so thet I might git to see the town nurse."

Belinda blushed but brushed his teasing aside. "I haven't even been seein' my own ma and pa for jest ages," she confessed.

"Well, we'll take care of thet on Saturday," promised Rand.

And Belinda smiled. She really looked forward to the day off.

Belinda was able to arrange for Saturday off, and she left with Mrs. Stafford-Smyth's orders to "have fun as young girls were meant to do," and prepared for Rand's coming with extra care.

Such a long time since I've been on an outing, she exulted as she bathed and groomed her hair.

Light-hearted, she chose her favorite dress, a full-skirted soft blue gingham with lots of bows and flouncy frills. *It kinda matches my feelin's,* she decided as she held it up to herself in front of her bedroom mirror.

She was ready with time to spare, so spent the extra moments playing with Ruthie. She had missed having time with her little niece.

They were busy with a game of peek-a-boo when a male voice interrupted them. "Now, if that doesn't make some picture," he said.

Belinda's head swung up. She had not heard anyone knock on the front door.

But it was in the entrance to Luke's office that the male figure stood. Belinda's eyes traveled upward over sharply pressed suit pants, white shirt with rolled up sleeves and broad young shoulders. Then she looked at his face and a little gasp escaped her lips. "Jackson! I didn't know ya were here yet." Luke had told her that Jackson was planning to join the practice, but she didn't realize it would be this soon. She could not remember his being so tall—so good-looking. She flushed in embarrassment and turned her eyes back to Ruthie.

"My niece," she said, disentangling Ruthie's small fist from her bodice frills as Jackson moved into the room.

"I've already met the little charmer," said Jackson evenly. "It's her aunt who has eluded me."

"I—I hadn't even heard ya were—were back," Belinda repeated in defense.

He crossed to sit down on the sofa beside her. "Actually," he said, "I just arrived on Thursday, and I spent a few days with my mother. Then Luke said I should pop in and take inventory of his office supplies to see if I have any ideas on what we might add."

"Luke will be so glad to have ya here," said Belinda. "He's been worked near off his feet."

"I heard that it's his nurse who puts in long hours."

Jackson studied Belinda's face and she found herself flushing again.

"Not—not really," she stammered. "I'm taking the whole day off today."

"You are?" said Jackson. "Splendid! The inventory can wait until another day. Mother said there's a picnic out at the church. I'd love to go and see how many of our old friends are still around."

"That's a great idea," put in Belinda. "Folks would all love to see ya."

"Then let's go," he prompted and stood, offering a hand to help Belinda to her feet.

"Well—I—I—I can't," she stammered, not accepting the hand.

"You can't go? But I thought you said—"

"I—I did. I mean—I—I am going but I—I already—"

A knock on the door saved her from explaining further. Belinda lifted small Ruthie into her arms and went to answer it. She felt quite sure that she knew who was there, but she wasn't sure he had come at the best of times.

When Belinda opened the door, Rand stepped inside without comment. But he whistled softly as he stood studying her in the blue gingham dress. It emphasized her wide blue eyes, fair skin and cheeks just touched with pink.

"My feelings exactly," said a deep male voice, and Rand lifted his eyes from Belinda to see a tall, well-dressed young stranger.

Belinda's cheeks turned even more pink as she looked from one to the other. "Rand," she said, "this—this is Dr. Jackson Brown. Jackson, please meet Rand O'Connel."

For a moment Rand stood in silence, measuring the man before him. Then he stepped forward, offered his hand and said,

"Welcome to town, Doctor. You might not know it, but seems I've been waitin' on ya fer a long, long time."

Jackson did not understand the implication of the words, but he took the offered hand and shook it firmly.

"If you'll excuse me," said Belinda, "I'll give Ruthie back to her mama and grab my shawl."

It was then that Jackson realized what was happening. His eyes clouded for a moment and then he straightened his shoulders. He was deeply disappointed, but he was not a man to give up easily.

"And if you'll excuse me," he said to Rand, "I have some inventory to care for. Nice meeting you, Mr. O'Connel," and he turned back to the office.

"And nice to meet you, Doctor," put in Rand just before Jackson closed the door.

The picnic outing did not go as well as Belinda had hoped. It was obvious to her that the relationship between her family had not healed. She had prayed that over the months things would have returned to normal. She could see at a glance that they had not. For the first time in her life, she thought that her mother looked old. There was a weariness about Marty that surprised Belinda. Her mama shouldn't have changed that much in a few months' time.

Then Belinda saw young Abe, and she could see further deterioration in his arm. Abe hardly used his left hand at all, and Belinda knew that Luke's worst fears were being realized.

As she gazed around at the laughing, chattering picnickers, she realized that most of the girls her age were already married or being courted. That left very few of her old friends with whom to sit and chat. And just seeing her old classmates made her miss Amy Jo and Melissa even more.

The quiet ride home was not the way Rand had planned it would be. He had dreamed of a far more intimate conversation. But he sensed that Belinda was troubled about something, and he held himself in check.

"Ya seem bothered," he did dare to comment.

Belinda responded with a sigh.

"I'm sorry to be such sour company," she responded. "It's nothing, really. Least not any one thing. Just a lot of little things all pressin' in together."

"Care to talk about 'em?" asked Rand. "All these 'little things'?"

Belinda smiled in appreciation. "Thanks," she said, "but I think not. Not right now, anyway. I haven't sorted through 'em myself yet."

Rand nodded in understanding and drove on in silence.

They were almost home when he startled her with a question. "This here new doctor—Dr. Brown? Ya knew 'im before?" He had seen open admiration for Belinda in the eyes of the young man, and he figured he'd better find out all he could.

"We—we went to school together," she answered. "His ma was my teacher. She still teaches our school. Been there for several years now."

Rand's eyes narrowed.

"An' he'll be workin' with ya now?"

"He's to be Luke's associate," she answered simply.

"How do you feel about thet?" asked Rand.

Belinda frowned slightly. She really wasn't sure, but she answered as truthfully as she could. "Luke has been countin' on it fer some time. He will have more time with his family now. Thet's what he's wanted fer such a long time."

"An' you?" asked Rand.

"I—I guess maybe I'll have more time, too," Belinda stammered.

Rand smiled. *That's* what he had wanted—for a long time.

He drove for a moment in silence. Then another thought came to mind.

"This here doctor—he's not married?"

"No—o," answered Belinda.

"Got 'im a girl?"

"I—I wouldn't know. We haven't been in touch fer—fer some time."

Rand's eyes darkened. It was just as he feared. The new young doctor would bear some watching.

Chapter 15

Confusion

"And how are ya feelin' this mornin'?" Belinda asked Mrs. Stafford-Smyth upon entering her room.

"Oh, it's good to see you!" exclaimed the elderly lady with feeling. "I've missed you all weekend."

"Problems?" questioned Belinda with a frown. She did hope nothing had gone wrong over the weekend.

The woman shook her head and waved a pale hand feebly in the air. "No, nothing—nothing specific," she admitted. "Flo does her best and so does that deah Mrs. What's-her-name, but it just isn't the same as when you are heah. They never seem to know . . ."

She went on and Belinda let her talk, much relieved to know that there really was nothing seriously wrong with the woman.

Belinda busied herself checking her patient's temperature and pulse as Mrs. Stafford-Smyth poured out her woes. Without comment about the complaints, Belinda fluffed up the pillows, politely asking, "Would ya like to sit up in a chair fer a few minutes?"

"Oh my, yes," responded the woman. "I am so sick, sick, sick of this bed." Then she hurried on. "You see, that's exactly what I mean. Those—those other two. They nevah think of things like that. They just do the 'necessaries.' It's as though they don't want to bothah—just want to get the day ovah with."

"I'm sure they don't feel thet way," Belinda assured the el-

116

derly lady. "It's jest thet they haven't had much experience in bedside nursing care. Mrs. Mills has nursed neighbors fer years, but most of her time has been helpin' mothers an' new-born babies. Flo is just being trained in nursin'. Luke wants to have a second nurse available so thet one doctor an' one of the nurses might get a break now an' then. He is even talkin' of trainin' a third girl to help jest so thet she'll have some knowledge if he ever needs to call on someone. Mrs. Mills is gettin' older an' won't want to nurse much longer."

"Well, I think it's a splendid idea to train others. Believe me, I do," insisted Mrs. Stafford-Smyth. "But you must admit that some folks are fah more adept at sensing needs than othah people are. You are one of those few, Belinda. You seem to feel for the patient—to understand the hardness of the bed and the misery of lying day after day on one's back."

She hurried on. "I know you need time off. No one can work day and night. But I do hate the days or nights when you are not heah. Things just always go so much—"

"And how is our patient this morning?" a man's voice asked along with a rap on the door for their attention.

Belinda recognized Jackson's voice before she turned around to bid the tall young man to enter. Mrs. Stafford-Smyth's face showed her surprise and her eyes were filled with questions.

"Mrs. Stafford-Smyth," said Belinda without really looking directly at Jackson, "this is Dr. Brown, Dr. Luke's new associate. Dr. Brown, Mrs. Stafford-Smyth of Boston."

Jackson crossed to the bedside and took one of the lady's weak hands in his, smiling at her warmly. And though she was not aware of it, his trained eyes were already picking up much information about her physical condition.

"And how are you feeling this morning?" he asked her sincerely.

She didn't answer his question. Instead, she studied him evenly, her eyes—as sharp in their own way as his—assessing everything about him. She saw a young man, carefully dressed and groomed, his eyes intent, his smile pleasant. His long, slender fingers suggested to her that he would be skillful in surgery.

His manner was not brisk or offensive. There was nothing cocky about him, nor did he seem in the least unsure of himself. Immediately she liked him—though she was quite sure that no one could ever possibly quite measure up to her Dr. Luke.

"You caught me by surprise," she finally responded slowly. "I was expecting my favorite Doctah Luke to be in to see me. Now I see a good-looking young man who appeahs to me to know what he is doing. How can such a small town have the honah of two such notable doctahs while the city of Boston suffahs with old has-beens and young, smug upstarts?"

Jackson laughed heartily, patting her hand as he did so.

"Doctah Brown, you say?" Mrs. Stafford-Smyth said, turning toward Belinda. "Where did you evah find him, my deah?"

Belinda could feel her cheeks flushing. She could also feel Jackson's eyes upon her. She did wish that Mrs. Stafford-Smyth were not quite so forthright.

"Dr. Brown grew up in our community," she explained, hoping her voice was even and controlled. "His mother is the school-teacher in our country school. Dr. Luke has been in touch with him all through his trainin', hopin' to entice him back to our little town."

The elderly lady's eyes again rested on Jackson. She hadn't missed the slight tension in the air.

"I still say it is unfai-ah," she protested good-naturedly.

Jackson became serious and all-doctor then, examining the patient, asking questions, and jotting items of note on the small pad he carried.

Mrs. Stafford-Smyth cooperated. Belinda had the impression that she rather liked doctors fussing over her.

"We have some new medication that I would like to try," Jackson told the woman. "It has been used with good success in the hospital where I took my training. I will explain to Nurse Davis the dosage and how it is to be administered."

Mrs. Stafford-Smyth nodded in agreement.

"Now I do believe," went on Jackson, "that when I arrived, I heard some talk about sitting up for a short time. I think that's a splendid idea. Could I help you to settle Mrs. Stafford-Smyth before I go, Nurse Davis?"

Belinda nodded and went to prepare the lady's chair by the window. Then, with Jackson's help, Mrs. Stafford-Smyth was carefully positioned on the chair, the draperies pulled back, and the window slightly raised so she might enjoy the freshness of the summer day.

Belinda thanked Jackson and was about to turn back to her patient when Jackson surprised her.

"May I see you for a moment please, Nurse?" he asked.

Belinda felt a twinge of concern. Had he noticed something about her patient that she had failed to see? And then she remembered the new medication—he had said that he would explain to her the proper use and dosage.

"I'll be right back," she assured Mrs. Stafford-Smyth, "and I will be jest outside yer door. If you should need me, I'll—"

"Nonsense," said the lady. "I'm fine. I haven't breathed such wonderful ai-ah for weeks."

Belinda smiled and followed Jackson to the hallway.

"She's really doing remarkably well," he commented after the door had closed gently behind them. "I am convinced that she has had first-rate care."

"Luke has—" began Belinda, but Jackson interrupted her.

"I know that Luke has handled her treatment well—but I was talking about nursing care."

Belinda could only flush at his compliment. "Thank you," she stammered, her eyes dropping.

Jackson stood for a moment looking down at her. He had waited for so many years for just such a moment. She was more charming than ever with her big blue eyes, her golden-brown hair and her air of complete modesty. He now knew that he had been right in not becoming enamored with the girls in the city where he had trained. *Not one of them can measure up to Belinda,* he thought. So many years had already slipped by. He felt an impatience stirring within him. He shifted slightly and then spoke softly.

"I was hoping that you'd have dinner with me this evening."

Belinda looked up quickly. The invitation had caught her completely by surprise.

"I—I thought you were goin' to explain the medication—to tell—" she stammered.

"I didn't bring it with me," hastened Jackson. "I have a supply at the office. I'll bring it this evening and explain it all to you then."

His eyes seemed to be pleading, and she wasn't sure just why. Was it necessary to meet over dinner to discuss the medication? Would a doctor ask his nurse to discuss cases over a meal? But she had worked only for Luke, and they were occupants of the same house. They could discuss cases any time. Maybe it wasn't unusual. How was she to know? She found her head nodding in agreement. Instinctively she knew that working with Jackson was going to be different than working with her brother Luke.

"Very well," she responded, licking her lips to moisten them.

"When are you off?" he asked next.

"Mrs. Mills comes at seven."

"Fine. I'll see you then."

"But—but—" argued Belinda. "I—I should freshen up some before—before dinner."

"Of course," he smiled. "I was thoughtless. How much time do you need?"

"It's going to make supper—er, dinner—very late," Belinda reasoned. "Ya'll be starved by then."

"Tell you what," he bargained; "why don't we both catch a little something to eat around four, and then we'll be able to wait until eight with no problem."

Belinda felt she had been invited into some kind of conspiracy—actually, it was rather exciting. She nodded, a smile playing about her lips.

"I'll leave orders downstairs to send something up to the room for you and Mrs. Stafford-Smyth," he went on, and when Belinda was about to protest he waved it aside.

"I'll see you later," he promised with a smile that both dismayed and warmed Belinda. He touched her arm gently and was gone.

Belinda stood shaking her head, watching his brisk strides take him down the corridor. Just before he rounded the corner, he turned slightly and gave her a little wave of his hand. She blushed, not expecting to get caught watching him walk away.

She pushed the door open gently and returned to her patient, glad to have something with which to occupy her time and attention.

"How are ya?" she asked solicitously. "Are ya tirin'?"

"Oh my, no," said the woman forcefully, "and don't you daiah try to put me back in that stuffy old bed yet."

Belinda smiled and went to freshen the bed while her patient was out of it.

"My," went on Mrs. Stafford-Smyth, "such a nice young man! You're a lucky girl."

Belinda lifted her eyes from the bed she was remaking, about to ask the lady what she had meant by her statement. But Mrs. Stafford-Smyth went on. "He likes you, you know. Anyone can see that. Have you known him long?"

Belinda wanted to deny the lady's assumption, but she wasn't sure she could truthfully do so, so she skipped it and went to the woman's question.

"We went to school together for a couple of years. He was a year ahead of me an' he left to go take his trainin'."

"And did you develop your interest in nursing before or aftah you met him?" questioned Mrs. Stafford-Smyth frankly.

Belinda felt her face coloring but she answered, perhaps a little too quickly, "Before. I guess I've always been interested in nursin'. When Luke discovered my eagerness to learn it, he promised to help me. I was only a little girl then."

The lady smiled, then nodded. "See! It's like I said. Good nurses are born, not made."

They were silent for a few moments. Belinda continued straightening up the room, and Mrs. Stafford-Smyth sat looking out upon the sun-drenched world beyond her bedroom.

"I must say, though," she mused, "it certainly has complicated things for me!"

"Complicated things? Meanin'?" Belinda asked offhandedly, not following the woman's train of thought.

"I had been hoping that I might soon be ready to make the train trip home."

"The new medication won't complicate thet, I'm sure," Belinda quickly assured her. "In fact, it might well hasten thet time fer ya."

Mrs. Stafford-Smyth's eyes began to shine with excitement, the first that Belinda had seen there. Then the woman sobered again.

"That wasn't just what I meant," she continued. "I had—had been planning for some time to ask if you would accompany me."

Belinda's breath caught in her throat in a little gasp. She had never even thought about such a thing. The enormity of it caught her totally by surprise.

"You mean—travel with ya by train—all the—the way to Boston?" she asked.

"If you would."

"Oh, my," said Belinda. "I never thought I'd see the likes of Boston."

"Would you consider it?" asked Mrs. Stafford-Smyth.

"I—I don't know. I'm not sure thet Luke could manage—"

"He would have Flo—and the new nurse he's training. You said so yourself."

"Yes, but—but Luke hasn't even started trainin' the second girl yet, an'—an' Flo—well, she's not ready yet to take over—"

"It wouldn't be for a week or so yet—and besides, there are two doctahs now. They can relieve each other."

That was true.

"Maybe they could—could manage for a short time," began Belinda. "How many days would the trip take?"

Mrs. Stafford-Smyth did not answer at once. She hesitated, studying Belinda's face. Then she spoke slowly. "That's the complication. I had wanted you to stay on with me in Boston—indefinitely—as my private nurse—and now—now this young, good-looking doctah appeahs—and it is very plain to me that—that he has othah plans for you."

Belinda began to flush deeply. "Oh—I—I believe you are—are mistakin' friendship fer—fer something more," she argued. "Jackson—Dr. Brown and I were classmates, not—not—" She faltered to a stop, feeling that she had already said too much.

Mrs. Stafford-Smyth did not appear to be convinced.

"Did you write?" she quizzed.

"Fer—fer a short while," answered Belinda honestly.

"Did he return a married man?"

"No—o—o."

"Has he ever spoken of anothah young woman?"

"No," Belinda quickly explained, "but we have not been writing lately. There might very well be a young woman—"

But Mrs. Stafford-Smyth just smiled a knowing smile.

"I rest my case," she said coyly.

Belinda's head began to whirl. What was Mrs. Stafford-Smyth telling her? Surely, after all these years Jackson could not still think—? Why had he invited her to dinner to discuss a case that could have been taken care of at the office or here in the sickroom? *What is going on? Oh, my!* she thought. *Oh, my!* But Mrs. Stafford-Smyth was speaking again.

"If I should be wrong—or if you should be interested," she began, "my offah stands. I would welcome you as my traveling companion and as my nurse in my home in Boston for as long as it would convenience both of us. The salary will be negotiated at such time as you decide. I will not pressure—but it would please me very much if you should decide to accept my proposal."

Belinda could only shake her head. It all seemed like a dream.

"Oh, my," she said hesitantly. "I—I think I would enjoy the trip—but to stay on—well—thet's quite different. I've never been away from my family—and—well, I guess I sorta feel I'm needed here. Luke needs me an'—an' Mama needs me. Now that things are—are—now that Dr. Brown is here an' you are feelin' much better—I—I plan to go home more. I—I jest don't know . . ." Her voice trailed off.

"We'll let it rest—for now," said Mrs. Stafford-Smyth.

Belinda was glad to dismiss the amazing idea from her mind and turn to other things.

At four o'clock sharp there was a rap on the door and a young girl from the kitchen staff stepped aside when Belinda opened it.

"I was ta bring this to yer room at four," she offered.

"Oh, my. Oh, oh yes," responded Belinda. She had quite forgotten Jackson's promise. She took the tray from the girl, thanked her sincerely and turned back to the room.

Mrs. Stafford-Smyth, who was tucked back in her bed propped up with pillows, looked quizzically at her.

"Dr.—Dr. Brown ordered it," explained Belinda. "He thought thet a bit of refreshment might be—might be a good idea."

"What a thoughtful young man," commented the elderly lady. She eyed the tray filled with hot tea, pastries and fresh fruit. "It does look good, doesn't it? Could you help me sit up just a bit more?"

Belinda looked in surprise at her patient. Mrs. Stafford-Smyth, who had needed to be coaxed and cajoled into eating even a small portion of her meals, was prepared to attack with enthusiasm the tray of afternoon tea things.

Perhaps we should have thought to try this long ago, Belinda told herself. *She might have taken to "tea" more quickly than to "dinner."*

Belinda poured two cups of the steaming tea, added sugar and cream to Mrs. Stafford-Smyth's at her bidding, and then the two ladies settled down to enjoy the dainties from the tea tray. It was almost like having a party, and Belinda enjoyed the bright chatter of Mrs. Stafford-Smyth as she recalled some of the teatimes she had shared with others in her home in Boston.

I must remember to tell Jackson—Dr. Brown—over supper— dinner—how good this has been for Mrs. Stafford-Smyth, Belinda told herself.

Perhaps it would not be long, after all, until the elderly lady would be able to return to her dearly loved Boston.

Chapter 16

Dinner

Belinda had ample time to bathe, do her hair, and dress carefully. She had gotten a bit of teasing from her two small nephews and a few good-natured remarks from her brother Luke when her plans for the evening were known. She tried to brush it all aside and convince them that this was nothing more than a doctor-nurse consultation in regard to a patient. But she had difficulty even convincing herself of that.

She told herself that she would not dress "special," but even as she thought the words she found herself lifting a soft, full-skirted pink taffeta from her closet. She knew it was by far the most becoming dress she owned. She slipped it over her head and studied herself in the mirror, determining just how she should style her hair to go with the gown.

She had just finished adding a touch of cologne to her wrists and temples when she heard the knock at the front door and Luke admitted Jackson to the family parlor. Belinda felt her pulse quicken—merely because this would be a special evening, and for Belinda those were few indeed. With heart pounding and cheeks warm, she waited for Luke's summons before leaving her room to meet her caller.

Jackson did not compliment her with words, but his eyes shone with appreciation as he looked at the becoming young lady before him. He was most anxious to be alone so he might express his pleasure at her appearance and her company.

Belinda walked sedately by his side, anxious to take her seat in the hotel dining room before the whole small town was abuzz with the fact that she was out strolling with the new doctor.

The dinner was an enjoyable experience for both of them. Jackson talked easily, sharing with Belinda stories of his experiences in medical training and his excitement over new medicines and treatments that were constantly being discovered.

"The field of medicine is moving forward so quickly that it is difficult for us doctors to keep up," he said, genuine awe in his voice.

Belinda could not help but feel some of his enthusiasm. For a moment her old wish came to mind. *I wish I'd been a boy. Then I could have been a doctor.* But she did not dwell on it for long.

When there was a bit of a lull in the conversation, Belinda dared present a question. She didn't know how Jackson would respond to being asked about a patient—by a mere nurse. She was so used to working with Luke and they discussed all cases openly.

"What—what do you think about Mrs. Stafford-Smyth and her progress?" she ventured rather timidly.

"From reading all Luke's reports and examining her today, I would say that she has made a remarkable recovery," he answered without hesitation.

Belinda relaxed. It was good to hear another doctor fresh from the latest in medical training agree with Luke about her patient. She had really become quite attached to the elderly lady in spite of the obvious difference in their social backgrounds.

"I think that getting her up for a brief time was an excellent idea," Jackson continued. "Did she tire quickly?"

"She surprised me. But I didn't leave her up quite as long as she would have liked. I was afraid thet she might overdo."

"Good for you," encouraged Jackson. "She should gain her strength back quickly now as long as she doesn't do something foolish and have a set-back."

"She is beginning to talk about traveling home to Boston," Belinda said slowly.

"Home? That might be rushing things a bit. Unless, of course, she has someone who will come and travel with her. Even then I would give it another week or two at the least."

A week or two. That really wasn't very long.

"Someone mentioned a traveling companion," went on Jackson.

"Yes," said Belinda, "but we just heard from her. She hasn't recovered well after her surgery. She isn't able to come."

"Well, Mrs. Stafford-Smyth definitely won't be able to travel by herself for some time yet," said Jackson soberly. Then he brightened. "But perhaps something else could be arranged. I would like to free you from your heavy responsibility as soon as possible."

Belinda looked up quickly. "I've rather enjoyed nursin' her," she said.

"I'm sure you have. And you have done a commendable job. But there comes a time when one must move on to other things—don't you think?" and Jackson smiled at Belinda in the soft light of the lamp.

She nodded. *Perhaps it is time to move on to other things,* she agreed, but she did not voice her thoughts to Jackson. Something told her that she and Jackson might not quite be thinking along the same lines. She wondered just what he might say if she were to tell him about Mrs. Stafford-Smyth's complimentary proposal. But she decided that this might not be the time. After all, the two doctors did need a nurse to assist in the office, and Flo was not yet knowledgeable enough to take over all the duties. She would not concern Jackson with the possibility that she might ask for a few months' leave. At least not just yet.

"Now, about that medication," Belinda began, but Jackson stopped her with a chuckle.

"In my hurry to pick up a very attractive young lady, I'm afraid I've forgotten to bring it," he said. Then he added quickly, "I'll be sure to bring it with me when I come to check Mrs. Stafford-Smyth in the morning."

"So—so you will be coming again tomorrow?" asked Belinda shyly.

"Luke and I went through all the patient files, and Mrs.

Stafford-Smyth is one of the patients that we agreed I will take," answered Jackson simply.

Belinda nodded. "And the—the directions for giving the medication?" she prompted.

"Very straightforward—nothing other than one tablet morning, noon and night—with water."

Belinda blinked. *Hadn't Jackson indicated complicated instructions when he'd mentioned the new medication earlier? Or had she imagined it?*

Jackson was talking about his desire to help bring culture, in some small measure, to their town.

"It would be so enriching and relaxing," he said, "to attend a play or a concert now and then," and though Belinda had never had the pleasure of either, she quite agreed.

"It would also help young suitors, such as myself," Jackson went on with a teasing smile. "What is there now to offer a young woman except a walk in the fresh air or a ride in the country?"

Is Jackson courting someone? He couldn't mean me! Belinda's thoughts rushed frantically through her mind. To cover her confusion, she tried to make a little joke with, "Well, there *are* the school programs each spring." She was very relieved when they laughed together and Jackson, as far as she was concerned, completely changed the conversation.

"Mr. O'Connel seems like a fine young man."

"Yes," agreed Belinda innocently. "He is."

"Is he from the area or did he move in?"

"He grew up here. Went to our school, in fact. But I guess thet was before you came. He was ahead of me. He left to go off to work fer his uncle down state."

"Was he just paying a visit in the area when—?"

"Oh, no. He's back to stay."

"What does he do?"

Belinda thought it was nice of Jackson to be so interested in Rand.

"He's a builder," she replied. Thinking of the fine house Rand had built for the Kirbys made her eyes brighten. "He built the most magnificent house," she continued enthusiastically.

"He had a fella come and help him with the most ornate parts—the gables and fancy trimmin's an' all—but he built most of it himself."

"Is it the building or the builder that makes your eyes shine?" Jackson asked softly.

Belinda flushed. "Maybe—maybe it's just the lamplight reflectin' in my eyes," she countered. Then she responded truthfully, "Rand is a good friend."

"Just a friend?"

"Of—of course," Belinda answered.

"Nothing more? Because, if you have an understanding—" Jackson spoke softly and left the sentence dangling.

"We have no understandin'," Belinda offered quietly, though she did wonder why it was necessary for her to explain this to Jackson. She was surprised at his look of relief. He nodded and smiled at her.

"Then," he said with mock formality, "since there is nothing else for one to do in this small town, may I escort you for a walk in the soft-gathering twilight?"

Belinda smiled at his playfulness and fell into the mood of the moment. "Thank you, kind sir," she answered and accepted his proffered arm for a leisurely stroll back to Luke's house.

Dusk gathered about them, making the dust and grit of the little town less noticeable. The scent of the garden flowers drifted out on the hint of a breeze, caressing the senses with feelings of warmth and good-will. Belinda breathed in deeply. It was good just to be alive on such an evening. She was glad Jackson was back, that she had been out for dinner and that the lovely evening was perfect for a walk.

They were nearing Luke's house, carefully picking their way along the wooden sidewalk, when they turned a corner and almost ran into a figure in the semidarkness.

"Excuse me," a voice said and Belinda recognized Rand at once.

"Rand!" she exclaimed without thinking, and his head abruptly came up.

"Belinda," he returned with equal surprise.

"I didn't expect to—" she began, but Rand interrupted her brusquely.

"Obviously not."

What does he mean by that? she found herself wondering, but Jackson was saying, "Miss Davis kindly consented to be my dinner guest."

"So I was told," Rand retorted.

"Have you been visitin' Luke?" Belinda asked, feeling her question quite a safe one, but to her amazement Rand answered that query curtly also.

"No. I was not calling on Luke." Then he added more quietly. "I went to see his sister."

"Oh! I'm—I'm sorry I wasn't home. I—I didn't know ya were plannin' to call. I—I—"

Rand softened then. He turned to Belinda with apology in his voice. "I'm sorry," he stammered. "I shouldn't have jest taken it fer granted. I jest never thought—had never—never concerned myself with—with makin' plans ahead before."

It was true. Rand had been accustomed to dropping over casually whenever his busy schedule would allow. If Belinda should happen to be busy with a patient, he would visit briefly with Luke and then go on back to the boardinghouse.

"But I see," went on Rand, "that from now on, I'll need to make my plans known."

He spoke to Belinda, but his eyes never left the face of Jackson. Belinda felt very uncomfortable and uncertain. *What is happening here?* she wondered.

Then Rand tipped his hat and bid them a good night, and Belinda felt Jackson's hold on her arm tighten as he guided her carefully over the uneven boards of the sidewalk.

Chapter 17

Looking for Answers

"I've missed you around here, Belinda," Luke said as he entered the office. Belinda was gathering her things before departing for her day of nursing at Mrs. Stafford-Smyth's hotel room.

Belinda smiled at her older brother. "I've been missin' you, too," she said honestly. "Fact is, I feel thet I haven't seen much of any family fer some time. I'm lookin' forward to Ma's birthday supper."

Belinda noticed the slight frown that creased Luke's forehead.

"Can't you make it to the birthday dinner?" she asked quickly.

He tried to smile at her. "I'll be there," he said simply.

Belinda's eyes were still full of questions, and Luke felt her studying him. He reached out and laid a hand gently on her carefully pinned hair. When she had been a little girl, he used to muss her curls, but he did not muss them now—they were too skillfully arranged.

"Sorry to be so—so obvious," he said. "It's just that family dinners aren't what they used to be."

"Ya—ya mean Arnie?"

Luke just nodded.

"Have ya—have ya seen Abe recently?" Belinda asked.

"It's just getting worse all the time."

"And Arnie still—?"

"I haven't talked to Arnie about it since I promised Ma I'd—" Luke stopped. He was silent for a few minutes and then continued. "It's not just Arnie. It's the whole family. Have you seen Ma and Pa lately? They both look like—well, like old, worn-out people. They look like they don't sleep nights or—or even eat properly."

"I don't think they do," said Belinda, her voice full of grief. "Last time I was home I heard them talkin' in their room in the middle of the night an'—an' when it came to mealtime, Ma mostly just pushed things back and forth on her plate."

"I worry about them. I took out some tonic to them—but I've no idea if they are taking it or not." Luke shook his head. "I worry—but worrying doesn't help. I pray—but I feel like my prayers are getting nowhere."

Belinda looked at her brother. His young shoulders seemed to sag beneath the heaviness of the load. For one brief instant she thought of trying to talk some sense into Arnie herself, but she quickly dismissed it. She wouldn't know what else to say and, besides, Ma had promised Arnie that no one would bring up the matter again.

"Wish I could get out to a few of the special meetings." Luke's statement surprised Belinda.

"Special meetin's?"

"You hadn't heard? They have a revivalist coming to the little church. It seems like it's just what I need. I feel—"

But Belinda interrupted, her eyes shining. "Thet's it! Thet's it!" she cried. "We need to get Arnie out to those meetings. Can't ya see? If Arnie would get things in his life straightened out an' let God lead him—then God could talk to him about young Abe, an' the family wouldn't need to. Oh, Luke, this whole thing—this whole tension and the heartache of Ma and Pa—it could all be straightened out if only—if only Arnie would let the Lord show him what to do."

Luke nodded thoughtfully.

"Oh, Luke! Let's pray and pray some more until Arnie goes," she pleaded.

Luke put his arm around her shoulder and gave her a squeeze. Belinda's excitement was infectious—or maybe it was her faith.

"Yes, let's pray," Luke agreed.

"So how was your dinnah with that new young doctah?" Mrs. Stafford-Smyth asked Belinda forthrightly.

Belinda felt the color rise in her cheeks but kept her back turned and her hands busy with morning duties. "Very nice," she answered evenly.

"Did you know that the young gentleman—the builder—stopped by heah a few moments after you had left last night? Said he had come to walk you home."

"Rand?"

"Yes—that Rand. He seemed terribly disappointed when we said you'd already left. Said he'd slip by your place a little latah in the evening."

Belinda wondered why Rand had been telling her his personal plans, but then she couldn't help but smile. With the direct questioning of Mrs. Stafford-Smyth, he very likely had little choice in the matter.

"He seems like a nice young man, too," went on Mrs. Stafford-Smyth.

"Too?" echoed Belinda.

"Well, the young doctah. Both of them seem like fine young men. I don't know how I would evah make the choice if I were you."

Belinda frowned.

"But girls have changed since the days when I was being courted," the frank woman went on. "Why, I knew a girl back in Boston—she had three beaus—all at once. She went with one to the opera, one to church doings, and the other out boating each Saturday afternoon. Managed all three of them—just as slick as you please. She said she enjoyed all of the activities, but the church-go-ah would nevah be seen at the opera—and the opera-go-ah didn't care for open air and sunshine, and the boat-ah refused to be seen in church. 'Course it was a bit difficult for her to arrange her days so that the one didn't meet the othah, but—"

But Belinda turned to her with flushed cheeks. "I'm afraid you have this all wrong," she said firmly. "The two young men in question are friends—both of 'em. I went to school with 'em as a—a child—and have no reason not to keep up their friendship. They are both fine young men, with high principles an' moral conduct, and I don't need to sneak around an'—an'— assign different days of the week or—or appropriate activities fer—fer—"

Mrs. Stafford-Smyth did not seem at all taken aback by Belinda's flushed cheeks and out-thrust chin. The lady smiled demurely. She loved to watch Belinda's face when she was worked up about something. The blue eyes snapped, the pink flush of the cheeks grew pinker, her chin lifted, and the intensity of her spirit shone through.

No wonder young men find her irresistible, thought Mrs. Stafford-Smyth, but to Belinda she said, "You needn't defend your actions to me, my deah. I understand perfectly that you look at things a bit differently than your young men do."

The phrase "your young men" bothered Belinda, and she was about to tell Mrs. Stafford-Smyth so when there was a gentle rap on the door. It opened and Jackson stepped into the room. In his hand he held the bottle of medication he had promised to bring. He greeted them both cheerfully and handed the bottle to Belinda with a wink. She felt her cheeks grow even hotter and turned to the window to let in a little of the morning sunshine and fresh air. Jackson moved on to the bedside of the patient. Soon the two were engaged in jovial banter, and Belinda, with attention diverted from her, was able to regain her composure.

"While you are here I'll slip down for Mrs. Stafford-Smyth's breakfast tray, if I may?" Belinda said to Jackson. When he nodded his agreement, she smoothed her white apron over her full skirts and left for the kitchen. She was glad to get out of the room. But even away from the sharp eyes of Mrs. Stafford-Smyth and the teasing smile of Jackson, she felt ill at ease.

What if—what if Mrs. Stafford-Smyth was right? What if both young men really did see themselves as suitors? Belinda enjoyed their company—their friendship, but she had no intentions of letting it go beyond that. Not with either of them. Surely they didn't think—? But Belinda shook her head in frustration and confusion. She did wish that men weren't so—so presumptuous.

That night Rand arrived at Luke's with a box of nicely wrapped candy and an invitation for supper the next Saturday night. Belinda smiled her thanks but she really wished she could refuse the gift. She liked candy but she did not want it from Rand. She wanted only his friendship—the outings and the long quiet talks and his listening ear. Why—why did he need to go and make things difficult?

The next morning when Belinda arrived at Mrs. Stafford-Smyth's room, she saw a pretty bouquet of flowers on the bedside table. She smiled at the elderly woman.

"Flowers," she commented. "Isn't that lovely—someone has brought ya flowers."

"Not so," said the elderly woman with a mischievous smile. "Read the note."

"With a puzzled frown Belinda moved to the bouquet and picked up the piece of paper beside it. "To the busiest little nurse in town," it read. "How about dinner on Saturday night? J.B."

Belinda's face burned with anger and embarrassment. Why would Jackson go and do such a thing so—so publicly? Why involve Mrs. Stafford-Smyth, who already was suspicious of his intent? Belinda's chin lifted as she moved to pull back the heavy drapes and open the window. *Things are getting out of hand,* she reasoned, and she didn't like it one little bit.

Belinda turned down both Saturday night dinner invitations. It was easy to come up with an excuse. She was going home to her ma and pa. Never had she felt a need to escape more than she did on that occasion. Never had she been so relieved to lay aside her traveling hat and pull up a chair in the quietness and peace of her mother's kitchen.

"You look tired, dear," Marty observed as she served the tea.

"I am. A bit," admitted Belinda. She sighed deeply and reached up to loosen the combs in her hair, letting the heavy, long tresses fall down about her shoulders. "It's been a long, long time since Mrs. Stafford-Smyth was brought to us," she observed.

"But I thought she was doin' much better."

"Oh, she is. She doesn't even need constant care now. We had a cot moved into the room an' Mrs. Mills is able to sleep at nights. And we are able to go for her meal trays, an' she can sit up for longer periods. She really is doin' jest fine—but I—I guess the strain of it all might be catchin' up with me."

"How much longer?" asked Marty.

"She's talkin' daily 'bout going home now. I don't think we'll be able to keep her much longer."

"Will she be able to travel alone?"

Belinda looked carefully at her mother. "She's—she's asked me to accompany her," she answered slowly, watching for Marty's reaction.

Marty took her time in responding. "An' ya think ya'd like to." It was more of a statement than a question. Marty knew her daughter well.

"I—I thought it would be a nice change. See a bit of the country. I've never been east before, and I—"

Belinda wished she could bring herself to say openly that she needed to get away—needed time to be able to think. The two young men in her life were crowding her, making her feel she was being pushed into a corner. She wanted to get away to where she had room to breathe. But Belinda said none of those things.

"I think thet it would be good fer ya," said Marty, tiredly pushing a stray strand of hair back from her face. "Days I wish thet I could jest do the same," she admitted, and Belinda turned a concerned face to her mother, then reached out a comforting hand and touched her cheek.

"Luke an' I are both prayin'—" she told Marty, "prayin' thet those special meetin's might turn things right around. God can, you know. Arnie can still—"

"It's more than jest our young Abe. Luke was right 'bout 'im, of course. The arm has gone bad. But it's—it's beyond thet now. Sometimes I look at Arnie an' I see such pain in his eyes thet I can scarcely stand it. I think thet he is hurtin' far more than thet boy."

"He still comes to church?" Belinda asked. Since being so busy and having so few weekends at home, she had been attending the little church in town rather than the one out near the farm.

"Oh, yes, he's there. Doesn't take part in anythin' though. Jest sits. I sometimes wonder iffen he's even listenin'." Marty sighed deeply.

"Is he still angry with Luke?" asked Belinda.

Marty shrugged her shoulders. "He doesn't say—but I'm guessin' he's still angry with Luke an' Clare—an'—maybe even with God. I don't know."

"We need to keep prayin'," insisted Belinda. "If we all jest pray—"

Marty nodded and managed a smile. "Prayin'? Thet seems to be all yer pa an' I do. Sometimes even in the middle of the night we spend us time a'prayin'. This has been hard on yer pa. I worry 'bout him sometimes."

Marty stopped and Belinda reached out again to take her hand. She worried about both of them. She had never seen anything as difficult for Clark and Marty as the rift in the family circle.

The meetings began with the special speaker in the small country church. Arnie went to the first meeting and then declared himself too busy to go back on successive nights. Anne could go if she wished, he said, but he had other things that he needed to do.

But Luke went. Every night he could possibly get away—even on those nights when his doctoring duties made him late for service—he rushed to finish his work, dressed quickly and went to join the others. He had been feeling a "dryness"—a need for spiritual refreshing. The strained relationship with Arnie had cut him deeply. He knew instinctively that only God could meet his inner need and, ultimately, mend the broken family relationships.

Chapter 18

Changes

As much as Belinda would have liked to, she could not avoid either Rand or Jackson. As soon as she was back in town, Jackson was either at the bedside of Mrs. Stafford-Smyth or in the small office where Belinda picked up her nursing needs and left her daily chart.

He always smiled and teased a bit, and asked for dinner dates or evening walks. Belinda put him off the best she could, but she knew that one day soon there would be some kind of showdown if she didn't escape.

Rand, too, was a problem. Nearing completion on another house, he had hinted once or twice that as soon as it was finished, he would like to begin work on a house of his own. At first Belinda had been surprised, but then it seemed reasonable enough that a builder would make himself a place to live rather than continue to pay rent at the local boardinghouse. She had smiled and commended him.

Then one day Rand followed up on his intentions, "Could I drop by some sketches, so thet ya can do some lookin'?"

"Well—I—I," she began, but Rand only smiled and said he'd bring over the sketches the next evening.

Belinda went to work the next morning feeling desperate. Had Rand really meant what she feared he might? Had she been giving him the wrong impression? She hadn't intended to.

She needed—she desperately needed some time away from all this.

She pushed her troubled thoughts aside as she entered her patient's room. She did not wish to bother Mrs. Stafford-Smyth with her problems. "Ya look very chipper this mornin'," she informed her charge, and Mrs. Stafford-Smyth responded that she was feeling much improved, too.

After Jackson came and had completed his regular morning check, Belinda turned to her patient. "I'm going to slip down to the dining room for a cup of coffee with Dr. Brown," she said very matter-of-factly, though Mrs. Stafford-Smyth smiled knowingly and Jackson gave her a broad grin as he held the door for her.

"What a pleasant surprise," he noted when they were alone in the hall.

Belinda only smiled. "I'd like a full and honest report on our patient," she informed him.

"Oh, my," he laughed. "I had hoped that you found my company irresistible."

Belinda did not say any more about Mrs. Stafford-Smyth until they were seated at a corner table with steaming cups of coffee and fresh morning muffins before them. "Mrs. Stafford-Smyth talks daily about returning to Boston," she began. "What I want to know is this: is she well enough to travel?"

Jackson's eyes lit up. He would never jeopardize the health of a patient, but he was anxious for Belinda to be back in the office with more time to make plans of her own.

"I'm sure that traveling would not in any way be a hazard," he answered truthfully, then hastened to add, "providing of course, she has able assistance."

"And would you call me 'able assistance'?" asked Belinda with a teasing tone.

Jackson set his coffee cup back down and stared at Belinda. "What are you saying?" he asked.

"Mrs. Stafford-Smyth has been after me for some time to travel home with her," responded Belinda. "I have been puttin' her off—but recently I've been thinkin' thet it might be a nice change."

Jackson looked shocked, but he quickly regained control and even managed a smile. "Perhaps it would," he answered. "You have been quite—quite confined, haven't you? A little break for you might be nice and then when you return . . ." Jackson did not finish his sentence.

"How long do you think you would be gone?" he said instead. "A couple of weeks?"

"Thet's—thet's not quite what Mrs. Stafford-Smyth has in mind," answered Belinda evenly. "She wishes me to stay on as her private nurse."

Belinda saw the shadow pass over Jackson's face and linger in the depths of his eyes. "But surely you're not even considering—?" he began.

"Yes," Belinda nodded. "Yes, I am."

"But—but—" began Jackson, "you can't be serious."

Belinda did not waver. "Why?" she asked simply. "I talked to Luke about it last night. He says thet Flo is quite able to handle the office duties now. He said thet you had been particularly intent on trainin' her—"

"I *was* intent on training her," Jackson said abruptly. "I've been most anxious to relieve you of your constant nursing—but not so that you could go to Boston. Only so you would be free to consider—consider other things."

The silence hung heavy between them. Belinda, uncomfortable, toyed with her teaspoon, unable to look up at Jackson.

"How long?" he asked at length.

"I don't know," she answered honestly. "It depends on how things go. Mrs. Stafford-Smyth has even mentioned my bein' a travelin' companion. She likes to go abroad—"

Jackson groaned. "After all these years," he said softly. "After all these years of waiting, and you are asking me to go on waiting while—"

Belinda's head came up. "No!" she said quickly. "No!"

She looked directly into Jackson's face. "I have *never* asked ya to wait, Jackson. Never. Waiting was—was yer idea. I'm—I'm dreadfully sorry if ya've had the wrong—the wrong impression about—about us. Yer a dear friend, Jackson, an'—I—care deeply fer ya, but I don't—haven't ever meant to make ya think thet—"

She stumbled to a stop. Jackson sat before her with an ashen face saying nothing. He reached a shaking hand up to rub his brow. At length he was able to lift his eyes again to Belinda's.

She also was sitting silently, the tears unwillingly forming in the corners of her eyes. She hadn't wanted to hurt Jackson. Hadn't planned to do so. She felt heartless even though she knew that the fault was not really hers.

"I—I'm sorry," she whispered softly.

Jackson reached across the table and took her hand gently in his. "My dear little Belinda," he said in not much more than a whisper. "You've always tried to tell me—haven't you? But I refused to listen. Refused to believe that it wouldn't work out—in time." He paused a moment to sort out his thoughts and then went on softly, "Go ahead. Go to Boston. And if you ever get tired of it—or if you ever change your mind, I'll—I'll be here—waiting."

"No, Jackson, please," broke in Belinda. "Please—please don't wait anymore. I—I couldn't bear it. I—I feel thet so much of yer life has already been spent in waitin'."

Jackson's laugh was strained, but the sound of it relieved the tension in the air. "You make me sound like an old, old man," he chided.

Belinda shook her head in confusion and flushed. "Of course I don't mean thet," she hastened to say, gently withdrawing her hand. "It's jest—jest—"

Jackson nodded, understanding what she was saying. He would say no more. But what difference did a few more years make? Perhaps Belinda would tire of Boston quickly and soon be back home again. He'd wait. He'd just wait and see.

It was no easier breaking the news to Rand. He had come over that evening with the sketches he had promised. After pouring two glasses of lemonade, Belinda reluctantly followed him, with his sketches, to the picnic table under the large elm trees. Rand spread the drawings out before them.

"I want ya to go over 'em carefully," he said, excitement in his voice. "Anythin' thet ya like, jest mark and then we'll do up another sketch combinin' it all together."

Belinda drew in her breath. "I'm—I'm really excited about yer house, Rand," she said slowly, "but I don't know how much help I'll be able to give."

At Rand's questioning gaze she hurried on, "You see, Mrs. Stafford-Smyth is able to travel now, and she has asked me to accompany her back to Boston."

"To Boston?" echoed Rand. "Thet's a fair piece, as I understand it. How long's it take anyway?"

"Fer the trip? I—I'm not sure but—"

Rand began to fold the sketches, then changed his mind and spread them out again. "Iffen we have it figured out before ya leave," he said, "I could start gettin' things under way whilst ya was gone. Then when ya git back—"

"But Mrs. Stafford-Smyth wants me to stay on," Belinda admitted hesitantly.

"Stay on? What ya meanin'? Stay on fer how long?"

"In—indefinitely," mumbled Belinda.

"But ya didn't agree to anythin' like thet, did ya?" asked Rand in disbelief.

"Well, I—I said that I would consider it and—and recently I have thought thet—thet I would like to," Belinda finished in a rush, her chin coming up.

"But—but what 'bout us?" Rand asked hoarsely.

"Us?"

"Us! Our plans?"

"Rand," Belinda said as softly as she could, "you and I have not talked about any 'plans.' "

Rand flushed and rustled his sketches. "Well—well, maybe not—yet," he stammered. "The timin' wasn't right. I had to git me some means first. But ya knew—ya knew how I felt about ya. Thet as soon as I was able I'd be askin'—"

Belinda shook her head slowly, her eyes clouded. "No, Rand. I'm afraid I didn't know. I've thought of you as a dear friend—"

"A friend?" hissed Rand. Then he drew himself up, a set look on his face. "It's the doctor, ain't it?" he insisted. "I knew—

I knew the minute thet I saw thet guy thet he was trouble." Rand's eyes sparked angrily.

Belinda reached out to lay a hand on Rand's sleeve. "No," she said abruptly. "No." She shook her head, the tears spilling down her cheeks. "Jackson has nothing to do with how I feel about you. I—I—care deeply about you, Rand. If there was—anyone—anyone thet I would—would like to share a home with—it would be you." Her lips trembled as she spoke. "But I'm not ready. I—I'm jest not ready."

"Yer two nieces have been married fer a couple'a years already," Rand reminded her, then added almost bitterly, "Seems thet by the time a woman reaches yer age, she should be most ready to settle down—to know 'er own mind."

Belinda turned away. His words seemed unfair—even if they were true. Most young women were married before they were her age. She thought of her nieces. By all reports Amy Jo and Melissa were both very happy. Belinda was happy for them. But she wasn't Amy Jo—and she wasn't Melissa. She still didn't feel ready for marriage. Or maybe she just hadn't met the right young man. She didn't know. She was so confused. Maybe there would never be a young man in her life. Well, that was better than trying to live her life with the wrong one. She turned back to Rand.

"I'm very sorry—really. I wouldn't have misled you for the world. I—I—you are special to me—as—a—friend. It's jest—jest thet I don't care in—in thet way."

Rand took Belinda's hand. He wished he could pull her close—hold her. He was sure that if she would just give him a chance, he could make her love him. But Belinda resisted his effort to draw her toward him.

"Okay," he finally conceded. "Go 'long to Boston. Guess I can busy myself on another house. No rush on this one. But when ya git back—we'll—we'll talk about it."

"Rand," argued Belinda. "I—I might stay for a long time—several years. I might not ever come back."

"We'll see," said Rand darkly as he rolled up the sketches. "We'll jest have to wait an' see."

"How soon can you be ready to go?" Belinda asked Mrs.

Stafford-Smyth the next morning.

"Am I being evicted?" the woman asked good-naturedly.

Belinda smiled. "No! I thought thet ya were anxious to be on yer way home, and I asked Dr. Brown yesterday over thet cup of coffee if ya were ready to travel. He assured me thet there was no reason for ya to stay on here one moment longer then ya want to."

By the time Belinda had finished her speech, Mrs. Stafford-Smyth was beaming. "And you'll go with me?" she asked.

"I'll go with ya," promised Belinda, feeling much relief in just saying the words.

"And stay?" asked the elderly woman.

"And stay!" responded Belinda. "At least fer a time."

"Good!" said Mrs. Stafford-Smyth. She looked forward to having Belinda with her. They got on well. She really hadn't expected the good fortune of being able to keep Belinda with her. A frown momentarily creased her forehead as she thought of the two young men whom she knew would like to keep Belinda here with them. She wondered what had happened, but for once she held her tongue. Perhaps someday she would dare to ask.

Luke went to the farm for a visit with Clark and Marty. Marty knew the moment she looked at his face that something important had happened, but it wasn't until they were seated around the comfortable kitchen table sharing their coffee and doughnuts that she dared to comment.

"Ya look like a heavy weight's been lifted off yer shoulders," she observed.

Luke smiled. "Not my shoulders—my heart," he said.

Marty's face brightened. She knew Luke had attended every meeting he could, staying behind to share in the prayer times whenever possible.

"Those meetings were just what I needed to get things back into proper focus again," he admitted.

Marty nodded. She had found the meetings a time of spiritual encouragement and refreshing as well. In fact, she and Clark had talked and prayed together one night until near morning, and finally had been able to leave the matter of the family tension in the hands of a masterful God.

"I'm on my way over to see Arnie," Luke went on and Marty looked at Clark, hardly able to contain her pleasure. God was already answering their prayer.

"To tell 'em ya forgive him?" she asked quickly, eagerly.

Luke looked surprised. "Forgive? I have nothing to forgive him for. No—I—I am going to beg my brother to forgive me," said Luke soberly and the tears began to fill his eyes.

"But—but I don't understand," said Marty. "Arnie was angry with you—"

"And for good reason," Luke explained. "I had no business to be butting into Arnie's life, assuming that I knew what was best for his son, demanding that he see things my way." By the time Luke had finished his speech the tears were coursing down his cheeks. "I didn't mean to be arrogant—and—and self-righteous, but I was. I just hope and pray that Arnie can find it in his heart to forgive me."

Marty looked at Clark. His eyes also were filled with tears. He reached out and took the slim, strong hand of his doctor son and squeezed it gently. He was unable to express his thoughts because of his deep emotions.

Marty wiped at her eyes and blew her nose. When she could speak again she took Luke's other hand. "We'll be prayin'," she said. "Yer pa an' me'll be prayin' the whole time it takes ya to talk to yer brother."

But Clark had found his voice. "I think we should start now," he stated simply, and bowing their heads together, Clark led the little group in prayer.

Luke and Arnie each talked about the incident later from his own perspective. Both said that the meeting of brother with brother was the most emotional thing they had ever been through. After Luke's initial confession and plea for Arnie to forgive him for his arrogance and interference, Luke suggested that they pray together. At first Arnie was guarded and defensive, but as Luke began to pray, Arnie too was touched with his need to restore his relationships—first of all with his God, and then with his family. Soon he too was crying out to God in repentance and contrition.

They wept and prayed together, arms around one another's shoulders. By the time they had sobbed it all out to God and to each other, they both felt spent but, at the same time, refreshed. Nothing was said about young Abe. Luke knew that it was not his decision, and Arnie knew that he would need to deal with the matter soon and honestly.

Arnie did not put off the matter of Abe's arm for very long. He realized that already too much time had passed since the accident and recognized himself that the arm was continually worsening. After talking it over with Anne, that evening, he called Abe to the kitchen where he and Anne sat at the family table.

Arnie swallowed hard. It was not easy for him to speak honestly with his son about a matter that was so painful and had caused so much heartache.

"Yer Uncle Luke has been to see us," he began. When he hesitated, Abe looked from his father to his mother with some fear in his eyes. With effort, Arnie hurried on. "He—he's—he's concerned 'bout yer arm."

Abe let his glance fall to the offending limb, but his gaze did not linger. Arnie noticed that the boy drew the arm closer to his side.

"Fact is—fact is—" Arnie found it hard to keep the tears from his eyes and voice. "We've known fer some time thet the arm wasn't healin' right. Luke tried to tell me—but I wouldn't listen." Arnie paused to clear his throat and then said, "Luke told me at the time thet ya needed surgery to—to right the arm—but I—I—"

But Abe stopped him, his eyes wide with amazement. "They can do thet?"

Arnie looked at the boy, not sure what he was asking.

"Can they, Pa?" Abe repeated. He let his eyes return to the crooked arm, locked into its constant position. "Can they right the arm?"

Arnie nodded slowly, blinking back the tears. "Luke says

they can," he said honestly. Then seeing the light suddenly come to the eyes of his son, he hastened on, "Oh, maybe not—not perfectly—but at least—at least they can help it a good deal—straighten it some and strengthen it some an'—an' give it some movement."

But Abe was not hearing his pa's words of caution. He was hearing words of hope. His eyes were bright with joy as he turned back to Arnie.

"When?" was all he asked.

Anne finally spoke, brushing away tears that lay on her cheeks and reaching to put an arm around her son. "Abe," she said slowly, softly, "I—I don't think thet ya understand. It's not gonna be thet easy to fix. Ya don't jest walk in the doctor's office an' have him—do—do yer arm. It means a trip to the city—examinations—decisions—then iffen the city doctors think thet it will work out okay—then they—they need to operate—to—to break the arm agin—an' then try to set it—mend it better."

"But—but—" Abe faltered, his eyes mirroring new despair. "But ya said, Pa, thet it would help some—thet Uncle Luke said—"

Arnie nodded solemnly.

"Then—then—?" But Abe stopped. His eyes misted for the first time. Arnie felt that his son now was understanding about the pain involved with the surgery. But when Abe spoke, the pain was not mentioned.

"It costs a lot, huh?"

The simple words cut Arnie to the quick. "No," he said quickly, shaking his head and starting to his feet. "No, son, thet's not the reason. We—we—" But Arnie could not go on and again Anne took over, reaching for Arnie's hand as she spoke to Abe.

"It was yer pain we feared—not the cost. We—we didn't want ya to suffer no more—yer pa an' me. We—we hoped thet the arm would git steadily better on its own, but—but—we think now thet it won't, not by itself." She stopped and, still clasping Arnie's hand, reached out her other hand to Abe.

"So—so," she went on hesitantly, "I guess it's really yer

decision. Now—now thet ya know about—about the—the surgery—the healing agin—what—what do you think we should do?"

Abe did not hurry with his answer. He looked steadily from one parent to the other. Then he looked down at his disabled limb. He swallowed hard and licked dry lips.

"Iffen ya don't mind—iffen it won't be—be—too much cost, then I'd like to try it—the surgery. Even iffen it jest makes it a little bit better, it would be—be good."

The words brought a flood of tears to Arnie. He reached out and drew Abe to him, burying his face against the leanness of the young body. Abe seemed confused by his father's response, but even in his youth he knew that Arnie needed him. Needed his love and his support.

"It's okay, Pa," he mumbled, his arms wrapped firmly around Arnie's neck. "It's okay. It won't hurt thet much."

"Don't ya see? Don't ya see?" sobbed Arnie. "Ya shoulda had it done first off. Luke tried to tell me—but I wouldn't listen. It woulda worked better—"

Abe pulled back far enough to look into the eyes of his father.

"Is thet what's been troublin' ya?" he asked candidly. Arnie only nodded. Abe moved to place his arm securely around his father's neck again.

"Oh, Pa," he said with tears in his eyes. "We've been so scared—so scared—all of us kids. We feared thet ya had some awful sickness an' might die—an' here—here it was jest my silly ol' arm. It's okay, Pa." The young boy patted his father's shoulder. "An' ya know what? Iffen ya'd asked me way back then 'bout breakin' my arm all over agin, I'da prob'ly been scared ta death an'—an' run off in the woods hopin' it'd heal by itself. Now we all know thet ain't gonna happen," he finished matter-of-factly. "I know ya love me. The pain—it—it won't be too bad," he reassured them.

Father and son held each other close, and Anne breathed a prayer to God as she wiped her tears. There was much ahead for all of them—for there would be surgery to be faced just as soon as Luke could make the arrangements.

Arnie went to see Luke the next morning, but on the way he stopped to ask forgiveness of Clare and to beg Clark and Marty to forgive him for all the suffering he had caused them in his bitterness. He pleaded to be restored to his old relationship within the family circle, and with tears of joy and prayers of thanksgiving he was drawn back into loving arms.

Chapter 19

Boston

"Are ya comfortable?" Belinda asked Mrs. Stafford-Smyth. They were settled on the eastbound train for Boston after an emotional and teary goodbye at the station. Most of Belinda's family had been there to see her off. She was glad that neither Rand nor Jackson had appeared, although she had received messages from each of them the night before her departure.

"May your trip to Boston be smooth, uneventful—and hasty," said Jackson's teasing note tucked into a basket of forget-me-nots. Belinda had not been able to hide her smile.

Rand's message had been more direct. "Sorry for any misunderstanding," it read. "Whenever you are ready to come back, I'll be here. Rand." This note came with a small packet of house plans, and etched in a corner in Rand's script was the terse comment, "Study at leisure."

Poor Rand, mused Belinda. It seemed that he refused to give up.

But now all of that was behind her. She leaned back against the velvet seat of the Pullman and tried to gather her thoughts into some kind of order.

I'm actually on my way—to Boston! Imagine! She had made the decision, arranged for her absence from her work, checked with her family, planned the departure, and sent word to her new employer's home in Boston. *I guess I'm really grown-up now!* she teased herself. She was on her own, bound for a city hundreds of miles from home—and with indefinite plans as to the length of her stay.

Marty had shed some tears, of course. Belinda had expected it. She was Marty's baby—the last of the children to go. Belinda knew it would be hard for her ma and pa, but she was so thankful that the clash between Arnie and the other family members had been healed before she left. Again she said a quick prayer of thanks to God. That morning at the station her mother had looked years younger and much more relaxed, even though she was bidding her youngest a tearful goodbye.

Belinda took a few moments to worry about the office. Would Flo really be able to take over all the tasks that had been Belinda's for so long? Would she be skilled enough to assist with the simple surgeries that were done in the little surgical room? Of course, now that Jackson was there, he would be able to assist Luke—or Luke assist Jackson, whichever way it went. Belinda, happy for that fact, was able to dismiss the office from her mind.

Next, Belinda considered her nieces and nephews. They grew so quickly. If she stayed away for any extended period of time, they would grow up without her. She pictured rambunctious Dack. It seemed like such a short time ago that he was a boisterous, sometimes in-the-way little preschooler, and now he was playing boyish games and doing lessons. Even Luke's three little ones were growing up so rapidly. Belinda found it hard to believe that Ruthie was already toddling about and chattering words that might not be understood but seemed to mean something to the pint-sized chatterer.

What will they be like when I get back home? she wondered. *They change so quickly.*

Then Belinda remembered Melissa and Amy Jo. Word had just arrived that Melissa was the mother of a baby boy, Clark Thomas, and that Amy Jo would have her turn at motherhood some time in November. It seemed unreal to Belinda. She thought again of Rand's angry words. He was right, Belinda admitted. *Most girls—women—do know their own minds by the time they're my age.*

For a minute Belinda's face reddened with the memory, and

then she straightened her shoulders, lifted her chin and assured herself, *And I know my own mind, too. I knew then and I know now that I'm not ready to marry either Rand O'Connel or Jackson Brown. It would be wrong, wrong, wrong for me to do so.*

Feeling better with that matter settled, Belinda turned her eyes back to her patient. "Would ya like another pillow?" she asked solicitously.

"Stop fussing so," scolded Mrs. Stafford-Smyth good-naturedly. "If I want something, I will let it be known. This is your first trip. Enjoy it. Look there—out the window. See that sleepy little town? The whole country is filled with one aftah the othah. I wondah how folks can tell them apart." She smiled. "Wondah just how many people get off at the wrong stop," she mused on, "thinking that they have arrived home?"

Belinda smiled. But she was sure that no homecoming included such a problem. She realized Mrs. Stafford-Smyth saw even her little town as one of tiny duplicate beads of a necklace stretching all across the great continent. Yet, if she, Belinda, were heading home, she knew that no other town would look the same to her as her own town would.

She decided to check with her patient one more time. "Ya promise ya'll ask if ya wish something?"

"I promise," laughed the woman.

Belinda shifted some hand luggage so she could move closer to the window.

"In that case," she said lightly, "I will be glad to accept yer invitation and enjoy the scenery. I've never traveled quite this far from home before," and Belinda settled down to follow the changing landscape as the train rocked and rattled its way east over the uneven tracks.

The landscape soon began to change. The trees were bigger and forests more dense. The farms looked different to Belinda than the farms at home. The small towns gave way to larger ones. They even passed through some cities. Belinda, face pressed to the window, found them especially intriguing and couldn't see enough of the people who lined the platforms or walked the streets. *This is a new world from the one I've known all my life,* she told herself. She could sense it even though the glass windowpane held her back from it.

They were obliged to make two train changes. Belinda worried that the procedure of getting resettled might be hard for her patient, but Mrs. Stafford-Smyth seemed to handle the situation well. They had plenty of help from the solicitous porters, who seemed to sense a good tip from the hand of the older woman.

On the third day Belinda noticed Mrs. Stafford-Smyth begin to lean forward in some agitation. At first Belinda wondered if her employer was experiencing some kind of pain or discomfort. Then she noticed the shining eyes, the flush of cheek. "We should be in Boston by teatime," the woman exulted, and Belinda understood her excitement.

Belinda tried to imagine what the home of Mrs. Stafford-Smyth was like. Whenever she had asked, the woman had refused to indulge her curiosity. "You shall see for yourself in due time," she answered comfortably, and so Belinda was forced to wait. Now that they were almost there, she found her own excitement mounting.

Just as Mrs. Stafford-Smyth had told her, shortly after two Belinda began to see buildings crowding in closely on both sides of the tracks. The shrill whistle of the train announced that they were coming to another city center, and then the conductor was walking the aisles crying his message of "Bos-ton. Bos-ton. Next stop, Bos-ton," and Mrs. Stafford-Smyth began to twitter and flutter and primp for their arrival.

Belinda felt a-twitter too. She peered from the train window for as long as she dared, trying hard to gather all the information she could by staring out into the busy city streets.

"This is the shoddy part of town," Mrs. Stafford-Smyth said with a wave of her hand. "We'll see the real Boston latah."

Belinda looked around. It did look rather shoddy, but she would not have said so to her elderly charge. She knew how much Mrs. Stafford-Smyth loved her city.

The train was decidedly slowing, and Belinda began to gather bags and packages together. She picked up the hat she had laid aside and carefully settled it back into position on her

golden-brown curls, pinning it securely into place with her hat
pins. Then she moved to assist Mrs. Stafford-Smyth, smoothing
her grayish hair into place and arranging her hat and veil securely.

"What do we do once we arrive?" she asked as she worked.

"Windsah will be theah with the carriage," replied the lady.

"Will you wish to lie down?" asked Belinda, wanting to
know how to prepare things for her patient.

"My word, no!" sniffed the woman. "I will ride through my
own town sitting up." Then her tone softened. "I'm not sure
that I will evah want to lie down again," she added. "Seems I
have been lying down for yeahs and yeahs."

Belinda smiled. "It has really been just months and
months," she corrected softly.

Windsor was there just as Mrs. Stafford-Smyth had said. He
came aboard and assisted his lady from the train, helping Belinda to settle her in the elaborately ornate carriage. Belinda
was so busy staring that she could hardly keep her wits about
her to do what was necessary. At length they were ready, Mrs.
Stafford-Smyth ensconced among many pillows, and Belinda
sedately seated opposite her beside the butler Windsor. The
driver was given the signal, the whip cracked and the impatient
horses were off with a flurry into the traffic of the downtown
streets.

Belinda longed to lean out the window to see all they were
passing, but she knew that it would not be ladylike. Instead,
she sat silently as the good man Windsor inquired about their
journey.

"And was the trip tedious, madam?" he was asking.

Mrs. Stafford-Smyth sighed. "Yes," she said simply, "quite
tedious. But it would have been much worse had it not been for
Belinda. She made me quite comfortable."

The butler did not turn to look at Belinda, but she could tell
that he was greatly relieved to know she had made things as
easy as possible for his madam.

"And how are things at home, Windsah?" asked Mrs. Stafford-Smyth.

"We have done ou-ah best in Madam's absence," he said
simply as she nodded.

Belinda turned her head slightly to gaze out the small window of the carriage. Would she ever have opportunity to see all the fascinating things they were whisking by in this wonderful city? Mrs. Stafford-Smyth and Windsor seemed not the least interested.

"Cook needs instructions," Windsor was telling her. "She wishes to know what diet regimen Madam might be on."

"Madam is on no diet," declared Mrs. Stafford-Smyth. "I am so sick of flat-tasting hotel food. I can scarcely wait for the flavahs of my own kitchen. You tell Cook to prepare the usual—and lots of it, because I plan to eat my fill ovah the next few days."

The butler's face barely hid his amusement. "Very well, madam," he said. "And where does Madam wish to be served? In your own chambers?"

"I shall take tea in the drawing room the moment we arrive," said Mrs. Stafford-Smyth; "then I wish to see my rose garden. I have missed it terribly. Then—"

"But Madam should rest after such a long and rigorous trip," Windsor chided her with just the proper amount of respect and liberty born out of long years of service.

To Belinda's surprise Mrs. Stafford-Smyth did not argue. "Perhaps," she consented, "for an hou-ah or two."

"And does Madam wish Miss Davis to occupy the Omberg suite?"

"No, she shall have the suite next to mine."

"The Rosewood?"

"The Rosewood."

How foreign these terms seemed to Belinda! This talk of "suites" instead of rooms, of names instead of locations. The Omberg suite! The Rosewood suite! It all sounded very mysterious—and so elegant.

But when Belinda got her first view of the mansion Mrs. Stafford-Smyth called home, she gasped and understood why they had to name rooms. She was sure they never would have kept things straight otherwise. Never had she seen so many rooms under one roof—not even at the Rose Palace Hotel.

The house was of brick and stone, and its extensions and

gables and additions seemed to go on and on. *I'm glad to be near Mrs. Stafford-Smyth,* she decided. She might never find her way otherwise.

The house was nestled on the wide expanse of carefully manicured green lawn, with flowerbeds filled with hollyhock, daisies and begonias. The driveway of red stone circled to the wide front step, and an arched brick canopy reached out to keep all who arrived protected from the weather.

Mrs. Stafford-Smyth was excited to be home, but she showed none of the awe Belinda felt as her eyes scanned the imposing sight.

"Welcome to Marshall Manor," said Mrs. Stafford-Smyth softly, smiling at Belinda.

"Oh, my!" was all Belinda could manage. She felt that she had just stepped into a fairy tale. She was glad Windsor, at least, had his wits about him. He stepped down from the carriage to help Mrs. Stafford-Smyth.

Two maids stood at the top of the stairs, ready to be of assistance at the least nod from the butler. Windsor spoke to the one nearest to him. "Madam wants her tea in the drawing room," he said, and the girl bustled off without so much as a nod.

Then Windsor spoke to the second girl. "Show Miss Davis the Rosewood Suite," he said, "so that she might freshen herself for tea. Then escort her back to the drawing room."

The girl nodded to Belinda and led the way through the doorway and up the long, circular staircase. Belinda was still gazing about her, enamored by the polished wood, the glistening chandeliers and the sparkling crystal. Never in all her wildest dreams could she have imagined that such a place existed. *No wonder Mrs. Stafford-Smyth was so anxious to get home!* The place was absolutely breathtaking.

Chapter 20

Getting Acquainted

The Rosewood Suite was like a dream room too. Belinda, expecting to find a pretty little room in a soft rose color, found instead a suite of rooms done in rich wood paneling, blue velvets, and white lace. Never had she seen anything so exquisite, not even in the picture books that Melissa had shared with her during their school days.

A large four-poster bed with a blue spread and lace overlay graced one wall of the large bedroom. The window drapes were also of blue velvet with white lace. On the other side of the room was a marble fireplace with a comfortable grouping of soft chairs surrounding a low, highly polished wooden table. An ornamental lamp was placed on white lace in the middle. At the window was a window seat covered with blue velvet, almost hidden from view by several pillows of blue print fabrics and lace work. The chest of drawers and the tall wardrobe matched the polished wood of the bed. The walls that were not paneled were covered with beautifully patterned wallpaper, with blue as the predominant color.

Belinda just stood there drinking it all in.

Wouldn't Mama love to see this, she breathed to herself, well aware of Marty's love for beautiful things.

"The bath is through there," indicated the young maid, pointing to a door off to the right. Her voice brought Belinda back to the present—she was supposed to be getting ready for

158

tea. She flushed and hurried forward.

"I'll wait for you in the hallway, miss," said the maid.

Belinda did not dare linger any longer, though she certainly wanted to. She looked quickly about her, promising herself a leisurely, thorough inspection later, and quickly went through to the small room off her bedroom.

The bath too was in blues, but here bright spots of pink and some ivory had been added in place of the whites in the bedroom. It was most becoming and Belinda wished that she could skip tea and just wander the suite at her own leisure.

She poured water from the pitcher to the basin and looked about her for a washcloth. The only ones in view looked so new and so ornate that she wondered if they were put there for use or for decoration. She had to use something, so at length she gingerly picked one up, dipped it carefully in the warm water and wiped her face. Alarmed at the travel grime that showed up on the cloth, Belinda carefully washed it out the best she could and then hung it back on its rack. Hurriedly she smoothed her hair and went to present herself to the maid.

She was led through a long hallway, past many doors, down long winding stairs and then through another hallway and finally into a room where a bright fire burned on the hearth. Here, too, homey, elegant furnishings seemed to abound. In the midst of her pillows sat Mrs. Stafford-Smyth, Windsor before her and an older lady standing back slightly, listening carefully to the Madam recounting tales of her illness in the little town out West. For a moment Belinda hesitated. It was only now that she fully appreciated the difference in what Mrs. Stafford-Smyth was accustomed to and what they had been able to offer her.

"Come in, my deah, come in," the lady said cheerily, motioning with her hand to Belinda.

Belinda felt suddenly shy. She could not refrain from looking dolefully down at her crumpled and slightly old-fashioned traveling gown. Surely it—or she—was out-of-place in this elegant home.

"Would you pou-ah, my deah," invited Mrs. Stafford-Smyth, not the least nonplussed by Belinda's appearance. Then she turned to the butler and the elderly woman in the room. "Belinda has spoiled me dreadfully, I'm afraid. She nursed me the total time I was ill. Oh, she had replacements at times, of course, but it was really Belinda who cared for me. I don't know what I should evah do without her. She knows exactly how I like my tea, the right amount of fluffing in the pillows, even how to make me smile when I get out of sorts."

Mrs. Stafford-Smyth gave Belinda an appreciative smile and waited for her "exactly right" tea.

"Ella showed you you-ah suite?" she asked as she accepted the cup.

Belinda could not keep the shine from her eyes. "It's lovely," she enthused.

"Good! Then you won't be quite so tempted to be running back to one of those young men you left behind."

Belinda could feel the color rising in her cheeks. She poured another cup of tea, and handed the cup to the lady who still stood by the serving tray. The woman was obviously flustered and she nervously indicated that the cup was not for her. Belinda was bewildered.

"Mrs. Pottah does not take tea in the drawing room," said Mrs. Stafford-Smyth simply. "She has her tea in the kitchen."

Now it was Belinda's turn to be flustered. She felt her gaze travel to Windsor. Mrs. Stafford-Smyth seemed to read her question.

"Windsah does not take tea with us eithah—unless on the rare occasion I can talk him into it."

"I see," murmured Belinda.

The woman called Mrs. Potter moved forward to serve Mrs. Stafford-Smyth some of the dainty sandwiches. She then hesitated, seeming not to know what to do next.

"Serve Miss Davis," instructed Mrs. Stafford-Smyth. "She will be taking tea with me daily."

The woman said nothing, just moved forward with the tray of sandwiches. Belinda was alert enough to realize that what was going on in the room was not the usual—but she had no idea what the usual might be.

After Mrs. Potter had served sandwiches and Belinda had

replenished the teacups, pastries were served. Belinda thought she should decline, but they looked so good and she was so hungry after three days of train fare that she could not resist. *I'll work it off later,* she promised herself, and then wondered just how she was to work it off. While Mrs. Stafford-Smyth rested, there would be nothing for her to do, unless of course she could be of assistance in the kitchen.

When Mrs. Stafford-Smyth declared that she couldn't eat another bite, Windsor took her arm. "You wanted to see your roses, madam?" he asked with proper respect.

"Oh, yes, Windsah, please," she returned and was led sedately toward another door.

Belinda stood, carefully set her teacup back on the tray, and began to help Mrs. Potter gather the tea things. She was stopped by a dark look of disapproval. Not knowing her offense, she drew back, her eyes offering apology.

"I'm—I'm sorry," she stammered. "I meant to be most careful."

"Nurse does not need to concern herself with the picking up," the woman said curtly. "We all know our stations, 'round heah."

Belinda frowned. It was all so strange. A room with people and you had to pick and choose who could be served. Work to do and only those designated for the certain job dared to do it. She had never heard tell of such a way to live.

"And what am I to do?" she dared ask.

"Madam gives your ordahs."

"But—but she hasn't given any," Belinda reminded the woman.

"Then I guess you wait until she does," the woman threw over her shoulder as she hoisted her tray and left through the side door.

Belinda, left alone in the room, didn't know whether she should exit through the door that had swallowed up Windsor and Mrs. Stafford-Smyth, try to find her way back to her own suite, or just wait right here where she was. It was all so puzzling.

She wandered slowly about the room, admiring each piece

of furniture, each ornately framed picture. Her eyes traveled over everything, drinking in the beauty of her surroundings.

Oh, she thought, *I never dreamed anything could be so lovely. I could jest look and look and look.* And except for wishing that she had her family near to share her adventure with, Belinda was full of excitement and satisfaction. *It won't be one bit hard to stay on here,* she told herself. *It's like living one's make-believe.* Then she turned to retrace her steps around the room one more time to make sure she didn't miss a single elegant item.

In the days that followed, Belinda became more acquainted with her surroundings. The suite she occupied also had an adjoining parlor room. Here again the basic color was blue, with a pattern of rose and touches of mint green enhancing the design. Belinda could not get her fill of the softness, the coolness, the harmony of the colors. The polished grain of the furniture and elegance of another marble fireplace added to the charm.

Off Belinda's sitting room was a door that led to Mrs. Stafford-Smyth's suite. A button on the lady's bedside table had been skillfully arranged to ring a buzzer in Belinda's room. Belinda soon discovered that there were many such buttons throughout the house. One in the parlor to ring for the maid. One in the drawing room to ring for the butler. One in the sunroom to ring for the cook. It seemed to Belinda that wherever Mrs. Stafford-Smyth took repose, a button was near her elbow.

But Belinda liked the button idea. It meant that she could attend the elderly lady without being with her every waking hour. She asked innocently for other duties about the house to make herself useful and was met with open-mouthed disbelief.

Do they think I'm capable of nothing but nursing? Belinda shrugged her shoulders and went to her own room to mind her own business. It wasn't as though Mrs. Stafford-Smyth kept ringing her buzzer. Belinda had plenty of free time that she could have used to lighten someone else's load.

Her dilemma was partly solved by Mrs. Stafford-Smyth when she sent Belinda to the library to get her a book or two. Belinda was told to go to the drawing room and ring the bell for Windsor. He would show her to the library and indicate which new books Mrs. Stafford-Smyth had not yet had the opportunity to read.

Belinda did as she was told, and Windsor led her directly to a room with high-paneled ceilings and shelves upon shelves of books. Belinda gasped at the find. Windsor selected a few volumes from a stack of books that appeared to have been set aside, and Belinda carried them, still gasping, to Mrs. Stafford-Smyth.

"I declare," she said as she entered the room, "I have never seen so many books in all my life. Are they all yers?"

The lady smiled. "Of course. But if you like, we will pretend that it is a lending library. You may help yourself to whatever you like, anytime you wish."

"Oh, may I?" Belinda could scarcely believe her good fortune.

"One hint. Don't evah put a book back where you found it. Leave the book on the big oak desk in the middle of the room. Windsah is absolutely convinced that he is the only person in this house—in the world, I'll wage-ah—who knows the proper place on the shelves for each book."

This seemed a bit foolish to Belinda, especially when she planned to read many of the books. But she did not argue. She would do as she was bidden. As soon as she was excused, she went directly to the library to browse among the books.

It was difficult for her to choose from among so many, but at length she selected three volumes and took them to her room. The rest of the day passed quickly as she became engrossed in a Charles Dickens novel. An American history and a lovely little book of poems were also inviting. She no longer fretted that her hands were not busy—she would keep at least her mind occupied.

Wouldn't it be wonderful, she thought, *to read every book in there before I go home again?* But she knew it would take years and years to devour all the contents of those ample shelves.

Belinda could sense a certain tension in the household. She wasn't sure what it was, but she had the feeling it might have something to do with her. She couldn't think of what she might have done to cause friction, but it was there, nonetheless.

One afternoon when Belinda and Mrs. Stafford-Smyth were enjoying tea in the east parlor, Mrs. Potter entered the room.

"Has Madam decided when she would like her dinnah party?" she asked.

Mrs. Stafford-Smyth did some thinking. "Bring me a calendah, Pottah," said Mrs. Stafford-Smyth, and the woman went to do her bidding.

While she was out, the lady turned to Belinda. "I plan to have some of my old friends in," she confided. "Not a large pahty, but my closest acquaintances. I haven't seen them for so long and it will be nice to catch up on the news of Boston."

She sat silently for a moment, then went on as though talking to herself. "Let's see . . . We arrived home on Monday. We are now to Saturday. We could nevah be ready for dinnah guests by tomorrow. What night would you suggest, my deah?"

Belinda had no idea what to suggest. "How—how much time does the staff need—?" she began. She had finally learned to refer to all of the household employees as staff.

"Windsah will take care of the invitations. The kitchen staff can be ready for the group I wish to have in two or three days."

"Then perhaps Wednesday evening," suggested Belinda, just as Mrs. Potter returned to the room carrying the needed calendar. Belinda felt the woman's cold eyes upon her. She wasn't sure what she had said or done that had angered her. Wasn't Wednesday giving the staff enough time?

"Or Thursday—or Friday," she added dumbly, watching for some sign of regained favor.

It did not come. But the woman did turn from Belinda and confer with Mrs. Stafford-Smyth. "What day were you thinking of, madam?"

"Wednesday," said Mrs. Stafford-Smyth without hesitation.

"Very good, madam," said Mrs. Potter. "Is there anything in particulah that you would like the kitchen to prepare?"

"I will leave that with you and Windsah," said Mrs. Stafford-Smyth. "You know my agitation at fussing over menus."

"Yes, madam," responded the woman.

"Ring for Windsah, would you please, my deah," Mrs. Stafford-Smyth said to Belinda and Belinda pressed the buzzer. Soon Windsor stood before them.

"Windsah, we are planning a small dinnah party for Wednesday night."

"Very good, madam," he said properly. "And how many will Madam be seating?"

"I would like you to invite Mrs. Prescott, and the Judge Allenbys, and—let's see. No, not the Forsyths this time. We'll save them for latah. Mr. Walsh. Celia loves to chattah with Mr. Walsh. And—one more couple, I should think. The Whitleys. That will do it. Yes, that should be just right, I think. That will mean eight at table. That should do."

"But Madam only named six guests. With herself at table, that leaves one short."

Mrs. Stafford-Smyth, with some impatience, listed off, "The Allenbys, Whitleys, Celia Prescott, Mr. Walsh, myself and Belinda. That's eight," she corrected.

Belinda had seen a flash of surprise in the butler's eyes when her name was given, though he did not flinch. But the expression on Mrs. Potter's face indicated open resentment.

Belinda had thought nothing of being included in the dinner list, for she had been taking all her meals with Mrs. Stafford-Smyth, but when she recognized the looks on the faces before her, she began to wonder about the arrangements. Was this why she felt hostility in the house?

She dared broach the subject with Mrs. Stafford-Smyth when they were once again alone in the room.

"Did yer old nurse—I've forgotten her name—did she dine with you?"

"Of course not," said the lady frankly. "She ate in the kitchen or in her own rooms. Mostly she had her meals taken up, I think."

Belinda waited for a moment. "Do you suppose it—it would be wiser if I had my meals in my own room?" she asked softly.

Mrs. Stafford-Smyth looked surprised. "Don't you like sharing your meals with me?" she asked.

"Of course I do—it's jest thet—well, I feel that yer staff

might think it's not quite appropriate, thet's all."

"Nonsense!" spoke the lady curtly. "This is my home and I can make my own rules." Belinda could see that the lady felt the matter was closed.

"But I *am* another employee," Belinda said candidly.

Mrs. Stafford-Smyth looked up from her needle work. "You are more like the daughter I nevah had," she replied softly and Belinda was touched. How could she argue against that?

Mrs. Stafford-Smyth had been paying Belinda generously throughout the months of her nursing care out West, and Belinda had tucked away most of the money rather than spending it. But with the Lord's Day and the dinner party coming upon them, she decided that the time might be right to relinquish some of her hoarded funds. She entered the hall that led to Mrs. Stafford-Smyth's rooms, walking quietly lest the woman was resting. As she knocked gently and was bidden to enter, Belinda slipped into the room.

"I do hope I'm not disturbin' ya," she spoke hurriedly, "but I was wonderin' about doing some shoppin'. Are there dress shops nearby that I could visit? I know that my dresses are dreadfully outdated and out-of-place here, and with tomorrow bein' church an' all, I—I thought thet perhaps—"

"Oh, my," said the lady, "I was hoping we could get by until I could go with you myself—but you are right. You would feel more comfortable with something new tomorrow. I should have thought of church. The fact that I am not quite up to going out yet myself should not preclude you from going. Of course you shall have a new dress—and hat—and a shawl too, I'm thinking. And then of course a pair of dressy high-topped shoes and perhaps a parasol . . ."

Belinda was about to slow the lady down. She hadn't intended to spend *that* much money.

"Windsah will have the carriage brought round and will direct you to LeSoud's," she instructed briskly. "It is the shop I had planned to take you to myself. Oh, my, I do wish I could go with you—but then we'll have othah outings. Bring me my writing pad, would you, deah? I'll just drop a little note to Madam Tilley."

And so saying, Mrs. Stafford-Smyth propped herself up on her pillows. Belinda meekly handed her the writing pad and the pen and ink and she began to write a letter for the lady called Madam Tilley. Belinda began to feel more and more anxious as the pen scratched on. It seemed the good lady was willing to spend all of Belinda's hard-earned money. Well, she would just put her foot down once she got to the store, she decided. Mrs. Stafford-Smyth would not be there to give orders then.

Belinda was sent to dress for her outing, and Windsor was given his orders and put his call through for the carriage. Before Belinda could catch her breath, she was traveling down the tree-lined streets on her way to the dress shop, with Windsor in attendance.

This time, without inhibitions, she stared openly from one side of the carriage to every mansion-like home, every expanse of green carpet, every hedge of roses, every fashionable carriage. *This truly is a magic kingdom—no wonder Mrs. Stafford-Smyth loves Boston!*

Chapter 21

A New Life

LeSoud's was not like any shop that Belinda had ever seen. Magnificent draperies and glass chandeliers made it seem like a lovely parlor, not a retail establishment. Ornate ivory brocade chairs were grouped around low tables holding silver dishes of sweets.

Windsor stepped forward and presented Madam Tilley with the lengthy instructions from Mrs. Stafford-Smyth and introduced Miss Belinda to the older woman. From there Madam took charge, indicating which chair Windsor should retire to and that Belinda was to follow her.

They passed through to another room, this one smaller but decorated with the same type of furnishings. Belinda looked around her in bewilderment. She could see no gowns for sale.

Madam seated her and then called to a young woman dressed in a stylish black gown, stark in its simplicity but attractive with its flowing lines. The two conferred softly for a few moments, and then the girl, referred to as Yvonne, left and was soon back with three gowns draped carefully over her arm.

From then on things moved quickly. Belinda was ordered to stand, then sit, twisted and fitted until her head was swimming. She had no idea what was being decided on her behalf. The two women were not speaking English. Madam would "tut" and "hmm" and Yvonne would "oh-h" and "ah-h" as Belinda lifted her arms to accept one gown after the other over her head.

Then there were shoes to try on along with gloves and shawls and coats until Belinda felt dizzy. In spite of all the commotion, she did spot a gown that she liked. A soft green voile that seemed to suit her slender build, it was attractive without being too fussy, and she could tell that it was something Marty would approve of her wearing when she went to church the next morning.

But that gown, too, was whisked away. Belinda knew not from whence they came or to whence they were returned. She tried to ask, but her voice was lost in the chatter of Madam and Yvonne.

When Belinda finally had her own gown on and had set her hat back on her head and drawn her gloves on her hands, she looked about her in bewilderment. She had come to buy a gown, and from the note Mrs. Stafford-Smyth had sent, she had feared she might have to argue her way out of numerous other purchases. But now it seemed she was not to be allowed even the one dress she had deemed necessary. She looked to Madam, hoping for some explanation.

"But the gown—the green voile—I—I liked—"

"You were pleased with it—no?" the woman said happily, her eyes taking on a shine.

"Yes. Yes," said Belinda. "I—was pleased with it."

"It will be delivered this evening," responded the woman.

Belinda was relieved. She must have somehow conveyed to them that she wished to purchase the green voile dress. It was to be delivered.

Belinda wished that she had been able to purchase a light shawl and perhaps some stylish shoes. *Well, I'll just have to get them later on,* she consoled herself. At least she had one dress. She was thankful for that.

Madam and Yvonne still scurried about the room gathering gowns and shoes and handbags.

Belinda hesitated.

"Was there something more, Miss Belinda?" the woman finally stopped long enough to ask.

Belinda flushed, reaching into her handbag. "The account," she faltered. "I need to pay you for the purchase."

Madam looked surprised. "The account is cared for," she said quickly, her left eyebrow shooting up. "It is all to go on Madam Stafford-Smyth's charge."

"Oh, but there must be some misunderstandin'," began Belinda. "The—the gown is personal—for me."

Madam reached down and picked up the lengthy instructions that Windsor had given her. "It is all right here," she explained. "Madam has ordered specifically that the purchase go on her account, and we at LeSoud's do not go contrary to Madam."

Belinda started to speak again but changed her mind. She didn't understand the workings of this new world, but perhaps Mrs. Stafford-Smyth felt that it would be less complicated to charge the items to her account and for Belinda to simply reimburse her. Still slightly confused, she followed Madam Tilley from the back room to rejoin Windsor.

As they traveled the route back to the Stafford-Smyth mansion, Belinda thought again about her purchase. She was pleased about the green voile. It would be becoming and appropriate for Sunday church-going. She had wanted to buy a second dress—one a bit more "frilly" for such occasions as the dinner party. But she had been unable to get that message across to the Madam. Belinda sighed. She guessed that the voile would have to do for the dinner party as well.

"How did you make out at LeSoud's?" asked Mrs. Stafford-Smyth at tea.

"Oh, my," answered Belinda, "I've never seen so many lovely things. It was most difficult to make up my mind. I did find a dress, though. It is to be delivered this evening." Belinda looked up from her teacup. "But I owe you for it. They—they wouldn't let me pay at the store. I—I don't even know how much it cost. I couldn't find a price tag on a single thing."

"No," said Mrs. Stafford-Smyth simply, "LeSoud's do not publicly price their items."

Belinda thought that strange, but she did not say so. There were many things done in strange ways in the city, she had concluded.

"And about the cost," went on Mrs. Stafford-Smyth simply,

"the wardrobe comes with the job. There will be no need for reimbursement."

"But—" argued Belinda.

"No 'buts,'" cut in the lady, raising a hand to hush Belinda. "I realize that you have a unique position. You are not just my nurse in the same fashion that Pottah is my housekeeper. No, you are also my companion—and as such I expect you to accompany me into society, to sit at my table and welcome my guests. Because of that, your wardrobe needs to be more—more extensive—and I would not ask you to pay such costs yourself. That would be unfai-ah. Do you understand, my deah?"

Belinda thought she did, but it still didn't seem quite right.

"Could I have another cup of tea, deah?" the good lady went on and passed Belinda her cup.

The voile dress arrived that evening. And along with it came boxes and boxes. Belinda gasped when a quick check showed they held a multitude of gowns and accessories. *Surely there's some mistake.* She must talk with Mrs. Stafford-Smyth quickly, before the delivery boy had a chance to return to the store. Most of what lay stacked about her room must go back with him.

Belinda was about to run to the suite next door when she nearly bumped into Mrs. Stafford-Smyth coming toward her rooms. The lady had an excited look about her.

"Did they arrive?" she asked Belinda. "I thought I heard commotion."

"Oh, yes—yes. But, my—there's been a mistake—a dreadful mistake. I ordered the green voile but—but I think they must have sent most everything that they had me try on."

Belinda was concerned that Mrs. Stafford-Smyth might think she'd had the audacity to take advantage of the charge account.

"I love looking at new things—don't you, deah?" smiled the woman. "Do you mind terribly if I watch you open all the boxes?"

"But you don't understand," insisted Belinda. "They have sent things I didn't order."

"*I* ordered them," Mrs. Stafford-Smyth said.

"But—but—" began Belinda.

"My deah, I thought I had explained," said the lady rather impatiently. "I wish to take you about with me—as soon as I am able to be about, that is—and I—I want you to look the part."

For the first time, Belinda really understood. She had never stopped to look at herself through Mrs. Stafford-Smyth's eyes before. Certainly her own worn and serviceable gowns were not in keeping with the elegance of the other woman's clothing. Belinda let her eyes fall to the dress she was wearing. Her best. And yet it was so inferior to the gown of the grand lady who stood before her.

"Now, let's see what you have here," said the older woman, her voice again filled with eagerness.

Belinda turned back to the boxes—but she could feel no matching excitement.

There were many pretty things in the boxes. Belinda could not help but appreciate their beauty. She ran a caressing hand over the silks, the satins, the voiles. They were beautiful. *But I'll always feel I'm in a borrowed dress,* she moaned to herself.

There were hats and shawls, a long coat of fine blue wool, parasols, gloves, handbags and delicate undergarments and sleepwear. Belinda had never in her life seen so much finery. She would have thrilled at it all had it been really *hers*.

Over and over she mumbled her thanks to Mrs. Stafford-Smyth, and the woman, not noticing Belinda's discomfort, glowed with the excitement of the new clothing.

"You will be the prettiest young lady in Boston," she informed Belinda, while Belinda wondered what bearing that had on anything.

When the last box had been opened and the last item was carefully put away in the wardrobe or bureau, Mrs. Stafford-Smyth turned to Belinda with a merry twinkle in her eyes.

"You will wear the blue silk on Wednesday evening," she said. "And do up your hair a bit loosah—Ella will help you. She's very good with hair."

Belinda just nodded. Now she was being told how to dress—

she who had often made decisions on her own that could mean life or death for a patient.

She looked at the older lady and nodded dumbly.

The next morning Windsor escorted Belinda to church. She had looked forward all week to this chance to meet with God's people on Sunday. Certainly she met with God every day of the week—but Sunday always seemed to her to be a special time. There was just something so uplifting about the service with hymn-singing together and hearing God's Word read and preached. Belinda thought of her family as they would gather back home, and for a few moments she felt homesick.

But the Boston church was nothing like the little country church Belinda had been used to. Huge and made of stone, its spires seemed to reach almost to the clouds. Belinda gazed in awe, wishing she could just stand and take it all in. But Windsor was gently nudging her forward.

Inside, the building seemed even more massive. The people moving to take their places in the polished wooden pews looked small and insignificant in comparison.

There was not just *a* minister, but several men on the raised platform, all gowned in glorious colors that rippled and flowed as they moved about. Belinda smiled to herself. *And I feared thet my green voile might be too colorful,* she commented wryly to herself.

As the worshipers entered the building, strains of a giant organ rose and fell, wafting them up in lovely ecstasy and then bringing them back down to gentle peace again. Belinda turned her face to find the source and saw that the front of the church was filled with brass pipes of various sizes and lengths. She had never seen a pipe organ before, but recognized that she was seeing and hearing one now.

Her eyes traveled the rest of the way around the interior, appreciating each glass window. The morning sun caught the brilliant colors, making the artwork of the Good Shepherd reaching for a lamb, the dying Savior on the cross, the gentle Teacher cradling a child all look warm and alive to Belinda.

Her heart throbbed within her. The beauty and majesty of

the place! Oh, how easy it must be to worship God in such a setting! How easy it must be for the city-dwellers who met each Sunday in such magnificent buildings to feel close to the Lord!

Belinda could feel her heart swell and lift in sheer praise and gratitude to God for all His goodness. How she wished she could share this wonderful experience with her pa, her ma—with Luke. She looked about her at the congregation. The pews were far from filled, and among the ones gathered there, Belinda saw no shining eyes. Stiff-looking, well-dressed individuals with blank faces and fixed stares set in cultured rows. Belinda was shocked that they didn't look one bit excited about being in such a glorious place of worship. She felt a cold chill pass through her and made a conscious effort to reclaim her excitement of a few moments before. She turned her eyes eagerly to the platform. The robed men were so far away. She could scarcely see the expressions on their faces. She listened to voices that seemed to reach her only as an echo, and concentrated hard on what was being read from the large, open Bible.

The words were good. They were familiar. It was God's Word and it lifted her spirit. But the beautiful, large stone church still seemed cold and distant—the people masked and aloof. There were no welcoming smiles or gentle nods. Belinda wondered what was wrong with her and glanced anxiously down at her voile dress. But it really was not that much different from the dresses of the other women there.

No, thought Belinda, *I don't think it's the dress. It must be me. They must know—without me even sayin'—thet I come from the plains.* And Belinda felt alone and isolated among the Sunday church-goers.

Chapter 22

The Unexpected

In spite of the wonderful library, Belinda had more free time than she knew what to do with. Mrs. Stafford-Smyth, now that she was back in her own home with Windsor, the housekeeper Mrs. Potter, Cook, and the two housemaids, seemed quite able to care for herself. Belinda chafed, feeling she really was not needed there. About the only duty she performed daily was to pour Mrs. Stafford-Smyth's tea, and she reasoned that anyone should have been able to do that small chore.

So Belinda tried to find ways to occupy her days. She did read for a good portion of each day, but she had discovered that even reading has its limits. Belinda felt she must have some exercise, so she spoke with Mrs. Stafford-Smyth about it.

"Of course, my deah," said the woman. "An energetic young woman like you needs to get out. I should have thought of it myself. Just because I'm content to sit and vegetate does not mean that you are. Would you like to ride? I understand there is a good club—"

But Belinda shook her head. She couldn't imagine going off to ride horseback in some society club. She thought of Copper back home with a bit of a pang, then almost smiled to think of him sedately marching round and round a horse ring.

"Tennis? We do have good courts at the back—but of course one can hardly play tennis on one's own."

"Jest—jest walk, I think," responded Belinda.

175

"Oh, my," said Mrs. Stafford-Smyth. "You may walk about all you like. The streets belong to everyone and are quite safe, really."

So on Wednesday morning Belinda took to the rather quiet streets. It seemed that those who moved about did so by carriage. She had intended to walk briskly for a half hour or so, but there was so much to see that she kept finding herself loitering as she drank in the sights about her.

She returned to the house invigorated and ready for the luncheon that Cook had prepared. She freshened up and joined Mrs. Stafford-Smyth in the drawing room.

"Did you enjoy your walk?" the lady began and then quickly added, "Yes, I can see that you did. Your cheeks are quite flushed, your eyes glowing."

"It was lovely!" exclaimed Belinda. "A shame thet yer unable to join me."

Mrs. Stafford-Smyth chuckled. "There was a day when I might have fretted at being left behind—but no more," she said companionably.

They chatted about many things over their luncheon plates, and Mrs. Stafford-Smyth was again reminded of why she had cajoled and pressed for Belinda to return to Boston with her. The girl was so vitally alive that just being with her was uplifting to one's spirit. Mrs. Stafford-Smyth truly loved her home, she loved Boston, and she would miss it all terribly if anything should happen to change things for her. She was comfortable at home—with maids fussing about and Cook and Housekeeper and dear old Windsor hovering about to answer her every whim. But it was lonely in the big house. A staff of servants was not the same as having friends. And surprisingly, Mrs. Stafford-Smyth thought of Belinda as a friend.

She knew that Potter, with her rigid rules of what was right and proper, did not approve of the special status that was given the girl. Employees had no right to be served tea with the gentry, according to Mrs. Potter. There had been a time, even just a short time ago, that Mrs. Stafford-Smyth would have heartily agreed. But that was before she had met Belinda—before Belinda had tenderly and efficiently nursed her back to health.

Mrs. Stafford-Smyth had learned a new set of rules in the crude little prairie town. The rule of survival. There seemed to be no social status there, no class distinctions, and Mrs. Stafford-Smyth had discovered in Belinda an open, friendly, clear-thinking girl who would share her thoughts, her feelings and her humor. To the older lady's surprise she had enjoyed such exchanges. And now, back in Boston, she was not willing to give up what she had learned to appreciate.

She knew that the whole arrangement was a mystery to Belinda. She also knew that her household staff must titter and talk and exclaim over Madam's strange desire to treat the girl, an employee, as an equal—but in her own house she was mistress. *Let them talk and fuss,* she told herself. They'd eventually get used to the idea.

She turned her attention back to the attractive face before her.

"The blue silk will look lovely on you!" she exclaimed, surprising Belinda with her passion and her abrupt change of thought. They had been discussing a novel.

Belinda frowned. "You know," she said slowly, "things happened in such a flurry at thet—that dress shop," she corrected herself, "that my head was swimmin'. I don't even remember tryin' the blue silk on."

Mrs. Stafford-Smyth just smiled. She knew Belinda might not have tried the dress. Madam Tilley was a skilled woman. She would have known Belinda's size perfectly by the time she had fitted a few dresses. The blue silk was in answer to one of Mrs. Stafford-Smyth's specific instructions in the letter. But the dress was too expensive, too elegant, to be slipped over heads in the dressing room. Even in a place as refined as LeSoud's.

"What time is dinner?" Belinda asked.

"Seven-thirty," answered Mrs. Stafford-Smyth, "but the guests shall be arriving around seven. I should like you to be with me in the formal parlor by seven o'clock."

Belinda nodded.

"And I think that we shall take our tea in my suite this afternoon. We both will need to rest and prepare ourselves for tonight."

Again Belinda agreed, though she hardly felt in need of rest.

"I thought I might take a book and spend some time in the garden now," Belinda offered. "It's such a glorious day—and the flowers are so pretty."

"Thomas certainly does a nice job," Mrs. Stafford-Smyth acknowledged. "He's a good gardenah. Been with us for thirty-five yeahs. I don't know what I shall do when he wishes to retiah."

Belinda took her book and went to the gardens as planned, but she did little reading. The day was too beautiful, the flowers too enticing, the bees too busy for her to be able to concentrate on anything but the loveliness about her. She sat dreaming away her afternoon, enjoying the sights and scents around her.

"I don't believe I've had the pleasure of being introduced," spoke a male voice near Belinda's elbow, and she started forward and looked up.

A young man, his eyes deep-set and his dark mustache well-trimmed, stood looking at her. Belinda noticed his stylish clothing, and she knew that every item was carefully chosen—yet he managed to give an air of informality which she quickly gathered was the appearance he wished to present.

And then Belinda recognized him as one of the grandsons whose portraits graced the rooms of Mrs. Stafford-Smyth. They had talked about the boys on occasion. Belinda allowed a smile to greet the young man.

"I hadn't heard ya—you were expected," she said easily.

"S-h-h," said the young man, placing a finger to his lips. "I didn't send word on ahead. I wanted to surprise Grandmother."

Belinda laughed softly. "And so you will. She—she will be caught completely by surprise."

Then Belinda sobered. "I'm not sure but what she shouldn't have *some* warnin'," she continued. "She has recently been very ill, you know, and too much of a shock wouldn't be good—"

"She's used to us popping in and out," the young man said with a shrug. "I shouldn't think that this will bother much."

Belinda noticed a strange accent in his speech. She couldn't place it but assumed it had been picked up in his travels abroad.

It rather intrigued her. There was something mysterious and pleasing about the man.

He tossed his jacket carelessly on the velvet green of the lawn and sat down on it, close to Belinda's chair.

"You still haven't told me your name," he prompted.

"Belinda. Belinda Davis," she replied.

"*Miss* Belinda Davis?" he asked.

"Yes. Miss," returned Belinda and felt her cheeks flushing slightly under the intense scrutiny of the man.

They sat for a moment, and then Belinda spoke carefully. "You haven't said whether you're Peter or Frank."

He laughed. "Dear Grandmother! She insists upon calling us the American version of our real names. I'm Pierre. 'Peter,' if you wish. I don't mind."

"I'll call you Pierre if you prefer it," she answered simply.

He smiled. "Pierre, then. I do prefer it." Then he changed the direction of the conversation. "I was told by the watchdog Windsor that 'Madam is resting and not to be disturbed.' " He mimicked Windsor's voice as he spoke, and Belinda could not hide her smile. "How is Grandmother?"

"She's doing very well now."

Pierre seemed relieved at the news.

"So what are her plans? Is she going abroad for the winter as usual—or have you heard?"

Belinda shook her head. "I know nothing of plans that go beyond this evening's dinner party," she said.

"A dinner party? Oh, dear! How I dread Grandmother's dinner parties. Such stuffy occasions they are, with all those octogenarians. Have you heard her guest list?"

Belinda found herself enjoying the exchange. She had some of the same feelings that this young man was expressing; only she had hardly dared to think, let alone say them.

"I've heard the list—but I don't recall all of them. Let's see— a Prescott woman."

"Of course. Aunt Celia. She is always invited."

"Aunt Celia?" said Belinda in surprise. "I hadn't realized—"

"Oh, she's not really an aunt. We were just brought up to

refer to her as such. She's a good friend of Grandmother's from many years back."

"I see," said Belinda.

"Go on," he prompted.

"A gentleman to chat with Aunt Celia," smiled Belinda. "Mr.—Mr. Walls—?"

"Walsh," Pierre laughed. "Those two have been openly and shamelessly flirting with each other for thirty years. Don't know why they haven't done something about it."

Belinda's blue eyes opened wide at his frankness.

"And—?" he urged.

"Two other couples—one is a judge—the other I don't remember."

"No young people?"

"I—I don't know any of the guests. I have no way of knowing if they are young or old," Belinda reminded him.

"Let me assure you," he said as he stood from the ground and brushed gently at the sharply creased slacks, "none of them are under one hundred and five."

Belinda could not keep the twinkle from her eyes.

"I'm tempted to sneak away before Grandmother discovers me," he continued. And then he looked directly at Belinda. "You'll be there?" he asked.

She nodded in answer.

"Then the evening will not be a total loss," he said smugly. And with a slight smile, he gave her a nod and departed.

Belinda watched him go. How would Mrs. Stafford-Smyth feel about having her grandson home? What kind of a person was he? Surely he had been teasing about his perception of his grandmother's "stuffy" lifestyle. No one could help but love the house in Boston. *The days ahead might turn out to be most interesting,* she told herself as she closed the book she hadn't had a chance to read and stood to her feet. It was almost teatime and Mrs. Stafford-Smyth would expect her there.

Belinda was pouring tea when she heard a sharp gasp and looked up quickly to see Mrs. Stafford-Smyth lift a lacy handkerchief to her lips. Following her gaze, Belinda turned to the door behind her and saw the young man standing there, a strange smile on his face.

"Hello, Grandmother," he said. "I heard that you have been ill."

Belinda turned back to her patient, worried that the sudden appearance of Pierre might be too much for the woman. But after the initial shock she seemed to regain her composure.

"Petah!" she cried, holding out her arms. "Petah!"

He went to her and knelt before her. She reached out a hand to stroke his cheek and he patted her arm affectionately. Belinda thought it all very touching.

"It's so good to see you, deah. My, you've—you've become quite a man," the grandmother offered with pride.

Pierre just nodded.

"And where is Frank?"

"Still in France," answered Pierre. "He has a girl, you know. He is rather smitten, I'm afraid. He sent his love."

"Sit down. Sit down. Tell us all about yourself," Mrs. Stafford-Smyth urged the boy, and then she turned to Belinda. "This is Belinda," she hastened to explain.

The young man smiled and nodded. "I met Miss Davis in the garden," he offered.

"Good! Good!" Then the woman turned moist eyes back to her grandson. "I'm glad you've come. It's awfully good to see you—and Belinda needs some youngah company. You can accompany her to dinnah tonight. We're having guests. Just a few old friends—but Belinda could use someone her own age. I don't go out yet. She really has seen very little of Boston, and I wanted her to get to know the town. Of course we have been back only for a little ovah a week, but it would be so nice for her if—"

The young man chuckled and placed a hand on his grandmother's arm again. "I promise, Grandmother. I'll stay long enough to show Miss Davis the whole town. And I will be at dinner. And I will not run off and desert you without fair warning. Now—may I have some tea? I missed my lunch and I'm starving."

Mrs. Stafford-Smyth reached out and pressed her buzzer.

From the quickness with which he reached the room, Belinda wondered if Windsor had been standing outside in the hall.

"Bring anothah cup and more tea, Windsah, and have Cook make some sandwiches for Petah," she ordered in an excited tone, then turned back to her grandson to ply him with questions and offer her own bits of news. Belinda had never seen her so animated.

This is good for her, she thought to herself. *I'm glad he's home. She must have missed him very much.*

After what Belinda considered an appropriate time, she excused herself to her own suite. *The two need time to get to know each other again,* she reasoned.

Belinda was excited as she lifted the blue silk carefully from her wardrobe and laid it gently on her bed. She had never worn such a dress before. She caressed the soft material and then held a fold to her cheek. Ella would be coming any minute to fix her hair. She must hurry. She wanted to be ready on time. Mrs. Stafford-Smyth was counting on her to help greet guests as they arrived.

And then Belinda remembered Pierre. *Maybe things have changed now . . .* she pondered. Perhaps Mrs. Stafford-Smyth would wish her grandson at her side to perform the role of host. Well, she could always slip out to the garden if she was in the way. She still would be ready on time.

Belinda lifted the silk and let it slide down over her head and settle over her shoulders. She shrugged and shifted, puzzling as she attempted to adjust it. Something was wrong. The dress didn't fit as it should. She hoisted it slightly, thinking that it might be caught. It wasn't. She could not understand it. She looked about. Perhaps there was a piece missing. Surely there was an accompanying neck piece or an attached shawl. But there was nothing else on the satin-covered hanger. Belinda was still puzzling when Ella entered the room.

"What a beautiful dress, miss!" she enthused.

Belinda managed a smile, but she was still perplexed.

"But it—it doesn't fit right. Look. The front of it. It's scooped way down."

"That's the way it's cut, miss," explained Ella. "It's supposed to be like that."

Belinda was astounded. She wanted to argue—to protest.

"All the girls are wearing them like that, miss," said Ella, responding to Belinda's bewilderment.

"Well, I won't! I can't!" stated Belinda firmly. "It's most—most improper! Why, I'm—I'm indecent."

Little did Belinda know that by the standards of the city dress shops, her gown was modest for evening attire.

Ella smiled. "It fits you real nice, miss. Madam will be pleased."

Madam? Yes, the dress had been Madam's doing. She had ordered it. Belinda had *not* tried it on before. She would surely have remembered such a—a—daring gown. She felt most uncomfortable in it. Why had Mrs. Stafford-Smyth ever purchased such a dress? Surely she had been unaware of its skimpiness.

Sure now that Mrs. Stafford-Smyth had not known of the actual design of the dress, Belinda knew that she must talk with her employer—quickly. She hurried down the short hallway that led to the older woman's suite. She did not intend to appear at the dinner table wearing such a revealing garment, and she was sure that Mrs. Stafford-Smyth would not wish her to do so.

She stopped at the adjoining door only long enough to rap lightly and then went on in. Mrs. Stafford-Smyth had Sarah rushing about the room in last-minute preparations.

Without saying a word, Belinda stopped in front of the older woman and slowly turned completely around so that she could see the low-cut dress, both the back and the front.

She had expected to hear a gasp of shock. Instead, a murmur of approval stunned Belinda's ears. "Lovely! Just lovely. It was meant for you. Madam Tilley knew exactly what I wanted."

Belinda whirled around to see shining eyes and a broad smile.

"But—but—" Belinda began and then realized that her protests would not be heeded nor understood by the older woman. *She will think I'm just a simple prairie girl who doesn't know about such matters*, Belinda thought, her cheeks burning.

"Now hurry, deah," Mrs. Stafford-Smyth continued. "Petah will be waiting for us. He's going to help us with the guests." Her face was radiant.

Without another word Belinda returned to her own room and allowed Ella to pin her hair "becomingly." She hoped the evening might pass quickly.

Chapter 23

Pierre

Belinda stole down the stairs quietly, hoping not to be noticed. *What else can I do?* she debated inwardly. *My employer ordered the dress for me, paid for it and told me to wear it tonight!* It flashed into her mind that maybe she could have borrowed a shawl, *but it's too late now,* she told herself. Perhaps in the excitement of the expected dinner guests, she could slip in unobtrusively and Mrs. Stafford-Smyth and her grandson would hardly realize she was there.

It was not to be. The minute the swish at the door of the formal parlor announced her arrival, Mrs. Stafford-Smyth turned toward her. Her smile spoke even more than her words. She held out her hands to Belinda and urged her forward.

"Ah, yes," she said, slowly studying the picture that Belinda made in her blue gown. "It becomes you. The colah is just right for your eyes. And your hair—perfect! Ella does such a good job in styling."

Pierre made no comment, for which Belinda was thankful, but his eyes did study her carefully. Belinda felt dreadfully uncomfortable. *With all the material in this full skirt, you'd have thought they could have spared a bit to cover the bodice,* she fretted, but she did not voice her thoughts as she moved away from the probing eyes in pretense of pouring punch.

"May I bring you a drink?" she asked Mrs. Stafford-Smyth.

"That would be nice, my deah," the elderly lady responded

and seated herself in a green brocaded chair opposite the entrance to the hall, so she could face the doorway when the guests arrived.

The Allenbys were the first to appear. He was a very dignified older gentleman, befitting his honored position. She was a wizened little woman, her face pinched and her eyes sunken and sharp. Belinda could feel herself withdrawing from the open stare of the woman. She learned quickly that Mrs. Allenby's tongue was just as sharp as her eyes.

"And who is *she*?" Belinda heard her say to Mrs. Stafford-Smyth after their greetings were over. Belinda moved out of earshot so she wouldn't have to hear her employer trying to explain their relationship.

Mr. Walsh arrived a few moments later, chuckling over some unshared joke, and spent the entire evening laughing over one thing or another. Belinda did not pretend to understand his strange humor, but she did find him fairly pleasant company.

The Whitleys were admitted by Windsor at seven-thirty, the hour of dinner. He let it be known that he never had been one for pre-dinner chit-chat. After all, wasn't the purpose of dining together so one could visit over the shared meal? His wife said nothing, just looked a bit embarrassed by his blustering.

The minutes ticked slowly by with no moves toward the dining room, so the guests knew that someone else was expected. Once or twice Mr. Whitley took his gold watch from his pocket and studied it openly.

Since the guests' arrival, Windsor had taken over the duties of serving punch. Belinda knew without being told that she was now to allow things to proceed in "proper" fashion, and she withdrew to one of the matched green chairs.

Pierre eased his way over to where Belinda was fidgeting. "Isn't this fun?" he whispered, with a slight nod toward the older guests clustered about talking of weather and health problems.

Belinda only smiled.

"We could walk in the garden," he added.

"But she will be here any minute," offered Belinda.

Pierre laughed. "Aunt Celia? She's never on time for anything. When Aunt Celia is expected at seven-thirty, the only thing you don't know is whether she will arrive at eight or ten."

Belinda looked at him in surprise.

"Mark my word," he challenged, but just then the doorbell rang.

"Ah," he said, pulling out his pocket watch, "she's early— it's only ten minutes of eight."

Mrs. Celia Prescott came in with a flurry of excited comments and overdone apologies. She and Mrs. Stafford-Smyth hugged each other warmly, and then greetings passed all about the room. Mr. Walsh chuckled over each remark and Mrs. Celia Prescott tittered prettily in his direction. Pierre looked at Belinda with an I-told-you-so expression, and she had a hard time to keep from giggling herself.

"You know my Petah," said Mrs. Stafford-Smyth, and Pierre bowed to acknowledge the older woman.

"And this is Miss Belinda Davis," Mrs. Stafford-Smyth went on, and all eyes turned to Belinda.

"No wonder you've been off in hiding, young man," teased Aunt Celia with a twinkle. "In what part of Europe did you find her?"

Before either Pierre or Belinda could respond, Mrs. Stafford-Smyth interrupted with, "Belinda is American."

"Then perhaps we shall see more of your grandson in the future," observed Mr. Walsh with another chuckle.

Again Belinda could feel Mrs. Allenby's sharp eyes on her. She wished with all her heart that she could crawl more deeply into her blue silk dress. To Belinda's relief, the woman said nothing.

Aunt Celia reached over to pat Pierre's cheek. "I admire your taste, deah," she gushed. "I always knew you were discerning."

Belinda opened her mouth to say something, but when she saw Pierre shake his head, she closed it. They all had misunderstood the situation entirely. Was no one going to explain?

Belinda shrugged slim shoulders and allowed Pierre to lead her in to dinner.

As the meal progressed Belinda was glad for Pierre's presence at her side. She usually had no problem chatting with older people, but the conversation around the table was all foreign to her. They spoke of people she did not know, places she had never seen and events that were somewhere in their past.

Pierre let them chatter on. He directed the conversation to things he hoped would be of interest to Belinda. He found her charming and very attractive. He wished to ask her all sorts of questions, but he held himself in check. Where had his grandmother found such a lovely girl, and why was Belinda willing to spend time in a house with only an older woman?

The thought did occur to him that his grandmother was a very wealthy woman and that Belinda might have interest in her money. But even Pierre, with a somewhat suspicious turn of mind, dismissed that thought. She just didn't seem the type, unless she had everyone fooled.

After dinner the men retired to the library for a brandy and cigar, and the ladies went to the drawing room for another cup of coffee. Belinda was concerned about all the wonderful books that she had adopted as her own. *They will saturate the whole library with their smelly smoke,* she protested inwardly, and then reminded herself that this was Mrs. Stafford-Smyth's home, not hers.

She supposed she was expected to trot along with the ladies and was not looking forward to the idea. She cast one look of appeal toward Pierre and rose to follow the women.

"Perhaps you wouldn't mind if Belinda and I took a walk in the garden?" Pierre asked his grandmother.

Belinda drew a thankful breath.

"Run along," encouraged his grandmother, beaming as though the idea had been hers. She did not say it, but she was pleased with the interest her Peter seemed to have in Belinda. Perhaps, as Mrs. Walsh had said, this would have the unexpected advantage of keeping her boy in America. *Yes,* thought Mrs. Stafford-Smyth, *this could turn out even better than I had dared to hope.* She smiled secretly to herself as she led the way to the drawing room.

Belinda went for a wrap, though the night was still young and comfortably warm; she knew she would feel more comfortable with a bit more covering. She breathed deeply as she stepped out onto the terrace.

"Thank you," she whispered to Pierre, and he nodded in understanding.

"You mean you didn't look forward to the gossip of the old ladies any more than I did to the stale smell of cigars?" he asked lightly and Belinda chuckled.

"Actually," he said after a few minutes of walking in silence, "I wasn't trying to be a hero. I just wanted to have a very pretty girl all to myself."

He watched carefully for Belinda's reaction. She did not seem flustered. *She's had compliments before,* he observed, but she did not seem to take him too seriously either.

"I've chatted on about myself enough," he continued. "Now I think it's your turn."

She turned to him and smiled slightly. "I have nothing nearly as exciting to tell," she answered evenly. "I was born, grew up and lived right in one little town on the plains. And that's about all there is."

He laughed. "I think I am being effectively put off," he said good-naturedly.

"Not really," she assured him.

"You've not traveled?"

"Not a bit till I came to Boston."

"No interests?"

"Oh, I've lots of interests. No means." She spoke frankly, unembarrassed. His eyes narrowed. Maybe he had been right. Maybe this girl was after his grandmother's money.

"Where did you meet my grandmother?" he questioned.

"She was on a trip—out to San Francisco."

"You were on the same train?"

"Oh, no," Belinda hastened to add. "She took ill. Had to stop at our town until she recovered."

"I see," he said. But he really didn't.

"Grandmother spoke to me again about showing you Boston," he went on. "Would you be interested?"

Belinda's eyes took on a shine. "I'd like that," she said honestly.

"I'd like that too," he echoed. "Where do you want to start?"

"I—I know nothin' about the city. Best you do the choosin'. You'd know what we should see."

He smiled. "Fine," he said. "You'll have your first lesson at nine tomorrow."

Belinda returned his smile. She was looking forward to seeing more of this beautiful city, to learn of its history and its intrigue.

"I'll be ready at nine," she answered, then added with a little laugh, "Not Aunt Celia's nine—but clock-time nine."

Pierre chuckled with her. It was going to be fun to show her Boston.

"Are you—are you planning to be with Grandmother for—for some time?"

Belinda sobered. "I love it here," she admitted. "I've been here only a week and already I love it. Just like yer—your grandmother said I would. But how long I stay"—she gave her shoulders a gentle shrug—"that depends," she added.

"Depends? On what?"

"Your grandmother. Me. How we get on together."

"I see," he said slowly.

"Are you staying long?" she turned the tables by asking.

Her words brought him up sharply. Couldn't he answer in the same way? *It depends! On how Grandmother and I get on together!* In actual fact that was why he had come home. He was quite sure that his grandmother's will was still unsettled. She had wanted first to "try" her grandsons. Now that Franz was about to settle in France with his new love, Pierre felt it to be an opportune time for him to "get in good" with his grandmother. Why should this beautiful home, this notable estate, be left to someone quite outside the family? Yet his grandmother was independent—verging on the eccentric. She was likely to do just that if neither of her grandsons showed any interest in the place—or in her.

So Pierre had decided to leave his European playground temporarily and come home to "court" his grandmother. Oh, he had never admitted the truth—not even to himself. But as Belinda asked her question, the reality of the situation hit the young man. He was here to get what he could from his grand-mother's will. *Perhaps we are not so different after all,* he con-cluded with a careful look at the attractive girl by his side. The only fact in his favor was that he was kin.

Belinda sensed his hesitation, but she had no idea of the thoughts being sorted through by the young man. At length he turned again to her, smiled and shrugged much as she had done. "That, too, depends," he said honestly.

Pierre did not sleep well that night. To himself he admitted that he found Belinda attractive. She seemed so honest, so sin-cere—so—unsophisticated. Yet she had somehow managed to fool his shrewd grandmother. *She must be far more skilled at deceit than I can credit her with.*

He struggled with what to do. He saw his grandmother's deep devotion to Belinda. If he were to question her concerning Belinda's integrity, would she become upset? Would it be better to forget the possibility that Belinda might be after the elderly lady's money and take no chances of alienating his grand-mother? Did he really care so much about the estate that he would risk a rift with the elderly woman? After all, he knew that as things now stood, he and his brother would inherit at least some of her money. Perhaps he should be content with that.

And then Pierre thought about Belinda. *What if—what if she inherits the bulk of the estate?* Was there another way for him to solve his dilemma? After all, she was pretty and pleasing to be with. She had not seemed immune to his charms. Perhaps they could share the estate in another fashion. But Pierre felt uncomfortable with that. If Belinda was so sly as to ingratiate herself with his grandmother only for personal gain, was she to be trusted as a marriage partner? As any kind of partner? And hadn't he sensed an undercurrent in the room when the staff had been present? Did they know something about Belinda that was not yet exposed?

Pierre tossed and turned and tried to sort the whole thing through, but an answer escaped him.

Finally he decided that he must have an open talk with his

grandmother. He knew it was risky, but he had to chance it. With the resolution made, he settled down to a few hours of sleep.

He had already made his appointment to meet Belinda at nine, so at eight o'clock, Pierre knocked on his grandmother's door. She was already seated at her small corner desk, her breakfast tray left almost untouched on a low table by her bed.

She smiled when she saw him and leaned to accept his kiss on her cheek.

"Good morning," she welcomed him. "Belinda tells me that you are becoming a tour guide this morning."

He attempted a smile. He had little time, so he decided not to spend it in small talk. "That's who I came to talk about, Grandmother," he admitted.

She smiled at him. "You seem to be off to a good start," she beamed. "Isn't she delightful?"

He did not answer her question. "Where did you meet her, Grandmother?"

"I thought you knew. I took a train trip west, and on the way home I fell quite ill. A stroke, they said. I would have died had it not been for the care I received."

"Died?" he echoed, thinking that his grandmother was perhaps being a bit melodramatic.

"Belinda and her brothah, who is a doctah—and a very good one, by the way—stayed with me day and night for the first few weeks. Then Belinda continued to give me nursing care for several more months."

Pierre thought he could understand why his grandmother felt indebted to the girl, but he was still puzzled.

"So, in gratitude, you invited her here as your guest," he prompted, hoping to get more information.

"Belinda? Oh my, no. She traveled back with me to nurse me on the train if need be. I was still very weak. Still am." She stopped and chuckled softly. "She still insists that I get propah rest and—why, she's already been in heah this morning fussing and—"

"Nurse?" said Pierre. He still did not grasp the situation.

"Nurse!" his grandmother repeated, and seeing the frown

on his face, she continued. "Not all nurses are old grannies with head scarves, you know."

"You mean Belinda Davis is a *nurse*?"

"Yes, of course. Didn't you know? That's what I've been telling you."

"She's—she's in your *employ*?" He was aghast at the very thought.

Mrs. Stafford-Smyth laid down her pen and looked at her grandson.

"What is it that's bothering you?" she asked him. "Are you as stuffy and narrow-minded as Pottah or Windsah? Are you, too, going to insist that because Belinda is an employee, she can't be my deah, deah friend? If I want—"

But Pierre stopped her. "But the place as a *guest* at dinner? The—the expensive gown? Surely a working girl—?"

"I've just told you," the woman insisted. "Belinda is *more* than a nurse. She is good company."

"And you purchased her gown?"

Mrs. Stafford-Smyth shuffled angrily at her papers. "Yes," she answered sharply. "I purchased the gown. I didn't want her feeling uncomfortable in the presence of those who call. She's a sensitive little thing. She already feels upset about the coolness of the staff. They feel that she should be treated as one of them."

"But that's exactly what she is. Staff! An employee! Your nurse!"

"She is," admitted the woman.

"But—but—you led me to believe that she was your—your guest."

"I did no such thing," denied the woman. "You jumped to your own conclusions."

"But you—you asked me to—to escort her about town."

The dark eyes of Mrs. Stafford-Smyth sharpened and focused on the face of her grandson. "I did," she said evenly. "And you should bless me for it! Belinda is an intelligent, independent, sensitive and attractive young lady. Something that you haven't seen in one little lady for all your lifetime, I'll wagah. If you are so put off by the fact that she has no mansions, no family jewels, then you are not the man I had hoped you to be."

Pierre took a step backward. He knew better than to challenge his grandmother when she was in such a mood.

"Yet you seriously wish me—?"

"Yes," she said sharply. "Yes, I wish you to treat her like the lady that she is. Belinda deserves to see Boston—to have fun. And you should be thankful that you have the opportunity to be the one to escort her."

Her dark eyes snapped with intense feeling and Pierre closed his lips tightly against the words he wished to speak. Two pairs of eyes measured each other, and then Pierre took a deep breath and shrugged his shoulders.

"All right," he said resignedly. "All right, Grandmother. I'll play your little game. But if word gets out that your grandson is busy escorting a member of the household staff, you could well be the laughing stock of your friends."

"Then perhaps they have no business being called my friends," she retorted, and Pierre knew that he was dismissed—and defeated.

Chapter 24

Extended Horizons

True to his word, Pierre showed Belinda Boston. He took her to all the parks, museums and historical sites. They attended plays and musicals. He even accompanied her to church on Sundays. Belinda enjoyed it immensely. She appreciated his company and at times felt that he was happy with hers. But she had the feeling that in spite of the good times they had together, he held himself aloof.

Mrs. Stafford-Smyth was elated. The two young people did seem to be enjoying themselves. She hoped the relationship would quickly develop into something deeper than friendship. She urged them on to new sights and experiences, slipping Pierre the funds to show Belinda a lavish look at Boston.

Pierre was troubled. He did find enjoyment in the times with Belinda. He no longer worried that she was after his grandmother's money. In fact, Belinda was so naive that she scarcely knew what money was. She viewed it as something to be slipped to newsboys on the street corners or placed in the offering receptacle on Sunday. No, Belinda was not at Marshall Manor for selfish reasons.

But Pierre still puzzled over it all. Did Belinda, could Belinda, ever really fit into the life of high society? She was so open, so unsophisticated, and he knew she understood little of the social classes that existed all about her. No, he concluded, Belinda was really from a different world than the one he knew.

He decided to enjoy their outings, their friendship, and leave their relationship at that, even though he was aware that much of Boston's society already accepted the Stafford-Smyth grandson and the attractive young guest as an established pair.

Mrs. Stafford-Smyth was resting when there came a gentle tapping on her door.

"Yes," she called softly. "Come in."

Windsor entered and stood at rigid attention. "Mrs. Celia Prescott is heah to see you, madam." Then he added in a confidential tone meant only for the ears of his lady, "I must say, she seems to have herself in quite a tizzy."

The good lady smiled. Her friend Celia was often in quite a tizzy over one thing or another.

"Would you take her to the drawing room, Windsah, and have Pottah fix tea? I'll be right down."

"Yes, madam," answered Windsor with a click of his heels. Mrs. Stafford-Smyth smiled. Poor Windsor. He did insist on being socially correct in spite of their long-term friendship.

When Mrs. Stafford-Smyth entered the drawing room a few moments later, she found Celia Prescott pacing back and forth in front of the marble fireplace. A lace handkerchief was being brutally attacked in two agitated hands.

"Celia! So good to see you. Please, won't you sit down?" she greeted her friend.

"Virgie, you'll never guess what they are saying," began Mrs. Prescott excitedly. "It's slanderous, that's what it is. Just slanderous! And you must put a stop to it at once."

"Why whatevah are they saying?" asked Mrs. Stafford-Smyth in bewilderment, wondering if there was some news of her far-off grandson that had not yet reached her ears.

"Miss Belinda—that fine young lady you have staying heah—?"

"Yes," said Mrs. Stafford-Smyth hesitantly. Surely Peter had not gone and done some foolish thing and unwittingly besmirched Belinda's name.

"They are saying—"

"*Who* are saying?" cut in Mrs. Stafford-Smyth. If she needed to deal with gossip mongers, she wanted to know exactly whom she was dealing with.

Celia Prescott became all waving hands and fluttering handkerchiefs. "I don't know who said it," she replied offensively. "I heard it from Alvira Allenby and she heard it from— Oh, I don't know."

"And what are 'they' saying? Go on."

"They are saying that the young woman, Miss Davis, is— is *hired help*," finished Celia in a horrified whisper.

"And so she is," responded Virginia Stafford-Smyth calmly.

"Well, you must put a stop to it. Your grandson's name and your—she *what*?" shrieked Celia Prescott, finally hearing the words that had been spoken.

"Belinda is my nurse. And a most excellent one, too. Is there a problem with that, Celia?"

"Well, I—well, your—your grandson is—is escorting her about town, and folks assumed that he had your blessing and—"

"And so he has. I know of no young woman that I would rathah see my grandson spend his time with," said Mrs. Stafford-Smyth with spirit.

Mrs. Celia Prescott did not know how to respond.

"Ah," said Mrs. Stafford-Smyth. "Here's our tea. Would you pou-ah for us please, Pottah?"

Mrs. Celia Prescott lowered herself to the chair across from Mrs. Virginia Stafford-Smyth and fanned herself with her lace hankie. She had received quite a shock. First had come the bit of gossip that the Stafford-Smyth grandson was escorting "common household help." A rumor that Celia would have staked her life on being just a spiteful bit of gossip. And now when Virgie was confronted with the story, she calmly said that it was true, and furthermore did not seem the least concerned that her family name might be tarnished because of it.

Potter served and then retreated and Virginia Stafford-Smyth picked up the conversation. "Belinda was the one who nursed me back to health when I was so close to dying," she said simply. "I love the girl like I would my own daughtah. In fact, I've often considered adopting her." She paused and seemed to be off in thought. "I would, too, if I thought for a minute that she would allow it." Then she turned again to her guest. "I've seen a few of the young women that my two grandsons have shown interest in," she confided. "Monied families—looking for more money. Showpieces without an intelligent thought in their empty heads. Society girls! Oh, yes! Their family history can be traced back nearly to Adam. But shallow, selfish"—she hesitated, seeking for the proper word—"Nothing," she finally sputtered. "Just ornamental bits of fluffy nothing.

"Well, Celia," she continued, "as far as I'm concerned, I would as soon see my grandson marry an intelligent char as an emptyheaded socialite."

Mrs. Celia Prescott gasped in horror. Surely her friend's long illness had severely damaged her reason.

"There now! I've said my piece—now we will have no more of it," said Mrs. Stafford-Smyth and she changed the topic to what play was on at the local theater.

As summer turned to fall, Belinda enjoyed the briskness in the wind and the turning of the maple trees. Never had she seen such glorious fall colors. *The golds and browns back home are no match for these,* she concluded. Pierre often took a team and the small carriage, and they went for drives down tree-lined residential streets and sometimes even out into the nearby countryside. Belinda had passing moments of guilt. She had come to Boston to be nurse and companion to Mrs. Stafford-Smyth. She was the first to be thankful that the lady no longer needed strict nursing care; still it did seem to Belinda that as long as she was salaried, she should be doing something further to earn her wage.

But it was Mrs. Stafford-Smyth herself who kept urging the outings. She took great pleasure in Belinda being shown their beautiful city and surrounding area. Each night she would demand to hear Belinda's full report of what they had seen and where they had gone that day.

Belinda did not realize the secret hopes that the lady fostered. Mrs. Stafford-Smyth had been lonely for years. She dreaded the thought of Pierre becoming restless and leaving her to go abroad once more. She hated even more the thought that Belinda might decide she wanted to leave the quietness of the old manor to return home or someplace more exciting. So Mrs. Stafford-Smyth continued to urge the two young people to find excitement in the town and friendship with each other.

The autumn winds became chilly and trips in the open carriage were not as frequent. When the snowstorms moved in, one following the other, Belinda checked her calendar. They had moved into winter. She could scarcely believe that she had been gone from her home for several months.

Whenever she received a letter from Marty, homesickness struck her, a bit stronger each time. She missed her family so much. If only there were some way to combine the two worlds. She tried to compensate by throwing herself into each activity that Mrs. Stafford-Smyth suggested. Every day of the week, it seemed, she and Pierre found something more exciting to occupy their time. Eventually there was not even time to fit in Sunday church services. The day was spent instead with plays or concerts. Belinda had never had such full, fun days in all her life.

But then one day Belinda unexpectedly was called in to see the older woman. She was shocked to find her taken to her bed, her face ashen, her lips tightly drawn. Belinda berated herself. What had happened? Had the elderly lady had a setback? Why hadn't she, her nurse, seen it coming?

"What is it? Another attack?" she asked anxiously, placing a hand on the woman's brow.

"I'm fine. Really. I just—I just am a foolish old woman, that's all."

"Whatever do you mean?" asked the puzzled Belinda.

"I was—was hoping I'd found a way to hold him this time," Mrs. Stafford-Smyth said wearily.

"Hold him? Hold who?"

"Pierre. My Petah."

Alarmed, Belinda said, "What do ya mean?" fearing what the answer might be.

"He's leaving. He just came to tell me. He says he can't bear Boston wintahs. He's—he's going back to France."

Belinda had no voice to respond to the woman. She simply stood beside her, her hand gently stroking the cheeks, the brow, the silver hair.

"I thought—I thought he seemed happiah this time. That now, with anothah young person in the house, he—he might stay."

Belinda still said nothing.

"You—you didn't have a lov-ah's quarrel, now did you, deah?" asked the woman.

Belinda found her voice then. "Oh my, no! Why—why we've been nothing more than friends—just friends."

The woman looked sorrowful. "I—I was hoping—" she began, but she did not finish her statement.

With the chill that gripped Belinda's heart, she wondered if she unconsciously had been hoping to hold Pierre herself, but she did not confess as much to her employer.

"When—when is he leavin'?" she asked quietly.

"He has already booked passage. He sails on Friday."

Friday! That was two days hence. That didn't give one much time for goodbyes. But perhaps that was the way Pierre wanted it.

Mrs. Stafford-Smyth sighed wearily. "You don't understand, deah," she said. "I realize now that I have no way to hold him heah. No way. If I want to see him and Frank, then I must go to them. They will nevah, nevah come home to me."

Belinda nodded. She thought she did understand.

Belinda tried hard not to let her emotions show as she bade Pierre goodbye.

"I can never thank you for all the—the sharing of Boston," she told him. "Ya—you made the city live for me."

Pierre took her hand and held it firmly. She had made the city live for him as well, but he did not tell her so.

"It's going to be so—so dreary without you," she admitted. "I don't know how your grandmother and I shall ever bear it."

"Take care of her, Belinda," he said, earnestness in his tone. "I know that it is unfair of me to even ask it of you when I— when I should be staying here, doing it myself. But I can't. Not just now. I know—I know you can't understand that, but I beg you not to think too unkindly of me."

"I could never think unkindly of you," Belinda said sincerely. "And as far as your grandmother is concerned—I'll—I'll try," Belinda promised. "I know that she will miss you terribly. That she misses Franz. She would love to see Franz and his new—new—" Belinda floundered.

"New love," prompted Pierre. "Though I am the first to admit that Franz may well have changed loves once or twice since I left him. He has changed often in the past, you know. Although this time, he insists it is different."

Belinda smiled.

"Safe journey," Belinda said simply.

"In France we say, 'Bon voyage,' " he reminded her.

"Bon voyage," repeated Belinda.

He gave her a quick, rather brotherly hug and then he was gone. Belinda stood and watched the carriage until it was out of sight, a tightness in her throat. She had liked Pierre. She had even thought that he might care for her, just a little—but now he had turned and casually walked out of her life.

Little did Belinda know that Pierre was running away. He was beginning to care too much for Belinda but, unlike his grandmother, Pierre was convinced that the two vastly different worlds would not mix. Pierre did not wish to give up his world as he knew it, nor did he feel comfortable about asking Belinda to give up hers. The only answer, in Pierre's thinking, was to put the ocean between them.

Chapter 25

A Taste of Travel

While one winter storm after another swept through the area, Belinda shivered and watched the wind pile banks of driven snow where banks of flowering begonias had so recently been.

No wonder Pierre escaped, she thought to herself. She would gladly have left for parts unknown herself.

"Dear Ma," she wrote, "I do miss you all just awfully. And sometimes I can't quite figure out what I'm doing way out here so far from home. But Mrs. Stafford-Smyth needs someone to be with her and be a friend—even more now that her grandson has returned to France . . ." And Marty's mother-heart read between the lines and yearned over her youngest. She prayed that God would be with Belinda in a special way to heal the disappointment over Pierre and to bring her safely home to them at just the right time. *Help her be jest what Mrs. Stafford-Smyth needs now, Lord,* Marty prayed.

Not all Belinda's days were chilly and bleak. On the nicer ones, she bundled up against the cold and went for walks or had the carriage brought round so she might do some shopping for Christmas gifts. She was looking forward to sending packages home for her family.

As Christmas drew closer, Belinda felt a renewed stirring of homesickness. The letters from her mother continued to arrive regularly, and occasionally Belinda received notes from other members of the family as well.

Luke wrote with news of the medical practice. Belinda was pleased to learn that they had decided to have Rand build them an office—separate and complete, giving Abbie back the privacy of her home. Luke then planned to convert the old office in the house into a large room for the two growing boys.

The up-to-date reports on Abe's arm informed Belinda that he had been away for surgery—two surgeries, in fact—and though the arm was still not completely restored, it was vastly improved over what it had been. "Abe beams when he shows it off to the family members," Belinda read.

Arnie was back in church—and not just sitting stolidly on a pew. He was involved again, and his faith had conquered the last trace of bitterness.

But not all the news was good news. There had been deaths among neighboring families, and Luke had lost a baby in delivery—the first in his experience—and had very nearly lost the young mother, too. He felt the tragedy keenly, and Belinda, understanding her brother, ached for him.

The partnership with Dr. Jackson Brown had been a good one. Luke, from the beginning deeply involved with the practice of medicine, was now able to spend more time with Abbie and their growing family.

Ruthie's chattering had turned into understandable language. Thomas had been teaching her to say "Aunt Belinda," and Ruthie seemed to think their little game was fun. Luke wrote that the sound came out more like "Aw Binna." Belinda both laughed and wept over the little story. It was awfully nice to know she had not been forgotten at home.

Actually, both Rand and Jackson had written to Belinda too. But when she responded with short, friendly but matter-of-fact notes, each fellow had come to the conclusion that it no doubt was the better part of wisdom to "lay low" for the present and not continue the correspondence. Luke had reported in his letter that "Rand stopped by last Saturday to invite Thomas and Aaron on a little fishing trip—and were they ever excited!" Belinda smiled to herself as she imagined their enthusiastic chatter.

When Belinda had all her shopping done, her parcels wrapped and her gifts on their way, there seemed to be nothing left to do except to wait out the days until Christmas finally arrived.

Belinda had never spent Christmas away from home before. She wondered just how Mrs. Stafford-Smyth celebrated the day. Surely one could not expect much in festivities with only two people.

Other than Pierre, Belinda still had not made any friends of her own age. True, there were a few young people whom she had met in his company, but now that he was gone, she had really lost contact with them. She supposed that if things had been different and she had been included as staff in the big house as Potter seemed to feel was proper, she might have become friendly with Ella and Sarah. As it was, the girls spoke to her politely and did their talking and tittering over bits of neighborhood gossip when they met each other in the halls or kitchen. Though she had tried to engage them in conversation, Belinda was not considered to be one of them.

The guests who joined Mrs. Stafford-Smyth for afternoon tea or an elaborate dinner were all older folk, and though Belinda was always expected to join them, she really did not feel part of those gatherings either.

She took up handwork along with her walking and reading, and managed to tick the slow-moving days from her calendar, one by one.

Every day she spent some time with Mrs. Stafford-Smyth. She knew that the older lady was as much in need of companionship as she herself. Usually they sipped tea, chatted and did some kind of needlework before an open fire.

In a way it was cozy—at least to an onlooker it would have seemed so. But Belinda knew that deep down inside she felt a restlessness—a loneliness—and she wasn't sure just what to do about it.

On one such day—Mrs. Stafford-Smyth was working skillfully on a silk sampler while Belinda embroidered a pair of cotton pillowcases—they chatted easily about many things.

"It's hard to believe that next week is Christmas," Belinda observed. Mrs. Stafford-Smyth did not even lift her eyes from her needlework. Belinda thought at first that she had not even heard the comment. She was about to speak further when Mrs. Stafford-Smyth answered, still without lifting her head.

"There was a time when Christmas brought a flurry of excitement in this house," she remarked. Then she added slowly, almost tiredly, "But no more."

Belinda felt her heart sink. It sounded as though the lady was dismissing Christmas as of no consequence.

"How do you celebrate Christmas?" Belinda dared to ask.

"Celebrate it? 'Spend it,' you mean. Much as we are spending today, I expect."

Belinda's eyes lifted from the pillowcases to study her older companion. She saw a droop to the shoulders and resignation in her face.

"But—but it's Christ's birthday!" Belinda could not help but exclaim.

Mrs. Stafford-Smyth faced her then and her eyes brightened for a moment. "Oh, we go to the church service—to be sure. But there are no more stuffed stockings and tinseled tree."

Belinda had a sudden resolve. She needed Christmas. Mrs. Stafford-Smyth needed Christmas. She laid aside her needlework and quickly stood to her feet.

"Let's!" she said excitedly.

The older woman's head jerked up and she stared as though Belinda had lost her senses.

"Let's!" said Belinda again.

"What are you—?" began Mrs. Stafford-Smyth, but Belinda interrupted, her eyes shining and her hands clasped.

"Let's have Christmas again! You and me. Let's have the tree and the tinsel and the stockings."

"But—but—"

"No 'buts.' We need Christmas. I've never *not* had Christmas. Why, I would mope and cry all day without it. I just know I would. We can have Windsor get us a tree, and I'll decorate and Cook can make plum pudding or butter tarts or whatever you are liking, and we'll share gifts with Staff and—"

The older woman began to chuckle softly. Belinda's fire seemed to have ignited something in her soul as well. She gently laid down her silk piece and rubbed her hands together.

"If it means so much to you—"

"Oh, it does. It does!" cried Belinda.

"Then go ahead. Do whatever you like."

"No! No, not me. Us! Us! You need Christmas just as much as I do. We'll plan it together."

Mrs. Stafford-Smyth chuckled again. "My, you do go on, don't you? Well, if it pleases you—then of course we'll have Christmas. Ring for Windsah and Pottah. We'd best tell them of our plans as soon as possible. Staff will think I've gone completely mad—but—" She smiled. "Better a little mad than a lot lonely," she finished.

The next few days were spent in frenzied but joyful activity. After a trip out in the country, Windsor produced a magnificent tree. Potter rummaged in the attic and storage rooms until she discovered boxes of old garlands and tinseled decorations. Belinda shook the dust from them and trimmed the tree and hung streamers and garlands. From the kitchen came the scents of spices and baking as Cook prepared festive dishes. Mrs. Stafford-Smyth ordered the carriage and began returning from shopping outings with mysterious parcels and packages. A whole new air of excitement pervaded the house that had for so long been silent and empty. They were going to have Christmas.

"I think we need some guests," said Belinda.

"Guests? But all my friends spend Christmas with family— or abroad," responded Mrs. Stafford-Smyth.

"Then we need new friends," said Belinda, biting her lip in concentration.

Mrs. Stafford-Smyth just looked at her in bewilderment.

"I know," said Belinda. "I'll stop by the church and see if one of the ministers knows of any new folks in town who are away from their families. How many should we ask for?"

Mrs. Stafford-Smyth began to chuckle. "I don't know. As

many as you like, I guess. The formal dining table seats twelve."

"Then we'll need ten more," concluded Belinda matter-of-factly.

When Christmas Day dawned cold and windy, Belinda thought about their plans as she prepared for the morning worship service. *Will there be any guests on such a day?* She had asked one of the ministers, and he had agreed to seek out guests to fill their table. But with the weather so cold, Belinda began to have doubts. She also was concerned about Mrs. Stafford-Smyth going to the church—should she be chancing an outing this morning? Perhaps she would prefer to stay at home by the fire.

But when Belinda descended the stairs, she found the lady already bundled in her warm woolens and furs and ready for the carriage trip to the large stone church.

Belinda thought that the music of Christmas was especially beautiful as the well-trained church choir sang the story of Christmas. The deep recesses of the building seemed to echo back the praises. Her eyes filled with tears as she thought of her little church back home and the handful of faithful worshipers who would be gathered there singing Christmas carols and hearing the story of Jesus' birth.

The ride back home was a silent one, with both Mrs. Stafford-Smyth and Belinda busy with their own thoughts.

Tea was served in the drawing room and all of the staff was in attendance. The gifts that had been tucked under the festooned tree were distributed amid cries of appreciation and gleeful laughter. It was a good time, and Belinda felt a closeness to the staff she had never sensed before.

As the five o'clock dinner hour approached, Belinda paced the room, looking first at the clock and then at the frosted windows beyond which the snow still blew in fitful gusts. *We'll be all alone unless the weather improves,* she warned herself. But at ten of five the knocker sounded and Windsor admitted a young couple who had been married only a few months. New to Boston, this was their first Christmas away from their families. Shortly after, a family of three arrived. The little boy, Robert, stared in wide-eyed fascination at the decorated tree. His parents had not yet been able to afford such "luxuries." Then a young teacher with her father, and another woman, newly widowed, brought the guest list to ten, just as Belinda had required. None of them were previously known to the household or to one another. Coming from various stations in life by manner and clothing, they very quickly sensed their common bond. It was Christmas and they were lonely. They needed one another.

After the meal and an evening of fellowship with a small gift distributed to each one, farewells were said, and Belinda looked out on the wintry evening with deep satisfaction. *It was a great success!* she exulted inwardly. *And the wind has died down.* It would not be as bone-chilling for those who drove or trudged home through the snow.

After Windsor had seen the last guest to the door, Mrs. Stafford-Smyth and Belinda settled before the crackling fire in the marble fireplace for a last cup of hot cider and a few more minutes together to review the day.

"Thank you," said Mrs. Stafford-Smyth softly, and Belinda turned to look at her.

"Thank you for giving me anothah Christmas," the older woman said, and Belinda saw the glitter of tears in her eyes.

"Oh, but I didn't give Christmas," Belinda corrected gently. "He did. We just accepted His gift."

Belinda felt a bit let down after Christmas was "packed away" in the storage boxes and put back in the attic. The old house seemed to settle back into its normal quiet with only the sighing wind or the rustling fir trees to stir one's thoughts. Belinda was tired of reading—tired of needlework and more than tired of winter. Mrs. Stafford-Smyth must have felt the same way.

"I've been thinking," she mused one day as they sat by the fire, "I think that it's time to take a trip again."

Belinda's eyes lifted quickly from her knitting.

"I'm feeling perfectly well enough to travel now," the woman continued. "There's no need for us to sit heah listening to the wind day after day. We could be out seeing new things and meeting new people."

Belinda's heart quickened in her chest. *Oh, yes!* she wanted to cry. *Let's. Let's!*

Instead, she held her peace—and her breath—and let the woman go on. "I think the south . . . Maybe Italy or Spain. It's always nice there this time of year."

Italy or Spain? Belinda could not believe she was hearing correctly. She had only dreamed of such places.

"Then we will swing up into France. Visit the boys. I wonder if Frank has married that young woman. We could spend spring there—in France. I like France in spring. We might even slip over to Germany or Austria for a few days. You've never seen Austria, have you? No, I thought not. You'd like it there, I think. The mountains are quite magnificent."

Belinda wanted to jump to her feet and cry, *When? When?* but she sat silently, stilling her wildly thumping heart and listening to Mrs. Stafford-Smyth muse on with her travel plans.

"Yes," she finally said, turning to Belinda. "Let's do that. Ring for Windsah, deah."

Never had Belinda seen Mrs. Stafford-Smyth more eager— more alive. The very thought of going abroad and seeing her grandsons had put color in her cheeks and a new spring to her step. Windsor, with years of experience in such matters, took care of every detail in booking passage and reserving hotel rooms.

LeSoud's provided numerous new items for both travelers, and this time Belinda did not even attempt a protest. She knew so little about travel. How would she know what a young lady needed to be properly outfitted when going abroad? Having no desire to embarrass her employer, she decided to dress herself according to Madam's wishes.

The day of sailing finally arrived, and amid steamer trunks and hatboxes and carry-ons, Mrs. Stafford-Smyth and Belinda were transported to the dock where the S.S. *Victor* lay in the harbor. Belinda, excitement coursing through her veins, kept telling herself, *I'm going abroad!* She was actually going to see some of the places that she had only read of, dreamed of. *Imagine!* She, Belinda Davis, small-town girl from the prairie, was going abroad! Why, maybe—maybe she'd even be like Pierre and Franz and never want to come back.

Chapter 26

A Discovery

Belinda and Mrs. Stafford-Smyth shared a stateroom, but Belinda could hardly bear to spend any time in it when it was so much more entertaining to be on deck, walking about the ship or enjoying the fine meals in the dining room.

Belinda did not push herself in making new acquaintances. She realized that she was considered "staff" and held herself in check lest others should think she was being forward and presumptuous. But she did enjoy watching and listening to the varied and distinguished company among the passengers.

They had been at sea four days when a strong wind came up, driving many of the travelers to their cabins. Belinda hung over the railings, fascinated by her first storm at sea. She worried that the storm might make Mrs. Stafford-Smyth seasick, then reminded herself that she had come as a nurse and might be able to "earn her keep," after all. But it was Belinda who eventually came reeling into their stateroom needing nursing, and Mrs. Stafford-Smyth who was the nurse.

"Some people have a difficult time with the rolling and pitching," the kind woman said in good humor. "It has nevah bothered me," and so saying she tucked Belinda into her bed and arranged for medication from the ship's physician.

Belinda was awfully glad when the rolling finally subsided and she was able to eat again. Soon she was back on deck, enjoying the fresh sting of the salty air and walking the well-scrubbed planks to get her strength back.

A small town on the coast of Spain was their first stop. Belinda was so anxious to see this new country that she had to consciously slow her step to accommodate Mrs. Stafford-Smyth. The sights, sounds and smells of the small Spanish port were every bit as exciting as she had imagined. They settled into a small villa with white-washed walls and a red tile roof. Greenery crowded in close about it, giving it a protected air. Belinda loved it. The best part of all was that they were still within walking distance of the sea, and Belinda took long strolls daily, breathing deeply of the tangy air and watching the roll of the waves.

They managed frequent shopping trips through the quaint streets. Belinda loved to walk slowly through the aisles or stalls, fingering soft fabrics or admiring fine metal work. She made few purchases, but she spent hours thinking, *Wouldn't Ma like that,* or *That color would suit Abbie,* and on and on with each family member.

And then the two moved on by train to Barcelona, Madrid, Rome, Venice—from city to ancient city—where new sights, new people, and new experiences awaited them. Belinda could not immediately recall whether it was Friday or Saturday. There was so much to do and see that she rushed about from morning to evening trying to crowd it all in. Often Mrs. Stafford-Smyth stayed at the hotel, but she usually knew someone in the city who was willing to show Belinda the tourist sights. And Belinda was quite willing to let her traveling companion rest.

"I think I would like to be in France by mid-May," announced Mrs. Stafford-Smyth one evening, and Belinda nodded, knowing that the woman's heart was already in that country with her two grandsons. France in May would be fine. But she intended to thoroughly enjoy each stop along the way.

But as the days added up to weeks, Belinda began to feel a strange kind of restlessness. Each new city was no longer as captivating. There came days when she didn't bother going out for long strolls to study architecture or visit museums. She sat quietly and listened to the distant church bells, or lay on her bed staring silently at the plastered ceiling.

She tried to sort through her thoughts to understand what was happening to her, but she could find no reason for her lethargy.

Mrs. Stafford-Smyth noticed it, too. "Are you feeling ill, deah?" she asked anxiously one day at luncheon.

"No. No, I'm fine," answered Belinda, pushing aside the food still remaining on her plate.

But Mrs. Stafford-Smyth was not convinced.

"Maybe we've taken things too fast," she offered. "Tried to see too many cities in too short a time."

Belinda thought about that. Certainly they had covered a lot of ground. But she wasn't sure there were any cities she would have left out.

"I—I don't think so," she responded. "I liked each one—really I did."

"A little lonesome maybe?" prompted Mrs. Stafford-Smyth. Belinda thought about it. Certainly she missed her family. Over and over she thought of them—wishing she could share her experiences with them. In fact, her journal entries were to help her to do that very thing the moment she got home. She wrote them lengthy letters as well, posting them from various countries. But as much as she missed them all, Belinda didn't feel that that was the reason for her low spirits.

"I'm fine, really," she protested, then added with a laugh, "Maybe I'm like you. Just anxious to see France."

"Well, let's be on with it then," said Mrs. Stafford-Smyth. "There's no reason we have to wait until May. Let's go directly."

And so they did, arriving in Paris the last day of April. Belinda felt her excitement mount again. Maybe this was just what she needed.

Settled in the hotel room, Mrs. Stafford-Smyth stood at the window holding back the drapery with one hand and looking out over the city that stretched before her.

"It seems so strange," she murmured. "It is the same—and yet so different. It's like having someone you deeply love return after being gone for years and years. You know them—and yet you don't."

Belinda stirred uncomfortably. Mrs. Stafford-Smyth's words had a strange effect on her. *That's the way I feel about myself,* she thought restlessly. *Like I don't know me anymore. Have I lost myself somewhere along this journey?* Then Belinda pushed the thought aside and went to join her employer at the window with the twinkling lights of Paris stretching to the horizon.

From somewhere below them, music floated out on the evening air. Belinda could hear laughter and chattering voices in a language she could not understand. Then a dog barked and angry shouts answered and the dog yipped in pain or anger and faded away into the distance.

From somewhere far away bells began to toll. *A church,* thought Belinda. *A church somewhere nearby. Can we go to church come Sunday morning?* And Belinda found herself wondering how many Sundays it had been since she had been in church.

They often traveled on Sunday—or were tired, just having arrived from somewhere, or didn't know where the nearest church was. There was also the language problem. "Why go just to sit?" asked Mrs. Stafford-Smyth. "We can't understand one word of what they are saying," and though Belinda knew it was true, she still missed church. Perhaps now that they were here in Paris, Pierre would take them to a church. Belinda smiled in anticipation.

"I wonder if Frank is married?" Mrs. Stafford-Smyth interrupted her thoughts. Then she went on as though to herself rather than to Belinda. "He was always the ladies' man. He had a new friend every time I heard from him. But Petah said that this one seemed to be different. Well, perhaps my boy is growing up aftah all. Maybe by now he is settled down to married life."

But a surprise awaited them. When they, as arranged, met the two grandsons the next afternoon, it was Pierre who introduced his new wife.

"I sent word to you in Boston," he explained to his grandmother. "Windsor informed me that you had left to travel abroad, but I had no idea where to find you."

Belinda extended her sincere congratulations. Quickly putting their previous friendship in proper perspective, she could be happy for Pierre. The young woman was pretty, quiet and very devoted to her new husband. Belinda did not ask Pierre for an escort to church for fear Anne-Marie could misunderstand the request. She did not want to give the impression that she had any claim on the time or friendship of the newly married young man.

Franz, not at all like his brother, was dashing, bold, reckless in his behavior and dress and dreamy in his approach to life. He was not married, but he was planning soon to be, and his eyes seemed to see only his young Yvette.

Belinda felt that Mrs. Stafford-Smyth expressed the thoughts of both of them when she said, "Well, it seems that if we are to enjoy the sights of Paris, we must do so on our own. I believe that my two grandsons are living in their own private worlds."

Belinda tried to enjoy Paris. It was nice to visit museums and historical sites and shops with Mrs. Stafford-Smyth, who knew the city well, but soon Paris too was just another city. The streets were filled with people, not friends, and the noise was simply chatter, not words, and the bells that rang in the distance belonged only to stone buildings, not houses of God.

"Back home, spring will have come," Belinda said listlessly, as they sat in an open-air cafe one day.

"Ah, yes," said Mrs. Stafford-Smyth, lifting her head from her delicate French pastry. Belinda couldn't stop the sigh that escaped her.

Mrs. Stafford-Smyth went on. "I do hope that Thomas continues to work the gardens. I don't know what I shall evah do when he leaves me."

"It was so beautiful last year," Belinda thought out loud.

Mrs. Stafford-Smyth sat in silence fidgeting with her lorgnette.

"Should we return, Belinda?" she asked suddenly. "Perhaps

we have 'gadded about'—as Windsah puts it—for quite long enough."

"I'd like that," said Belinda softly.

And so they made the arrangements, packed their trunks and boxes and were delivered to a departing ship.

All the days at sea Belinda paced restlessly. Now she did not find even the other passengers of particular interest and barely noticed them. But someone noticed her. An older man in clergy attire watched Belinda as she walked the deck or sat morosely staring out to sea. One day he dared to join her, pulling up a deck chair and seating himself.

"Ah," he said softly, "do ye kin the sound of the waves like the soft flutter of angel wings?"

Belinda's head turned toward him and she smiled at his poetic musing. He took her acknowledgment as permission to continue.

"Are ye goin' home or away?" he asked her.

Belinda sat up a bit straighter in her chair. "Home," she said simply and wondered why the words didn't stir her more.

"It's away 'tis for me," the man continued with a heavy Irish brogue. "Me friends 'ave been sayin' for years, 'Come to America, Mattie,' an' I've been stallin' an' stallin', but then I said, 'Mattie, ye'll niver know lest ye go.' "

Belinda smiled.

"But first I went on to see me sister in Paris," he continued as though Belinda would be interested in all the details of his story. " 'Ye niver know if ye might niver be back,' I told myself."

Belinda nodded and tried to smile.

" 'Tis scary, goin' to a new country," the man continued soberly. "An' at my age too. I worried some, ye can be sure. But then I said, 'Mattie, why all the fussin'? Ye needn't leave God on here behind ye now. Ye ken take 'im with ye.' "

Something in what the kindly man said stirred a response within Belinda. Was that what she had done? Left God back in her homeland? Was that why her trip abroad had become so dismal, so unsatisfying? She knew she had missed attending church, but had she misplaced God, too? After all, God was not limited to buildings. His true dwelling was in hearts. Had Belinda shut the door of her heart when she stepped on the deck of the sailing vessel? If God had no place in her thoughts or plans from that time on, no wonder she had been miserable.

No! No, that wasn't when it happened, Belinda reasoned further. She had left God out of her life even before leaving Boston. Perhaps the downward slide had begun before she left her own small town, maybe starting with her restlessness. Had the restlessness been a result of her constant care of Mrs. Stafford-Smyth? She had allowed her nursing duties to keep her from daily quiet times of prayer and Bible reading. *And I was getting all nervous and upset about Rand and Jackson,* she remembered.

Things had only worsened in the flurry of activity in Boston with Pierre. They had been so busy running here and there that Belinda had put aside her Sunday church attendance as well. Gradually, thoughtlessly, she had drifted into a life that didn't include God.

Belinda looked across at the gentleman beside her. She did not wish to be rude, but she needed some time alone. No—no, she needed time with her God. She had been floundering—starving—and not even realizing why.

"Excuse me, please," she said to the man. "I've enjoyed meeting you, but I—I—need to return to my stateroom."

Belinda was thankful that Mrs. Stafford-Smyth was not there. She needed privacy. With almost frantic gestures she began to rummage through the baggage stored beneath her bunk. Where was her Bible? She who had read her Bible daily had not held it in her hands for weeks.

At last she drew it forth from the bottom of a suitcase. With tears streaming down her face she clasped the book to her bosom.

"Oh, God," she prayed, "God, I'm so sorry. Forgive me. Forgive me for forsaking you. I—I've been so lonely and in my foolishness I did not even know why." Belinda fell on her knees and cried out to a forgiving Father.

It was a while before the storm was spent and peace again entered Belinda's heart. She rose to sit on her berth and opened her Bible. She sat reading favorite portions from her precious book, thankfully noticing how each passage met her need, and wondering how she could have ever become so careless as to have neglected it.

She had been raised with Bible reading. Her earliest memories were of sitting on Clark's lap as he read to the family from the Bible each morning. She had always been impressed with the importance of Bible reading and time spent in prayer. She knew! She knew! She had learned it well. She had become a believer herself when she was but a girl and had allowed God to lead and direct her life throughout her growing years. How was it possible for her to let the pleasures of the world and the deceitfulness of living a life of leisure and wealth lead her so far off course? How could Satan so subtly and slowly have drawn her away from her source of spiritual life? It had developed so gradually that Belinda had been unaware of its happening.

It's not that the Lord doesn't want me to enjoy beautiful things and interesting places, Belinda decided. *But He wants me to do those things with Him, not without Him.* Thankful that through the kind words of an elderly man God had jarred her back to the truth, she read on, refreshing her parched soul.

At last, feeling renewed and alive again, she laid her Bible gently on the bedside table. She smiled softly to herself, hardly able to wait to share her new discovery with Mrs. Stafford-Smyth. She had not been the Christian witness to the woman that she should have been. She prayed that God would help her to change all that. And feeling assured that she served a merciful and understanding God, Belinda was confident that she would be given ample opportunity to share her faith properly in the future.

The future! Suddenly the thought seemed awfully good to Belinda. She had so much to look forward to—so many decisions of life still to be made. She no longer felt crowded—pushed against a wall. Why, even the thought of Jackson and Rand brought no accompanying anxiety. Belinda felt she was ready to offer honest friendship to both of them. *Friendship—but no more—at least at present,* she told herself and felt no guilt concerning her decision. She smiled again, thankful for the feeling of peace.

She felt no pressure to know what her future held. Perhaps—just perhaps God did have a home and family somewhere ahead for her. Belinda would like that, but she was willing to take one step at a time.

A wave of loneliness for the ones at home swept over her. She would love to see them—to see them all. To be held in her father's secure arms again—to share private thoughts with her mother over a cup of tea—to watch Luke's steady hand as he held syringe or needle—to chat, to hold, to laugh and cry with her family.

And then Belinda's thoughts turned to Mrs. Stafford-Smyth—the wealthy woman who was in reality so poor—and Belinda's heart ached for the woman. For the first time in her young life, Belinda began to sense what it would be like to be alone—really alone. The thought sobered and chilled her. She must do more with her—be more thoughtful and loving. More sharing and giving. The lonely woman needed her, not as nursemaid, but as friend. Belinda knew that at least for now, she would not—could not—desert her.

"God," she whispered, "I'll need your leading. Your direction. I want to do the right thing—an' I trust you to let me know just what that might be. Oh—not all at once—but step by step. Help me to be patient with what you have for me now—an' ready to move on when you give me a nudge. Don't let me rush the future—but help me to claim it." Belinda breathed deeply, at peace with herself. "An' thank you, God—for a future—for the knowledge that you have it all in your control."

Belinda smoothed her dress and raised a hand to tidy her hair, then moved forward to take the first step in her new walk with God.

I must find him an' tell him, she said to herself with a smile. *He's a rather strange little man—but his words changed my life.*

*I must tell him—an' then welcome him to America. "Mattie"—
he said his name was—but it's hardly proper for me to be callin'
him that. I must ask his name.* Belinda opened the cabin door
and stepped out into the bright sunshine and tangy sea air.

Barcelona—Rome—Paris—steamship—Boston? What does
it really matter? For as the kind man has pointed out, " 'Ye
needn't leave God behind ye now,' " and wherever one goes—
wherever God is, the heart can be at peace, at home.